M000218880

PRAISE FOR TO STARVE AN EMBER

TO STARVE AN EMBER

LISA HATFIELD

HIGH PLAINS WORDSMITH

High Plains Wordsmith LLC

To Starve an Ember

Paperback ISBN 978-1-7368941-0-1

Hardback ISBN 978-1-7368941-2-5

Ebook ISBN 978-1-7368941-1-8

Audiobook ISBN 978-1-7368941-3-2

Published by High Plains Wordsmith LLC

First edition October 2021

Book design by Gordon Saunders

LisaHatfieldWriter.com

This book is dedicated to:
Mark Carlyle Hatfield - husband, gentleman, and geographer

www.Tinderbox.tips - Factors that Control Wildland Fire Behavior:

- Fuel
- Weather
- Topography

Wildfire dominated the morning headlines again, and the TV on the wall glowed with images of recently burned-out homes as Prentice sat in his usual booth in the Rocky Mountain Diner. A thousand miles west of him, black, white, and gray ruins made scars against the intense blue sky.

The deep voice of the local Colorado morning news anchor narrated the devastation. "Residents in the Sierra Nevada mountains of California have begun surveying the damage from most recent severe wildfire." The screen shifted to show car-skeletons lined up on a paved road and acres of tall conifers reduced to black toothpicks.

The anchor continued. "On a hot August morning last week, this significant wildfire spewed fireballs the size of tennis balls, igniting spot fires in neighborhoods miles away from the main blaze. Within a matter of hours, the fires destroyed four California towns. Flying embers carried by the wind landed in the forest and on homes. The fire leapfrogged ten miles in less than two hours, taking everyone by surprise."

"Children on one school playground ran inside screaming that burning branches fell from the sky." The video showed a school bus unloading exhausted teachers and young children with soot-stained faces into a parking lot somewhere away from danger. "Traffic and smoke trapped this bus for six hours." The desolate images scrolled by.

"The fire spread as fast as ... wildfire. The number of 9-1-1 calls reporting the fire overwhelmed dispatchers across two remote California counties. Evacuees who made it down the mountain said dispatchers had asked them, 'Where did you say the fire was? How could the fire be there?' and then replied they couldn't send any help. They had to just get themselves out of there."

The news anchor paused and the television screen filled with images captured by a firefighter on his phone. A double stream of cars headed slowly down a two-lane mountain road away from the disaster. Although it was midmorning, headlights glowed in the eerie darkness, barely able to cut through the smoke.

"Towering flames blocked two of the four escape routes. Almost one hundred people died in last week's fire, and

18,000 buildings were destroyed. The
thousand people from their homes....

Prentice Keene watched the rep
this would make more residents prepare
build their homes in wildfire territory.
to his gut. He never seemed to distance himself from the
devastation, no matter how far away it was. *Fires are a vital*
part of nature, but people don't seem to realize that's where they
live.

The diner's young owner, Elva, brought him his big
breakfast with a side order of banter, as usual. She'd graduated in the same class as Prentice at Garnet High School,
less than a decade ago.

"How's the weather down there, shorty?" she always
asked.

He sat up, shrugged, and took the plate, acknowledging
Elva with a sideways smile. Elva was a foot taller than he
was. He was also the shortest guy in the Garnet Fire Department, and his shift didn't let him forget it. Only Engineer
Owens was shorter than Prentice, but she drove the 30-foot
pumper as if it were a limousine.

"Thanks, Elva." He dug into spicy Mexican chilaquiles -
fried tortillas and salsa verde made of green tomatillos and
poblano peppers. The heat made his forehead sweat, but he
was addicted to the endorphins the spicy food brought on.
Hot peppers count as vegetables, right?

He glanced at the television screen as he finished his meal.
The news anchor was gone and a woman appeared. He'd nick-
named her the weather chick months ago, since she acted and
dressed more like a high school cheerleader than a meteorolo-
gist. "The skies will be hazy again today due to smoke from the
fires traveling a thousand miles to reach us here in central

," she exclaimed. "That's what's making the sunset a pretty orange every evening. But let's skip those picnics d 5Ks for a few more days until the air quality improves."

"Honestly, that's all you can say?" he muttered. *Why don't you tell people how to get ready for when a fire comes here?* Every day, the local news anchors dished out passive information about wildfires when they could've been explaining how to reduce the potential for unnecessary destruction. *People can live with fire, but they need to play by its rules.*

A trio of elderly ladies sat in the booth in front of Prentice. At one time or another each of them had been his teacher in the Garnet school system. Their paths often crossed in town, and they usually asked about his dad, or if he was eating right or had a girlfriend. This morning he kept his head down, but he caught snippets of their conversation as they clucked about the fires in California.

"Isn't it awful!" one said, with her back to him.

"The smoke makes my asthma act up," said the second lady, Mrs. Smith, who'd been his teacher in first grade. "I wish it would rain so we wouldn't have to worry about a fire here."

Prentice's shoulders tensed up under his blue station-uniform t-shirt. "All we need is some rain" was one misconception he battled about wildfire risks. "No," he said. But he hadn't meant to say it aloud.

"What's that?" asked a third lady, Mrs. Everett. She'd taught him in elementary school too. "Prentice, did you say something?"

He shook his head. *Why don't I just wait until a person actually asks me a question?* But he met her gaze. "Colorado's wildfire season is year 'round. It'll burn any time there's no snow on the ground and it's not currently raining." He spoke with energy, trying to turn it into a teachable moment. "It's the fuel in your yard you have to worry about."

"What do you mean? I don't have fuel in my yard." Mrs. Smith argued.

He nodded and applied what he hoped was a positive expression to his face. "Sure you do. Most everyone does."

She shook her head.

He went on, focusing on keeping his voice under control. "I've seen your yard, Mrs. Smith. It's full of flammable junipers and ten times more pine trees than the soil can support."

"My goodness Prentice," she retorted. "You talk as if we're in danger from our own beautiful trees!"

He worked at maintaining the smile, but his hazel eyes were serious. *Why don't I just leave right now and go to the station?* But no, he had to finish this. He kept talking. "When it rains, it just postpones the inevitable. It all dries out again in hours or days. The vegetation keeps growing—"

She interrupted him. "Yes, that's how nature works."

His jaw tightened at her casual dismissal of his point. "Yeah, and nature wants to send fire through, on a regular basis, to clean out the understory. If not, you have to manage it yourself by cutting back brush and thinning the saplings."

The first lady turned around on the bench now and said, "That's enough of this. We're just here having breakfast."

Pressure blinked hard. "You're not listening!" He spoke loudly enough that the other diner patrons glanced over, and Elva peered out from the kitchen.

"Prentice Keene, you're getting yourself all worked up." Mrs. Everett spoke in her calmest grade-school teacher voice. "We know how fires upset you. You and your father have been through so much..."

Why do they always have to bring that up? "That's not it," he said in a voice he hoped was calm and professional. Removing a twenty-dollar bill from his wallet, he set it on the table and slid out of the booth. "You ladies taught me in school," he said, standing near them. "But now I need to educate you. We're definitely gonna have a wildfire here. This town is a tinderbox."

The ladies' eyes widened. Mrs. Everett said, "I'm sure you don't mean—"

"I sure do! There's tons more action you can take to be safer than to cross your fingers and hope it rains. We live in the high desert, a desert full of trees and grass. Why don't people wake up and smell the coff– no, the smoke in the air!"

He exhaled. His early life tragedies and their consequences would be the topic of their conversation as soon as he left.

Clearing his throat, he spoke with quiet authority. "We're surrounded by the potential for extreme wildfire. We all need to manage the forests on our land, not just let them grow wild." He saw by the glances they exchanged that his lesson had missed its mark. They couldn't see him as an adult with knowledge that could help them.

He made it out the door. In the parking lot, he spotted the stray gray cat peeking out from behind the dumpster. "Hey, cat. I forgot to save you some food. I'll make it up to you tomorrow." Then he headed to his shift at the station.

THAT NIGHT IN THE BUNK ROOM, HE DREAMED HE WAS IN A scraggly oak and pine forest filled with spot fires. Prentice was a kid, holding a blue plastic bucket with a white handle, like he and his brother used to play with at the lakeshore where their mom took them so long ago.

His dad's voice echoed all around him, scolding him to stay out of trouble, but he couldn't see him. He called out, "Where are you? Are you okay?" No one answered.

Alone and surrounded by flames popping up around him, he tipped the bucket out, but it was empty.

He woke up in a sweat, gasping for air, fighting to connect with reality. Getting off his bunk, he went down the hall to the fire station's kitchen, drank a glass of water, and polished off half a bag of Fritos before he realized what he was doing. He didn't want the junk. Why was he eating it?

So of course, he grabbed two Ding-Dongs from the white-and-blue box and ate them without tasting, staring into space. It was a while before the sugar took hold and numbed his brain enough to go back to bed.

He didn't know how much time passed before the crackle of the dispatch radio on the loudspeakers roused the crew. It was time to go. Medical call. Firefighters and paramedics got into their turnout gear. They moved like water flowing into the bay, into the trucks, and out into the night.

Fire danger in Garnet was a reality almost every day in the summer, and in recent years, fire season pushed into the other three seasons, too. In winter the threat loomed if there was no snow, and the wind desiccated the vegetation. Spring rain only delayed the danger. Green plants eventually browned and dried out, adding to the accumulation of fuel.

The National Weather Service posted a Red Flag warning again on Wednesday, as it had every other day for the last few weeks of August. Sustained drying winds, low humidity, and high temperatures increased risks. The warning meant, "We really mean it now! No slip-ups!" No lawnmower sparks, no cigarettes, no fooling.

Although Prentice made sure the arrow on the "Today's Fire Danger" sign board in front of Station #1 still pointed to "Extreme," people didn't notice it as they drove by on the way to live their lives. He and the crew worked through the shift. More medical calls. Some vehicle maintenance. Exercise in the weight room. Lots of time to think. Too much. It was better when he stayed busy and didn't think.

As he washed lunch dishes, he took in the view out the window at Two-Mile Lake, the same one where his mom used to bring him and William. He shook off remnants of last night's dream, just another variation on an endless theme: Prentice alone, trying to connect with his distant dad.

He put the last pot on the rack, watered the basil plant on the windowsill, and looked out the window again.

What the....! A little plume of smoke! It was a grass fire, right behind the station, at the picnic area at the north end of the lake. Grabbing two pots off the rack, Prentice banged them together three times, shouting, "Fire! Wildfire at the lake!" He ran toward the bay, yelling at the top of his voice, "We've gotta go right now, B Shift! There's a fire at the lake! This is not a drill!"

Keene, Owens, Wisniewski, Minetti, Nguyen and Lt. Grimaldi hit the ground, pulling on their wildland gear over their station wear. On the short drive to the lake, the guys in the engine reviewed their planned tactics and how grass fires behaved. This department's training focused mainly on structure fires, despite their location in the dry high plains. Prentice, however, had his Red Card and more training in wildland fires. He'd fought small grass fires like this before, but he'd never been deployed to a severe one.

Lt. Grimaldi called dispatch to document the action and the location of their rigs. His innate calm and cool authority rang through his booming voice as he handled the call. He'd told Prentice once, briefly, about his response to the 9/11 attacks and his subsequent departure from the New York Fire Department in search of peace. He seemed to have found it, too, in the wide open spaces of Colorado. Prentice was always glad to see Grimaldi relax. When he smiled, his white teeth contrasted with his deep black skin, and his eyes shone. Generous with his praise to the firefighters when they deserved it, he was a genuinely caring man. The crew looked up to him.

B Shift got to the lake in a few minutes. Two young women in jogging outfits were trying to stamp out the grass fire with their sneakers. Black soot covered their shoes, and they both coughed. One of them was on the line with 9-1-1. "It's okay, thank God. They're already here," she told the dispatcher and hung up.

The joggers got into their car but just moved it to the corner of the parking lot out of the firefighters' way, then sat with the windows open, watching and taking photos as the firefighters took over and worked to contain the fire.

Four of them dug a fire line to stop its spread through the grass. The wind blew from the southwest, pushing the fire from the picnic area toward the parking lot, and soon the fire ran out of grass to burn. Wisniewski used a shovel to smother sparks blowing to the far side of the lot.

Prentice's job was to run the hose from the engine's tank. On this small fire, attacked early, it was enough to put out hot spots.

Soon, a circle of blackened grass was all that remained

of the fire. One of the joggers approached the crew again as they packed up and asked, " A boy dropped a lit cigarette into the grass."

"Any idea who it was?" Lt. Grimaldi asked.

"No, there were three of them. Maybe high school or college age."

"Well, school's in session today," he said. "If they were cutting class from Garnet High, we might be able to track them down."

The other lady said, "It's amazing you got here so fast with the fire engine to put the fire out."

Prentice spoke up. "Well, if you noticed, we really used the fire line and the parking lot to contain this one. We don't generally fight wildfires with water."

The lady looked at him as if he had two heads, just like his teachers had yesterday in the diner. The public perception was that wildfires were fought the same as house fires, with water.

On the way back to the station, Lt. Grimaldi grinned at Prentice, and said, "Good eyes, Smokey. That's why we named you Smokey Bear."

Oh, I hate that nickname. Prentice shrugged but he made himself receive the praise, "Thanks, Lieutenant. Good luck rounding up the kids that started it." *But see how much the Red Flag warning actually changes people's behavior?*

www.Tinderbox.tips - Class A Roofs:

- If a three-inch chunk of burning charcoal lands on a roof, what happens?
- Roofs made of non-flammable materials have the least chance of igniting.
- Good examples: slate, clay, stone-coated steel, fiberglass asphalt composition shingles.
- Even a Class A Roof won't help if the ember lands in leaf litter in a gutter or next to flammable siding.

The primary mission of an urban firefighter is structure fires and emergency medical services. Prentice was in Garnet again today but not as a firefighter. He spent most of his off-duty time with his Tinderbox side business doing chainsaw and wood chipping work, helping people deal with overgrown vegetation on their land. And, as insurance against having any down time beyond that, he also earned money giving people transportation via a ride-share app.

As he breakfasted in the diner, he was pretty sure the coast was clear of past teachers since they only met once a month. Today, his first Tinderbox appointment wasn't until nine, when he would do a property evaluation, so he logged into the ride-share app to look for a client.

A local client popped up right away, a lady needing a ride from Garnet to Pioneersburg. He could drive her there and be back north in time for his appointment. He clicked to accept it.

On his way out to the truck, the gray cat let Prentice find her, and he set a paper napkin full of scrambled eggs next to the dumpster for her to eat. She meowed at him and then acted like she'd rustled it up herself.

The address on Crystal Street was a few blocks from the diner on the west side of historic Garnet. Parking on the street, the first thing he noticed was the tall grass around the house. He doubted anyone had mowed it all summer. Leggy evergreen bushes crammed the space below the front picture window. Metal sculptures of daisies and sunflowers poked up through the ragged grass in a crooked line. It was artsy. A dog's happy bark echoed from inside the house.

A petite lady came out onto the weathered porch. She was in her mid-twenties, he guessed, and noticeably pretty, even from a distance. She had tied her long, light-brown hair back in a ponytail. Dressed business-casual, with a light purple button-down shirt tucked neatly into khaki pants that highlighted her attractive curves.

He got out and said, "Hi, I'm Prentice. Did you call for a ride?"

"Yep," she answered as she compared the information on

her phone to the illuminated ride-share sign on the dashboard and the license plate and picked up her briefcase. She called through the open living room window. "Bye, Mom. See you tonight."

He went to the passenger side and opened the door for her as she walked out to his truck.

"Thanks for helping me get to work." She climbed up, using the running board as a step, and closed the door, smiling at him as he looked at her in the passenger window. He noticed her eyes were brown like milk chocolate and their shape hinted at some Asian ancestry. Black eyeliner, which only showed when she blinked, accented the outside corners.

Walking around to the driver's side of the cab, Prentice was distracted, and it unnerved him. He prided himself on being a no-nonsense guy, a first responder, cool under pressure. Well, at work that was true, but out in the world, he wasn't confident at all. *She could be a model. She's so out of my league.*

The app had already given him the address where she needed to go, a big government contractor at the north end of Pioneersburg, the city ten miles south of Garnet. "I was visiting my mom up here last night, but this morning my car wouldn't start. I'll deal with it later. Big stuff to do today."

Her mouth crinkled up at the corners when she smiled, nicely complimenting her nose, which was prominent in a more European way. The combination of her narrow eyes and wide smile captivated him. Prentice glanced at her and quickly away again. Better to just be himself, the quiet version of himself, and let her into and back out of his life.

However, as he put the truck in gear, he completely surprised himself by asking her, "What do you do?"

She lowered her voice in mock seriousness. "Vital national security work! Email accounts to set up. Backups to retrieve, you know." She smiled again.

Who knew if that was really it, or a more serious job? He realized he just liked hearing her talk, that it didn't matter what she was saying. She had the kind of voice that would make it worth listening to her read the dictionary aloud.

"You're Prentice? I'm Jessie. Named after my Grandmother Jiexen. She came here from China. Jessie was her English name." She laughed. "Why'd I just tell you all that?"

He chuckled too. "Yeah, Prentice. I don't have any relatives from China. Just America," he offered. It was a dumb comment, but she laughed anyway.

She asked, "Where are you from? Where's your family?"

"Oh, we moved to Garnet when I was four. A few years after that my dad retired from the Air Force."

"You were pretty young to have a retired dad."

"Yeah, in the military you can retire after twenty years and get a whole 'nother career. He still lives here, works as an accountant. I live in Pioneersburg now. That's about it." *Phew. That does pretty much cover it.*

"That's a problem when you meet a squirrel like me. I always ask too many questions."

"Nah, it's fine."

He wanted to ask her more, but she got more questions in first. "How about you? You're dressed for hard work, not driving."

"Right. I'm doing a wildfire evaluation and some chainsaw work today. I'm not due in Garnet until later."

"Wow, a lumberjack?"

He laughed. "I work for the fire department, but I'm not on shift today."

"So, why're you doing chainsaw work?" she asked.

"Oh, I have my own company. I help people reduce wild-fire risk and improve forest health." He went on, despite his intention to not talk too much, telling her a little about benign neglect of vegetation. She joked about the tall, dry grass at her mom's place having rattlesnakes in it.

"Tall grass is actually one of the easiest risks to reduce. But..." He didn't want to ruin things by trying to convince her of anything.

"But what?" she persisted.

"It's just that tall grasses make fuel for a fire too. It's better to keep it mowed close to your house."

"Hm," she mused. "Dad won't like hearing that. Seri-ously, that's a lot of responsibility you've taken on. Fire department. Chainsaws. And driving people like me around."

"Yep, I keep pretty busy. Keep moving."

"I'm that way too, and I have to remind myself to stop and have fun," she said.

He exited the interstate and soon pulled up in the drop-off zone in front of the modern white building on Contractor Boulevard. "Do you need a ride home, too?"

"Yeah, I was about to ask you. That would be great. Can you be here at 5:30?"

"Sure thing. I'll meet you right here." *She could never be interested in me. Just forget it.*

He watched until she'd disappeared inside the building, and then, shaking his head, he put the truck into gear and left the city to do the wildfire risk evaluation and then a day full of tree thinning work in Garnet.

⌒

He stopped the chainsaw job a little early. It was only 4 p.m., but he wanted to clean up the work area and stow the equipment into his truck, packing it neatly, taking his time, trying to be as methodical as always. He'd tried, unsuccessfully, not to think about Jessie all day while he worked. Finally, he'd decided that he'd go a few miles out of his way to his apartment in Pioneersburg to get cleaned up before his scheduled 5:30 p.m. pick-up.

Jessie hopped up into the truck and said, "Thanks for taking me back up to Garnet. This is a big help." He nodded, looking at her, smiling a little, and he was gratified when she returned his smile. He wished he could think of something clever to ask her but then realized he didn't need to worry about it.

In the background, the classic rock band Boston came on the radio. Without prologue, Jessie reached over to turn up the volume and sang all the words in a beautiful voice, an octave higher than the singers. It was about having a higher power and beginning another day. At the end, she turned the volume down again and addressed Prentice.

"That song is so deep," she said.

"One of my favorites, but I don't really get the lyrics," he said. "I think it came out the year before I was born, though. Old school."

"My mom and dad's influence on me too. They love the classics," she said. "So, we're heading back up to her place to get my car, but I still don't know what's wrong with it. That won't do me much good, will it?" She laughed.

"I know something about cars. Want me to take a look?" Prentice wanted to fix this for her.

"Sure," she said. "You know about cars too?"

"Yeah. I liked auto shop in high school."

She asked, "But you're a firefighter now?"

"I'm a structural firefighter, but I've also got my wildland fire certification and I'm an EMT."

"That's like a paramedic?" she asked.

"Sort of. I started out as a biology major. But I changed to forestry when we had that series of wildfires around Pioneersburg. My dad had a fit. He wanted me to go into a safer line of work and become a lab rat."

She nodded, looking ahead. "Parents are people too. They're so human sometimes it hurts." She glanced at Prentice, and he nodded with her, keeping his eyes on the road.

At the DeGroot family's house on Crystal Street, a dog's excited bark and more rock-n-roll boomed from the open living room windows. Behind the metal flower sculptures, the shutters were painted bright blue in the spirit of all the Victorian-style cottages in this part of town.

Jessie's mom was at the curb bringing in the empty trash cans. She wasn't much over five feet tall and wore comfortable, artsy work clothes. Prentice heard her singing along in a falsetto voice with the soprano's initial thrilling notes and mystery lyrics of Electric Light Orchestra's "Rockaria." Then the music jumped to electric guitars and drums.

Jessie said, "It's nice to see Mom. She's not always here. Dad's a trucker, and she goes on the road with him sometimes." She got out to give her a hug before she went back in the house, then returned to Prentice. "Her name's Anna. She'll be out again in a minute. And that dog you hear is Casey. He's friendly."

"It must be nice to spend time with your mom." A fuzzy memory of his own mom playing her guitar in the living room surfaced in his head. She opted for folk music in a minor key.

Then he got back to business. Jessie watched him as he got the multimeter out of the back of his truck so he could check the voltage in the battery. He answered her question about how to attach the red and black leads in their proper places.

Then he read the display. "It's in borderline territory. No wonder you don't have enough cranking amps."

"So I need to get a new battery?"

"Maybe. Probably. But you could try charging it and see if it holds the charge. I've got jumper cables."

"Awesome!"

"Once we get it started, you'd have to drive it for a half hour to get a proper charge from the alternator. I'll get it jumped now, and you can be on your way."

Jessie grinned, giving him a sidelong appraisal. Then she looked over at her mom, who now relaxed on the front porch in a patio chair, enjoying the evening and observing the two at work in the driveway. Casey had quieted down and lounged next to her on the porch.

"Well, you don't need to hurry, do you? What about ... before you charge it, what if we go for a walk? Two-Mile Lake isn't far from here. We could drive up there. If you have time, I mean."

He wasn't going to say no to spending a little more time with her, so he smiled in agreement. Jessie said to Anna on the porch, "Mom, we'll be back in a bit, and then I'll drive my car home."

It took a few minutes to drive up State Highway 55 and across the railroad tracks. The cars buzzed by on the interstate next to the lake. In the parking lot, she pointed at the burn scar with a question in her eyes, and he said, "We got here quickly, so this grass fire didn't turn into a major fire in town."

Jessie commented, "They can get out of control pretty fast. Like that one in California that surprised everyone last month."

"Right. One big danger is when they burn near towns and people haven't prepared for them. It's different when they're out in the middle of nowhere and they can just let them burn."

"I guess so," she said. "But right here in the middle of Garnet, it would be awful."

They walked on the path that circled the water, which was pretty low in August, as usual. The creek that ordinarily fed the lake was just a dry streambed full of weeds.

To change the subject, he asked her where she'd lived before.

"Mississippi," she answered. "We moved here after Hurricane Katrina destroyed our house on the Gulf Coast."

"That must've been terrible. How old were you?"

"Just starting seventh grade. Dad and Mom wanted to start over. They didn't ask me. My best friend stayed in Mississippi. Her family lived in a FEMA trailer for a long time. After we left, I could only email her from school and message her through Facebook."

He stayed quiet for a minute, thinking. "So you went to Garnet Middle School?"

"Yes... You did too? How old are you?"

"Twenty-six."

"Me too."

"How come I don't remember you?" he asked.

"We must have been on different teams in middle school. I hardly talked to anyone, anyway. Middle school was horrible."

"Yeah," Prentice agreed. "I didn't talk to people either.

25

That was when I first got into running...." His thoughts shifted back in time.

"Did you do cross-country?"

"Uh-huh. And track. It was good to have something to do after school. I loved it. Dad couldn't pick me up until after practice, so in high school I just walked home, up the mountain, or took the bus when I was off-season. Except one year I over-did it and got a stress fracture. Cut my season short."

"It's just you and your dad?"

"Yep." Prentice was looking in the distance as they walked. "But what about you? Where did you live?"

"Same house where you picked me up."

"Really? That's just a few miles from our house. Dad lives there." He pointed up the hill. "So why don't I know you from high school at least?"

"I went to the charter high school in Pioneersburg. Tiger Grandma made sure of that. She started living with us when I was in grade school, and she kind of took over raising me. I'm surprised she let me go to the regular middle school. But we had just moved then and it was complicated."

"What's a Tiger Grandma?"

"Have you heard of a Tiger Mom?" Prentice shook his head 'no,' and Jessie continued. "Well, my mom isn't a Tiger Mom, for sure. She's more like a Kitty-cat, a flower child from the '60s. I think it's because Grandma pushed her so hard." Prentice looked perplexed. "Some mothers in China just push and push for perfection. Grades are the most important thing. No free time. No fun. No individual choices. So, Tiger Grandma, there you go."

"Hm." He finally said. "Maybe my mom was a flower child too. And I must have a Tiger Dad. He's always stalking me." Prentice laughed, and it felt good. He grew serious again. "When I was growing up, I never knew when he was going to come out of the grass and pounce on me."

"What do you mean?"

"I got into the habit of second-guessing everything I did, wondering how he would react to it. After a long time, I realized he'd never be satisfied with anything I picked. I still keep trying, but it sucks the life outta me."

"That must be rough on you. With the firefighting thing..."

"I dunno. It's just the way it is." He shrugged and put his hands in his pockets.

Jessie stopped walking and looked at Prentice. She made air quotes with her fingers as she said, "We get guilt feelings when we stand up for ourselves instead of giving in to others. Right?"

He stopped too and nodded slowly, looking at her. "Yeah.... What? I never heard anything like that before. Who's 'we'?"

"It's a support group I'm in. Found it in college. It's really helping me breathe better, you know?"

Breathing. What a concept.

Back at Jessie's parents' house, Anna had moved her car to the street while they were gone so Prentice could charge Jessie's battery. He was starting to feel like his own internal battery wasn't dead anymore either.

Anna walked onto the porch and waved hello to Jessie and Prentice. Her big yellow dog barked a welcome but stayed by her side. Prentice noticed that an ash tree grew beside the porch and hung over the gutters. Junipers spread under the windows. *Turn off the analysis for once.*

Around her the music transitioned from the Moody Blues' "I'm Just a Singer in a Rock-n-roll Band" to The Eagles' "One of these Nights."

27

"I like those speakers," he said to her. "No distortion on the bass."

"Thanks for noticing." She leaned her hands on the railing, introducing herself. "Hi. I'm Anna." Her features seemed more Chinese than Jessie's did, but she and her daughter sounded the same when they laughed. She wore jeans and a t-shirt layered with a faded men's dress shirt covered in colorful paint splotches. It was voluminous, and while she had the cuffs rolled up, the sleeves were still too long.

"I'm Prentice. Helping Jessie with her car."

"So I see. That's really nice of you," she said. "I made iced tea. Jessie, why don't you and Prentice come inside and have some before you get started? You must be warm after your walk."

"All right," Jessie answered, and Prentice followed her into the small house. Right away, he appreciated the homey feeling of the little cabin with its bright colors. They sat in the kitchen and Prentice was drawn in by the cozy familiarity of the mother and daughter chatting with each other while making him feel welcome. Once they finished their tea, Jessie scratched Casey's soft ears and then led the way back outside.

Prentice used the jumper cables to get her car started, an easy fix.

She left the car running and went to her mom on the porch for a goodbye hug. "See you next weekend? Let's make wontons." Anna dipped her chin in agreement.

Jessie got in her car and closed the door, but then she rolled the window down so she could talk to Prentice. "She says you're a good guy."

Prentice laughed. "She can tell that after one glass of iced tea?"

"I'm glad for your help. This is a lot nicer than dealing with a tow truck driver."

"No problem." He smiled, a real smile, not like the smiles he put on his face to reassure accident victims or his old teachers.

Jessie started to back up again, but then stopped and leaned out the window. "How about tomorrow afternoon, you come by my apartment, and we'll see if the battery's still working?"

He stepped toward her. "Sure. I can do that."

She told him her address, and they realized their apartments were just a few miles apart in Pioneersburg. "Then maybe we could go for a real hike?"

"Sure," he said. *What am I gonna say, 'No, I'd rather go to the gym'?* He chuckled to himself.

She waved, and he watched her until she turned the corner.

He put the jumper cables in their designated spot, thinking to himself, *I'm probably being a total idiot.* Anna still sat on the porch, looking at the night sky and humming along with the music. "It was nice to meet you, Anna," he called over to her. A friendly wave sent him on his way.

Arriving at home a bit later, he surveyed his apartment. It seemed empty now, compared to Anna and her husband David's small, cozy house. For the first time, he noticed the walls, bare of posters and paintings. There was hardly any furniture. One white towel and a washcloth hung on a towel bar in the bathroom. Spares were folded in the little linen closet. It was just like the house he and Dad lived in, decorated in a Men-are-Practical-but-Not-Creative style.

He brushed his teeth, washed his face, then wiped down the bathroom sink, adding the cloth to the laundry basket already half full of old towels, his workout clothes, and his blue station pants and t-shirts. *Routines push back the chaos,* he thought as he fell into bed.

So what am I doing going for a hike with a lovely lady? That's definitely not part of my routine. He hoped tomorrow didn't end in chaos.

3

"Are you nuts? Where do you get off saying stuff like that?" The comment she'd just made vibrated in his mind like a gong. Prentice wanted to be furious at Jessie. "I'm not like my dad. You've never even met him."

It was Saturday afternoon, and they'd been hiking for an hour on a narrow dirt trail lined with sagebrush and scrub oak. Now they sat on a bench. Bright sunlight glared down on them since here there were no pines here to give shade. Despite his baseball cap, his eyes squinted into crescents against the bright August sun.

Jessie shook her head, emphasized by the sweep of her long brown ponytail. "No, I'm serious. It would be good if you let it out, all this history between you and your dad, and the fires that have affected your life"

Prentice interrupted. "I'm fine."

She had convinced him to go outside to enjoy the sunny day with her. Maybe he should've just gone to the gym this afternoon once they got her car battery fixed. But no, he'd let her drive him up here to the mesa for this hike. Now he was worried that maybe beneath the cute exterior was a lady who just wanted to talk about feelings all the time. *We got along so well yesterday.*

"Listen," she said in a careful voice. "If you face it, then all the junk stops smoldering inside you. You can breathe again."

He stayed quiet, curious about the point she was making. She continued, softly. "You're pretty buff, Prentice. You're ripped – on the outside."

He braced himself. Sentences starting like that always had a "but."

"But inside, and I'm talking from experience here, it seems like you're more concerned about fixing other people, like your dad, than you are about what you need to do for yourself." Leaning back, she crossed her arms.

Prentice didn't answer. He could tell she wasn't joking but spoke in earnest.

"So, want to keep hiking? Or... ditch me right here?" She gave him time to answer by leaning over to pull up a couple of knapweed plants next to the bench. She threw them toward the edge of the mesa.

Prentice yanked off his baseball hat and ruffled a hand through his sweaty blond hair, making it stand up even more than usual. He tried to think about what she just said. He'd met no one like Jessie before. She was so direct, so honest. She kept shining a spotlight into the dark corners of his soul he hadn't noticed were even there. She wasn't judging him but was helping point out hidden cobwebs.

"No," he said. "No, I don't know how you get it, but I think you're right. This is so weird. You might be onto something I've never thought about." This was really hard to say, but there it was, out in the open. "Let's keep walking."

She brightened. "All right."

He stood and flexed his short, muscular legs in a knee bend, then extended his hand to pull her up. She accepted, stood up, and held onto his hand a little longer than he expected. It was a great surprise. He adjusted the day pack on his strong shoulders, mostly to get some air underneath it and cool off. "Do you want to take the extra loop in the trail at the top of the mesa? Or is that smoky haze bothering you?"

She said, "No, it's fine. I'm just glad there aren't any fires burning closer to us right now."

"Not today, anyway," he couldn't help saying.

They moved on in silence until pausing in unison at an overlook on top of Blue Mesa. Spread out below was the little town of Garnet where he'd grown up and now worked. Far in the distance to the south was the city of Pioneersburg, nestled in next to the Front Range of the Rockies. A hot breeze gusted up the slope of the mesa. The strong winds, low humidity, and heat made it another Red Flag Warning Day, and he scanned the horizon for smoke.

Jessie said, "It's funny you live in the city but commute up to Garnet. I live down there so I can be closer to my work."

"I do a lot of things opposite of the way most people do 'em."

"I mean it. Do you ever feel like you don't quite fit in?" she asked. "Like maybe you missed a memo that everyone else in our age group got?"

He considered it. "When you put it that way, yeah. I totally thought I was the only one." He pointed over the mountains directly west of them. "Here's an example of how my serious nature doesn't fit in with the crowd," he tried to pass it off as a joke, but it failed. "You can't see it from here,

33

but in 2002 there was a record-setting fire that burned over 130,000 acres on the other side of those mountains."

"The mountains right next to us? I don't think I knew about that one," she said. "We still lived in Mississippi then."

Then he gestured southwest to the mountains at the edge of the city. "If you know what to look for, you can still see a burn scar even from this far away from the 2012 fire. More than 500,000 people could see that one from their living rooms, since it burned so high on the mountainside. When you get closer, you can see all the trees up there are just sticks now. But the grass has finally started to come back."

"That's when I was in college. Mom said she had ash and embers landing on her porch in Garnet." Jessie sighed. "And the next year, she had to evacuate because of another fire close by. She came up north to stay with me at my apartment that time."

"All the fires. That's why I can't take a day off," he said. "I think about 'em all the time. I'm always watching for smoke. But, like the other day, I was the first one to spot that grass fire at the lake. It could have really turned into something big, right in town, if we hadn't stopped it."

"You were on duty then, right?" she asked.

"Yeah. At least I get paid to be paranoid some of the time."

"It really comes naturally to you, doesn't it?"

"Yep."

They both looked into the distance. She said, "The blue sky gets hidden by that haze."

He agreed. "From the California fires burning now, the smoke reaches all the way here. Imagine what it's like out there today."

They surveyed the view, and she challenged him again.

"Old feelings, from childhood... Sometimes it hurts too much to admit they're even there. But if you don't, it's kind of like seeing a fire start and ignoring it." She spoke gently. "But I think right now you're ready for someone to listen to you."

There's nothing to tell, he said to himself. *Well, if there's nothing to tell, why is it so hard when I actually think about when our family fell apart?* He'd been trying to put everything back together ever since, but it was like a puzzle with missing pieces. His head ached.

He barely knew Jessie, and yet she had this effect on him, like beautiful, sweet truth serum. He was willing to talk, it dawned on him. They started walking again. She took his hand, a sign of encouragement, and then let go. He liked the fact that they were almost the same height. *Focus, Prentice.*

He puffed out a breath of air. "Okay. You asked for it. Here it is." He hesitated. "We had one really hard summer, when my mom left us and right after that my brother died."

"Oh my gosh. How old were you?"

"I was five. But I've moved past it now. I'm fine."

She paused before answering. "That's a lot to move past, Prentice."

He didn't answer immediately, and then tried to make it a joke. "It was probably hard for my dad, too. He was already divorced by his first wife before he married Mom. And then she left him too." Not so funny. "Anyway, in elementary school, they sent me to the counselor for a long time. She wanted me to talk about things I didn't want to think about."

"You were so young. That must have been hard."

"I didn't understand what had even happened." He felt comfortable with Jessie, at ease in a way that lowered his natural defenses. They rounded a bend in the trail. "Anyway, my brother William was two years older than me," Prentice heard himself say. "He stayed in his room. He read a lot. He didn't want to hang out with me."

"Oh?"

"William was so much like Dad, serious and smart. He got an airplane model for Christmas, and Dad actually spent time showing him how to paint it. I remember he told William he'd always wanted to do model building when he was little."

"Did he spend time with you?

"Nah. I was just too little to do those things. I tried to be like William doing his models, but with my coloring book. It wasn't enough for Dad. "

"Hm. That must have felt kind of unfair?"

"It sure did. Mom was alone a lot, too, or singing songs or reading books with me. It seemed like if Dad spent time away from work, it was with William. I played outside in a fort made of tree branches I found in the yard. I asked Dad to come out and see it, but he never did. He said maybe when I was older, we would have more in common." A bitter pill. "That hasn't worked out so well..."

"You mentioned coloring before. I liked coloring when I was little, too. It was something I could control," Jessie said. "I could scribble and scribble when I felt mad, and no one cared. Well, until my 'Tiger Grandma,' came to live with us."

Prentice said, "What you've told me about your grandma already sounds so much like my dad. He was all about coloring inside the lines, but I couldn't do that. I was a scribbler, believe it or not. Even though now I'm a neat-freak."

"Yep. But I get the feeling your mom wasn't as structured."

"No," he said. "She was creative and colorful, like your mom. I didn't understand it when I was little, but she was the one who brought all the warmth into the house. By the time our house... well, after it burned, she wasn't there to make it homey again. Dad got it repaired and bought new furniture, but he just left the walls blank."

Jessie whistled softly. "Oh, my gosh, and your mom left around the same time your house burned?"

"All in the same summer. Really heavy. I try not to think about it." He cleared his throat grasped for lighter topic. *I can't believe she got all that out of me.* "I really like your mom's house. Really welcoming."

Jessie didn't miss a beat but instead went along with his lead. "I'm glad she's painting again. She went through a rough time for a while, but she's doing better now."

Prentice smiled. "And her dog, he's so friendly. What breed is he, a Lab?"

"Yes, Casey's a cutie. He keeps her company while my dad's gone on a road trip."

"Maybe we should've had a dog when I was little. Then my mom would've had someone to talk to besides me and William." He attempted to joke his way out of another hole, but his brow furrowed. "My dad was hard to be around. He still is. You never know if he's going to say nothing at all, or lash out at me. You. Anyone, I mean."

"Sounds like you take the brunt of it now," she said. "That must've been hard for all of you when she left."

"My mom was the one who made it all work. She'd play her guitar in the evening. I could hear from upstairs when I was supposed to be sleeping." Now that he'd started talking, unexpectedly, it was hard to stop. It felt like rainwater racing down a burned hillside.

"The Christmas before she took off, I got a new 1998 calendar. It was the Magic School Bus." He grinned slightly. "Mom made a big deal about how I was turning five years old in July and I would go to kindergarten in the fall. We marked off the days on the calendar with colored pens, and these red heart stickers for special events. When she left, it was just a few days before the heart sticker that marked my birthday."

He gestured to a fallen log beside the trail so they could sit down in the shade. The hot Colorado wind had picked up. They drank from their water bottles, and as she listened, Jessie wrenched a few vines of bindweed from the ground with one hand.

"I was pretty young, but I knew she wasn't acting like her normal self. My biggest worry, though, was about my birthday cake. Usually, Mom made a big deal out of our cakes, but not that year." He looked at Jessie. "I asked William about it before my birthday came, and as usual he told me to leave him alone and just to go ask Mom."

"And?" she asked.

"I didn't want to ask her, because she'd already been acting so weird. Crying all the time. Not cooking dinner anymore. Stuff like that. But I puffed up and asked anyway, something about the kind of cake I wanted. She said, 'Maybe Dad will make your cake this year.' That's when I knew for sure something was wrong, because Dad never went in the kitchen." He paused. "Also, we never joke around in my family."

"So then she left?"

"Yep. One morning while my dad was at work, she put on her flowy yellow sundress, packed two suitcases and her guitar, and made us some sandwiches. She told us she had to go away for a while, and she would send us presents as soon as she got there. She said Dad would be home soon, and he would take care of us. She said to listen to Dad and help him out. Then she kissed us and left with a man who picked her up from the house."

"Wow," Jessie said softly. "Who was it? What did you do?"

"William and I were good kids. We sat in the driveway for a while, waiting I guess, to see if she'd come back. It just didn't seem real." He lapsed into silence, remembering it. "I never found out who he was."

"You must have been scared." Jessie loosened her chestnut brown hair from its ponytail, shook it out, and replaced the rubber band. "Did you call your dad?"

"No, we didn't. Dad came home after a while, just like she said he would. He must have left work early that day, though. I never thought of that."

Prentice watched Jessie for a few moments without continuing. Ever since he'd met her, he'd been wanting to really study her face, take her in, but it felt awkward. This kind of conversation had gotten so personal, and now it was awkward *not* to make eye contact. She had lively eyes and an inviting smile. Her nose was straight and perfect. She'd said her mom's family was from China, and her dad's parents both came from the Netherlands back in the day. *I could just sit and take her in.*

"And then?" she prompted.

"Oh." He came back to the present. "By then William and I were hungry, and we were sitting at the counter eating the sandwiches Mom made. Dad wasn't surprised to see us home by ourselves. He told us, 'Boys, your mom is gone. We're on our own now. You two need to stick together.' And that was about it." He paused. "I realized just now that he didn't say, 'We three need to stick together.' Hmm... Anyway, he found us a babysitter for the next day so he could go to work." Prentice cocked his head. "I wonder how he did that."

Jessie asked, "Maybe your mom found the babysitter before she left?"

"Maybe. that would make more sense. Mom was the social one with all the connections. And after the fire..." Prentice shook his head with some unspoken thought. "Mom was gone. William and I lost our routine. Dad had his work to do during the day at his office in the city. But in the evenings, he didn't know what to do with us. We all were just lost."

"It must have been so confusing."

"I didn't understand what was going on. Nobody explained anything. All I knew was that our normal life was blown to pieces. For dinner, Dad made macaroni and cheese from the box, and hot dogs. Lots of hot dogs."

"Food makes very strong memories..." Jessie mused.

"The babysitter we had for the weekdays did okay, but she wasn't my mom. This sounds stupid, but she cut up the apples the wrong way. She watched TV, soap operas. I watched them with her once. The announcer said it was 'All My Children,' but there weren't any children in it. I thought that was pretty dumb." Prentice laughed a little and Jessie joined him. "So William and I just did our own thing. He worked on his models or read books, and I went outside to the fort or played in the dirt."

He shrugged. "After a few days, I actually wished someone would make me take a bath or brush my teeth. So much chaos. I asked Dad when she was coming back and Dad went completely nuts. He lost his temper and yelled at me. Told me to grow up and figure out how to do those jobs myself. Zero to a hundred in three seconds." Prentice stood up.

Jessie joined him, and shouldering their packs they set off, continuing their hike.

"How was William handling all this?" Jessie asked. "You haven't said much about him."

"No. He was always quiet anyway. He was pretty freaked out by Dad that night, too. I knew it, because after Dad slammed his office door, William actually got a bath going for me and found the toys and stuff Mom always got out for me under the sink. He sat on the floor and read a book while I was in the tub. I asked him when Mom was coming back, too. He told me not to think about it."

"Denial is disastrous," Jessie said.

"I was always sure she left because I pestered her about my birthday cake."

"You really took a heavy load on yourself."

He sighed. "I probably did later on." He waved one hand in the air as if to shift gears. "But you'll like this. Dad basically forgot it was my birthday that weekend, until I asked him about the cake. He punted and took us to McDonald's like that'd been his plan all along."

"Do you ever hear from your mom?"

He slowed down, and Jessie matched his speed. "No. For a long time, I hoped I'd hear from her. She said she would come back. But I never saw her. No cards or presents."

"You must've felt so angry."

"I should be more angry, I guess. But I really just missed her. It was a mystery I never knew the answer to."

Jessie gave his shoulder a squeeze as they walked, which he surprised himself by leaning into.

"When I was in high school, I asked Dad if we could

paint the white walls in my room. I was hoping for black or something."

"Like a normal teenager," she smiled.

"But then completely out of nowhere, he said, 'Decorating was your mother's area of expertise, but she's never coming back.' And I said, 'What do you mean, never?' and he said, 'She's dead.'"

"What? Oh no!"

"Until then, I had imagined she was out there somewhere, and I might see her one day and find out why she never contacted me like she promised." Prentice put both his hands out wide in front of him in a gesture of frustration. "That was a horrible way to hear she was really gone."

"Oh my gosh!"

"Dad threw the words out like that and then pulled himself back into his shell. I never found out when she died or what happened. But that's when any anger I had left for her switched full-force to my dad."

"Oh, Prentice. I'm so sorry."

"It actually gets worse. Right after that was when William was killed. But I don't wanna talk about that right now." He shook his hands out in front of him again. Trying to lighten it up, he picked up the pace again and said, "I haven't thought about it in a long time."

"Really? Well, it's more than that. It's your own mom and brother you're talking about. Even your body remembers events from your childhood. When stuff like this happens to you when you're little, it continues to affect you as an adult."

Prentice slowed and gave her his full attention. "You sound like you've thought about this before."

She nodded. "Yep. It's been a big help to figure out what's hidden in there. Helps me deal with it now so I don't explode or fall apart."

He was surprised. "I haven't known you very long, but you seem pretty together."

"Thanks, but it's an illusion. You seem together too, on the surface." She paused. "Inside, it's a different story." He could tell she meant it just as a statement, not an indictment of herself. Or him.

"You said I'm always trying to fix things that are not mine to control," he said. They'd reached the steep switch-backs. Prentice reached for Jessie's hand again as they descended, and she accepted. The decomposed granite made their path slippery.

"Yes, I find myself doing that sometimes, too," she answered. "Does it sound true for you?"

"My dad still lives in Garnet, way on up the hill on the west side of town." He avoided answering her directly. "I convinced him to do wildfire mitigation in his yard. That was a mystery in itself. Oh, do you know what that is?"

"Not exactly."

"That's true of a lot of people, unfortunately," he said. "Mitigation is not clear-cutting all the trees like some people think. It just means making sure the zone around your house is less likely to ignite. You do it by thinning the trees and vegetation and keeping fuel, like branches and pine needles, away from your house. Mowing the grass. That kind of basic maintenance."

"That doesn't sound so hard," she said.

"No, especially if you keep at it," he went on. "If I hear one more person say, 'Oh, but I can't cut down a tree. I moved here for the trees,' I will puke on their shoes. They think they live in a suburban utopia and Mother Nature will take care of everything, so they don't have to thin out tree seedlings or rake leaves."

He continued. "The thing that frustrates me at Dad's is

I'm doing all the work for free, and all he does is question me, even though it's what I do for my career. But the other day I was there working, he acted odd, even for him. He never even came outside to see what I was doing or to remind me which trees he didn't want to cut."

She nodded. "Well, on one hand that's nice of you..." She trailed off. "I don't know, I haven't met him, but it does sound like you're trying to solve something for him."

It was getting hotter, and they sat down on a flat rock under a tree at the bottom of the hill. The grass at their feet was dry and crumbly.

She looked at him. "You're responsible for the whole world, aren't you, Prentice? You even have three jobs." She ticked them off on her fingers. "The ride-sharing app, to rescue stranded people. Firefighting. Property cleanup for wildfires. Trying to save people all the time. "

He deflected. "We live in such a beautiful place. But we need to be more responsible about maintaining it."

"Right, 'we' do need to be responsible for the wildfire risk." She put air quotes around the word 'we' as she said it. "Prentice, I'm talking about you taking on so much without setting boundaries for yourself. I used to be like that, but I'm trying not to anymore. The world is so much bigger than I am. I can't do it all by myself."

She kept speaking this new language that both annoyed and intrigued him. "Whaddaya mean?" he asked.

"I used to blame myself all the time for not being as good as Grandmother wanted me to be at school. My mom... it's funny, I know she spent her whole childhood being yelled at by Grandmother too, but when it came time for Grandmother to pick on me, Mom never defended me. She let her win, because Grandmother was in charge of the universe."

"Your mom seems pretty chill now."

Jessie nodded. "She's been working through a lot of her own issues. It's good to hear her playing her music again and doing her art."

"I was impressed with your mom's sound system the other day, I've gotta admit."

The afternoon sun beat down as they stood up and walked side by side on the flat, open trail. Prentice felt more tired than after a long day of cutting back bushes, trimming trees, and chipping slash. No guarantees if the work would save someone's house, but it was way more straightforward than talking about feelings and bad memories. This lady was full of surprises. She really made him think.

"Saving the world...." he said. "My mom told me a story once about a couple walking along the beach. The tide had stranded thousands of starfish on the sand, and they were going to dry out and die in the sun.

"The woman started picking them up and throwing the starfish back into the sea, one by one. The man said it wouldn't make any difference, since there were so many starfish and she couldn't save them all. She tossed another one in and told him, 'Well, it made a difference to that one.'" He removed his hat and raked his fingers through his hair. "It helps me remember my mom."

"She must have been a very kind person."

He ruminated out loud. "She was, but why did she tell me that story? It makes it hard to stop trying, even when I'm tired, and it seems like no one is listening." There were nights now when he couldn't sleep, thinking about all the starfish he wouldn't be able to save. All the people who refused to hear the simple message about being stewards of the forest.

"It's kind of like the way I can't stop pulling weeds," she admitted.

"Oh, I get that now..." He adjusted his pack straps. "People always say things like, 'It's a good thing it rained this *month*. Now the fire danger is gone.' But they're so wrong! The fuel is still there. As soon as it dries out again, like it always does in Colorado, we're back to Red Flag Warnings... even in winter."

Jessie said, "This is heavy. You're trying to carry all of this on your shoulders? It's a worldwide problem." She paused. "I see what you mean about the starfish. But it's such a big beach."

They approached the parking lot where Jessie's car was. Prentice almost didn't hear her, but pushed on. "Yeah, a big beach." He felt lighter as he said some of these thoughts out loud.

He said, "You know, once in middle school, we were all playing kickball in the gym. Everyone on my team was standing along the front of the stage, waiting for their turn to kick. I was standing off to the side, but no one from our team was ready to kick the ball. They pitched the ball to the middle of our group, and I ran out from the side of the group into the center, and I kicked it. The outfielder caught it on the fly. It was the third out. We lost."

"That's too bad...." She tipped her head to one side, and her ponytail swung out again.

"That's not the point. The stupid thing is, there actually was a guy from my team standing there, ready to kick it. I just couldn't see him. Afterwards, he grabbed me by the shirt and said, 'What the heck was that, Keene?' Then he punched me in the stomach and went into the locker room."

"That's called an overdeveloped sense of responsibility," she said, with another genuine smile. "You probably did it because you had so much crazy stuff happen when you were little." She shrugged and peered ahead to the end of the trail.

He forced a laugh. *She does know, somehow.* "You haven't heard the half of it," he said as they reached the gravel parking lot. "Hey, why're you smiling about it? It's depressing." He swatted her arm lightly with the back of his hand and smiled tentatively.

"I'm smiling because you're not doomed. And neither am I."

"I never said I was doomed." As they put their packs in the trunk, he said, "Jessie, I hate to tell you this, but you've got dirt on your nose." *It's so cute.*

"Oh gosh. Thanks for telling me. That's a real friend who'll tell you when you have something on your face." She looked in the side mirror and lifted the hem of her t-shirt to rub her nose. "There, better. Thanks."

They opened all the car doors, and Jessie turned the fan on to let out the heat. She drove back to Pioneersburg with the windows down. Except for the wind, it was quiet in the car, but not uncomfortable. Companionable silence.

When they got to her apartment, where Prentice had parked his white truck, she locked up her car and said, "I'm beat. Will you wait here a minute while I go get something I want to show you?"

"Sure." While she went inside, he transferred his pack full of empty water bottles to his truck.

In a few minutes she was back, holding a piece of paper printed in calligraphy.

Prentice glanced at it without really taking in what it said. It started with, "Family dysfunction rolls down from generation to generation, like a fire in the woods..."

"This looks heavy," he told her.

"I know," she said. "Will you save it for later?"

"Sure," and he started up the truck. *Weird.* Jessie waved at him. *She's cute and a breath of fresh air, but pretty intense.* He waved back.

As he drove home, more of Jessie's words bounced around in his head. "It's not your fault your dad's alone," and, "You can live your own life without feeling guilty."

"How do I do that?" he asked the sky.

www.Tinderbox.tips - Flying Embers, Part I:

- U.S. Forest Service official Dr. Jack D. Cohen says flying embers are burning pieces of wood blown by the wind.
- It's usually not a wall of fire that destroys homes during a wildfire.
- It's the flying embers which pile up in crevices, smolder, and trigger an ignition.

T he next day, he looked at the printout, shoved in the corner of the kitchen counter. He had to read it. "A fire in the woods... Face the flames...." The dark letters jumped off the page. *Thanks, I think.*

Prentice picked up the sheet of paper and added it to the tray that held a plate he'd stacked with crackers, salami and cheese. Sitting in the only chair he had, a zero-gravity chair, he pushed the buttons to elevate his feet and tip the seat back so he could think.

Jessie was so sincere about giving this to him. She even

seemed happy about it. Why? It was depressing! "Family dysfunction taking down everything in its path." *Honestly*?

Well, he *had* told her some things about his dad. "Rolls down from generation to generation"? *Big deal! That's just the way it is. You just go on and live your life, despite whatever junk happened to you.* That's what everyone does. Why write a poem about it?

"I can't set it aside, though," he said to the empty room. "There's something important here." He munched on the crackers and thought about what Jessie said about not trying to fix his dad.

"... Until one person in a generation has the courage to turn and face the flames."

Fueled by the few examples he'd shared with her, he analyzed his situation.

Was the way he lived now so bad? *Look at how great I'm doing!* He was a line firefighter. He and the crew saved people's lives. Trees were healthier because of his forest management. People were safer because of him. Three jobs. Plenty of money.

Yeah, and I argue with the chief every single shift. And I pick fights with little old ladies. It bothered him, but it also made him want to prove them wrong. Every single one of them.

Going home to an empty apartment. Calling his dad on weeknights to check on him. No social life. Trouble sleeping. Eating an entire bag of cookies in the middle of the night. Yes, it bothered him. He wasn't living to please his dad. He didn't even have a chance, with the ghost of William lurking around, making it hard for Prentice to succeed in his dad's eyes. *So why do I keep hoping for approval?*

His dad lived in the same little house perched on a hillside overflowing with pine trees, accessible only via a steep mountain road full of switchbacks. He drove religiously to work in the city every day and then hid in his nest in Garnet the rest of the time. Prentice had never been able to break into that fortress, the walls around his dad.

"That person brings peace to their ancestors and spares the children that follow," proclaimed the printout.

My God, how does she know these things about me?

He wanted to ask her more questions. What if she was right?

It was unreal that he'd only known her a few days. She was really pretty, and up-front. She wasn't crazy, either. She seemed to really understand him. *I'm not running away on this one. I've got to try something new.*

He grabbed his phone off the floor next to his chair and pressed her contact number. As it rang, he got up and paced around the room.

Jessie answered, "Hey Prentice. Glad you called. I was thinking of you."

"Oh. Really?" *That's a good sign.*

"Yes! At church this morning we talked about letting go of control. Letting God be in charge."

So much for something light. "I'm not really a church person."

"That's okay," she said breezily. "A lot of people say that. Anyway, it made me think about what you said about your dad. How he never talked to you about all the things that happened to you. To both of you."

Well, I guess she is reading my mind. "About that, I don't know why I told you all those things yesterday. It's in the past."

She laughed. "You can say that, but that's not how it works. Don't worry about it, though, okay?"

"I'm not. Honest."

"Have you ever thought how it's made you who you are today?"

"Huh?" *This is not going the way I planned.*

"It's the same with me. It's the same with all of us."

He paused. "What do you mean, 'us'?"

Rather than answer, she changed the subject. "What have you been up to today?"

He blinked, disconcerted. "Chores." He managed an answer. "Laundry and stuff. I shuttled a few clients..."

"I had a feeling... This is your day off, right?"

"Technically."

"It doesn't sound like a day off to me. It sounds like you're trying to prove something to somebody."

"Not really..."

She laughed. "I don't believe you. How about doing something spontaneous? I was just getting ready to go kayaking. Want to come along?"

"Oh! Sure." *How does she do this to me?*

"You've never been kayaking, have you?"

"No."

"Do you ever do anything just for fun, Prentice? Be honest."

"Fun. Hm." He chuckled softly. "Chainsawing is fun... in a way. I like lifting weights. I read a lot. Usually, I just try to be productive. Did you know, to have a healthy forest, you have to 'be' the fire if you're not going to let the fires burn through..." He trailed off. He could hear her rolling her eyes on the other end of the line.

"No firefighter talk today. Or wildfire talk either."

"I'm sort of out of practice on fun."

"You sure fit the picture, Prentice."

"What does that mean? What picture?"

She continued, "Never mind. Hey, I've already got my

kayak on the roof rack. I could come by and pick you up now. Sound good?"

Of course it sounds good. But what am I doing?

~

THEY WENT BACK TO TWO-MILE LAKE, NOT A BIG EXPEDITION. Just a windy afternoon under the same cloudless sky they'd had for weeks. Dust gusted up from the dry trail around the lake and the burn scar from the grass fire next to the parking lot.

They had to take turns with the single-person kayak, so after Jessie showed him how to operate it, she sat on the shore on a blanket. He experimented with the steering pedals and the two-bladed paddle, trying to travel in a straight line, and then a smooth loop. He got the hang of it after a while.

Then Jessie took a turn while Prentice sat on the blanket. The water dribbled off the paddle blades and caught the sunlight. She practiced flipping the kayak upside down and righting it again. She was soaked. Her hair was plastered to her head, and the ponytail dripped water down her back.

He tried to ignore the haze in the air from all the western wildfires in progress. The sun was hot and there was zero humidity, so by the time Prentice took another turn and came back in, Jessie was mostly dried off.

They sat together on the blanket. Prentice saw a pinpoint of sunlight prism-focused into a spot on the dry grass. It was a beam of sunlight going through the plastic water bottle. As he moved the bottle, he explained. "A guy told me once he saw a fire start in a dry stump. Get this, it was the same stump he was sitting on at the time!"

"A fire started because of a water bottle?"

"Yeah. Fuel is fuel. Smokey Bear can't stop all the fires."

"You're obsessed." she said.

"I know…"

"No, I kinda don't think you do. You work all the time. Why is that?"

"Why do you ask so many questions?"

She looked down at the blanket. "I'm sorry, Prentice. Sometimes I revert to my old over-responsible self and try to solve everyone else's problems."

"I can't believe I'm telling you so much…. But it's good. It's good to have someone listen, you know?" He said. "This is not like me," he added.

"I thought so. We have a lot in common." She hesitated. "I know I said no wildfire talk before, but maybe you could tell me how you got so obsessed with fires in the first place?"

Well, there was the fire when I was little, but there's no way I'm going to talk about that one. "It's a long list," he said. "The summer before fourth grade, 2002, a wildfire burned a hundred thousand acres up in the mountains."

She said, "That was the one you pointed out yesterday." She took two cans of pop from the cooler and offered him one.

"The wind blew storms of burning debris ahead of it. Leapfrog action, spot fires popped up. Hundreds of homes went up, one at a time." He ran his hand over his hair, remembering. "It wasn't the big wall of flames that people think of that was so destructive. It was the sparks in the fuel. We watched it every night on the news. It was the biggest fire on record for Colorado. Since then, we've had more, bigger wildfires all across the west, of course. And here, too." He sipped some of the cool drink.

"Your obsession makes sense. I can see why you're kind

of intense about it, the prevention part especially. I can identify."

He corrected her. "Not prevention, that's not reasonable. Just hoping people will plan ahead, so their houses can defend themselves when the owners have evacuated to safety."

"Right, instead of pretending a fire will never happen..." She pondered that. "You sound like me in some ways."

He sighed. "Being like you would be better than being like my dad." They shared a chuckle. "I wonder what you're obsessed with."

She said, "I'll tell you a lot more about me sometime when you have a year to spare."

"I bet you have quite a story, Jessie. Actually, I've been thinking a lot about what you said." He made air quotes in front of him as he said, "about the flames of family dysfunction." He laughed out loud now, hoping it would turn out to be a joke, and they could talk about something else.

No such luck. "I could tell something had upset you. It was worth the risk to share that with you."

Oh geez. "You're a mind reader? Trust me, talking about myself is not what I normally do."

"Yeah. I can tell that too."

He rubbed his eyes with his hands. "You must bring out the best in me."

Jessie inhaled. "I don't always invade people's personal space like this. You know that, right?"

"What, I'm just the lucky one?"

"No. I mean, yes. I just have this feeling you're ready to face some of those flames, like the ones between you and your dad yesterday, before we went to the lake? Just for example?"

He laid on his back on the blanket and bent his knees,

his arms behind his head. *Okay, fine.* "You know the cleanup work I've been doing at his house?"

"You said you were frustrated because he wouldn't help, didn't seem interested."

"Uh-huh. Yesterday I went over and finally got the last of it done, for this year anyway. It looks great. Last year, I even carved out an escape route through the trees to the gravel road up behind the property. It's a model wildfire risk reduction project. I even planted ignition-resistant plants along the driveway."

"Oh, that's a neat term."

"Plants like penstemon, rock soapwort—they're fire resistant." He raised his eyebrows at her amused expression and, laughing, said, "You know, Snow-in-summer? Blanket Flower? It's ready for a magazine layout, right?"

"Gotcha. I know those plants. So, what was the problem?" Jessie asked.

"He won't admit it's good. He didn't even thank me. He asked me who was gonna take care of it. Said he didn't want to be out there pulling weeds and stuff. He just keeps finding fault with what I do. Pushing me away."

"That *is* rough," Jessie said.

"He's probably thinking about William and how he would've turned out to be this perfect son. Just like him. I can't live up to that."

"How do you know that?" she asked. "Have you asked him?"

"No way, but I can't just give up on Dad, whatever he thinks of me. He doesn't have anyone else."

"Well, he's a grown man. He can take care of himself."

"That's the thing, he doesn't! He works all the time, and he's not eating right. He's a total couch potato. He doesn't have any friends. The only people he talks to are at work."

"That's not your fault."

"I didn't say it was. But the people at work are not going to check up on him."

"Nope. They're not. Not their job either," she said.

Prentice sat up again. "You're making it sound like I'm overdoing it."

"I'm not saying anything. You're saying it yourself."

Why am I explaining this to her? She doesn't know what it was like. "But I have to make sure everything is all right."

"Okay. If you say so." It could have been a taunt, but it wasn't. She was listening to him so intently.

"I don't wanna talk about this."

"I've gotta say, you do sound like him, Prentice."

He looked at her again. "That's ridiculous."

"He doesn't take care of himself. You don't either." She shrugged and smiled. "Why would I make that up?"

"I dunno." *Why am I trusting you, Jessie DeGroot?* He tried to relax his shoulders and neck. *Because everything you say sounds true once I think about it. I just never thought about it this way before.* "Here's the other thing from yesterday in particular. He really wasn't acting right. He didn't come outside to harass me, and when I went in the house, he was still in his pajamas. That's definitely not like him."

"Maybe he's turning over a new leaf and staying out of your way?"

"No, this was different. I noticed when I went into his office upstairs, he had trouble balancing when he stood up, and he had the computer screen enlarged so the text was huge. I asked him about it, but he said he was fine."

"Well, then he's probably fine."

"I don't think he would tell me if he wasn't. That's the problem."

Jessie scooted a quarter turn so she was sitting cross-legged, facing him. "Prentice, may I make an observation?" She proceeded as he agreed. "Over these last few days, I've thought of two words that describe you. Do you want to know what they are?"

He shrugged. *I knew I'd screw this up. Might as well get it over with.* "Why not?"

"The first word was, 'exhausted.'"

"What?" He squinted at her and pounded the ground next to him twice with his fist. "You've got to be kidding me." He sucked in a breath and looked away. "Exhausted? How can I be exhausted?"

Her milk-chocolate eyes brimmed with understanding.

This is ridiculous. Turning back to her, he said, "Dad's counting on me. I'm in great condition. I've been working out..." *She's right. I'm completely exhausted. That can't be. That won't work.*

He laid back on the blanket, closing his eyes, arm over his face to block out the sun. *I actually don't know anything about him or why he acts the way he does.* "Yeah..." He puffed air out of his lungs into the hot day. It was hard to draw in the next breath, and he didn't ask about the second word.

She waited a few minutes, then said, "I'm gonna do one more loop in the kayak, and then we can head back?" He nodded and didn't say more or open his eyes.

He didn't talk very much on the ride to Pioneersburg, but finally, the silence bothered him. "What you said... it wasn't mean, or rude. It was just... true. I need to think about it some more."

She said, "Okay, sounds good. Call me later if you want," but she didn't push it or ask more questions. "I'm going to D.C. this week for work, but I'll have my phone."

She pulled into the parking lot at his apartment complex and got out of her car to offer him a hug. He couldn't remember the last time anyone had hugged him with such warmth. She was so amazing, a serendipitous blessing. Despite the deep, uncomfortable questions. Instead of being repelled by the parts of him that were less than perfect, she took time to understand what he was saying.

Alone in his apartment, he collapsed into the zero-gravity chair. He didn't want it to be true, but she was right. Prentice Keene, the smart, strong firefighter, really was exhausted.

5

"The wild turkeys show up more often now," said Marlene. The homeowners association manager found Prentice as he worked in the neighborhood common area to let him know about positive comments she'd received from residents.

"That's no surprise," he said. "Now that the trees aren't jammed in close thickets, the ones that remain don't have to compete for moisture, sunlight, and soil nutrients." This was his favorite topic, and it was better when a willing student appeared. "Grass and herbaceous plants can come in, so the forest floor isn't a pine straw desert anymore."

Marlene agreed. "These trees don't have the three-foot diameter of a 'real' Ponderosa that smells like heaven, but in time, they will. And meanwhile, we have wild turkeys." She was one of the most positive people Prentice knew.

He enjoyed working on fire risk reduction in Gwilym Acres, cutting brush and stacking slash in a common area owned by the HOA. They had a standing contract with him, and it was evident it was paying off both for Prentice and the neighborhood, as more residents hired him for advice and work.

What drove wildfires was fuel, weather, and topography. People could only control the amount of fuel. They could do tree thinning and pine needle raking and make order from chaos. Simple property maintenance could make a difference when burning sticks and embers blew into their yards one day.

Educating people is the key, but how to get them to hear the simple message? He posted blurbs on his Tinderbox.tips website explaining basic concepts for those who'd listen.

People didn't even know they'd inherited a problem in their mountain town. The whole area had been logged in the 1850s to build Pioneersburg, and now the second-growth trees overcrowded a forest where the natural ten-year fire cycles had been suppressed. The result was a diseased, stunted, sad facsimile of what the forest should have looked like, except in subdivisions like Gwilym Acres, where he was working today.

This was all great. All goals he'd been striving for. Making order from chaos.

Orderly thinking calmed him down, making things line up where they used to be chaotic. *Like the trucks in the sand table in preschool. Building forts out of branches in the yard. That's when life wasn't out of control.* Mom hadn't left yet. All the other bad stuff hadn't caved in his life. *If William were here, I wonder what he would do about Dad being so stubborn.*

Today, everything Jessie had said kept ringing in his head and overshadowing the troubling memories. He needed time to think about what it meant. He was really glad to be able to just work and not talk to anyone for long stretches of time.

At the end of the day, he did a property evaluation for a

prospective residential client in the same neighborhood. He perched on an extension ladder, grabbed a handful of dry pine needles from the gutter and threw the clump two stories to the ground. This was a fun way to get their attention.

"I know that doesn't look like much," he told the home-owner, a middle-aged woman. He clambered down the rungs in his steel-toe boots, "accidentally" slipping off the last one as he descended. "Whoa!" He enjoyed the adrenaline rush.

In his head, his dad's voice blared. *Get serious, Prentice.*

He shook off the thought as he landed on the ground and addressed the woman standing near the ladder. "The National Fire Protection Association recommends that you clean out pine needles and leaves on a regular basis to make your house safer. There's no time to do that when the fire is already coming."

"I'm sure a few pine needles won't make a difference," she said.

"That's what a lot of people think," Prentice shook his head and held her glance. "But you know how you start a campfire with kindling and a spark? Same thing in a wildfire. When flying embers land on this fine, dry material in the gutter, it will ignite. It's not a good combination to allow flames to get near the wood siding near the gutter."

She frowned where he pointed at the roof valleys full of needles.

"Anything that encourages direct flame contact could cause real trouble." He went on. "When you're doing wildfire risk reduction, it's important to start with the house itself, so you don't get overwhelmed. Keep it free of fuel for the first five feet out from the house. That's easy work you and your husband can do yourselves, if you want to reduce your costs."

She nodded. "Start with the house and work out from there."

"Right!" *Yahoo!* "Next, let's examine the vegetation and trees around your house. You have fuel here, like the tall grass, that could draw a ground fire toward your house. And when burning firebrands land, they will find plenty to feed them and keep them alive."

Her smile went away. People seldom wanted to hear about changing their landscaping and didn't see how mowing the grass would help in a wildfire. "You boys will come help me if there's a fire," she said. "That's why I pay taxes."

"Yes, we'll sure try. But remember, there's thousands of houses in Garnet now, but we only have a few fire trucks. It would help if you raked the leaf litter out from under your steps and had some clear space around your house." He gestured at the scrub oak touching the wood siding.

She pursed her lips. "I guess you better show me what else you recommend." He made a note on his assessment sheet, and they headed around the house so he could finish explaining what concerned him and write up an estimate. *One more starfish headed back into the ocean.*

That night at home, he stayed up late to read more firebrands research and post summaries on the Tinderbox website late into the night. A Jessie-like voice in his head said, "Honestly? You're staying up to work? Or you're working late because you're so numb you can't fall asleep?" The Star Trek Vulcan Mind Meld was nothing compared to Jessie's intuition about him. She'd said she used to be more like him, so she understood, and he believed her. It was as if she'd opened him up and found a firepit full of glowing coals.

Exhausted. His throat felt tight again. *That can't be right. I'm just responsible. And detail-oriented. Good with money. Focused. Independent.* And in the edges of his consciousness, it crept up on him how much he was like his dad in certain ways.

Out loud, he said to himself in a joking tone, "It's a good thing she went out of town. She's wearing me out. I need a break."

His voice seemed loud in the spareness of his apartment. Who was he speaking to?

"All right, I'm exhausted. So why can't I get to sleep? I'm living the only life I know how to live. What am I supposed to change?"

Chief Rugen sat at his desk Wednesday afternoon. Prentice tried again to get through to him. Time for Round 9 of an ongoing fight. He took a deep breath and knocked on his door.

"Chief. Gotta minute?"

Rugen grunted a reply but didn't look up.

"Why don't we offer some workshops for residents to come to the station and learn from us firefighters about wildfire risk reduction? I could teach them. Maybe I could get some other guys to help. We can get brochures from the office of emergency management to hand out."

He turned to Prentice. "Hold on right there. I've told ya' a hundred times. We're not going to scare people into doing anything. They have a right to keep their properties the way they want. And I'm not going to go around telling anyone we can't save their house if there's a fire. Next year we're having a mill levy increase election, and if they don't have confidence in us, they'll vote it down."

"I know, Chief, but if the residents helped us, if they cleared out their extra trees, thought about their own evacuation planning..."

"This is what I mean about ya', Keene! If we get a wildfire through here, it'll be a total disaster no matter what we do. I don't want you bringing this up to people unless they're the ones asking you questions. Got it?"

"It doesn't have to be a total disaster if we get people to prepare for it. I've been trying to show you Cohen's research that proves that neighborhoods can be fire-adapted. Then more houses would survive!"

Rugen's eyes were steely. "I can't believe I have to say this, but I'd think of all people in this town, you'd be the one worrying the most about structure fires. You and your dad..."

He and Chief Rugen had this same argument about resident education all the time. However, this was the first time he mentioned Bill Keene. "What do you know about my dad? He doesn't have anything to do with you." Prentice blinked hard. He felt himself shooting backwards in time.

Suddenly, he was five years old again, sitting, shell-shocked, in the back of an ambulance. He remembered looking around. The babysitter was there too, lying very still on a white bed on wheels next to him. Her long black hair was so dark, all spread out on the white pillow. She was so pale.

A man wearing blue nitrile gloves put a plastic mask over Prentice's young face, with a clear thin tube attached to it. Everything smelled like acrid smoke. No idea where Dad was. *Whoa. Oh, my God.*

He had to sit down. He found a chair next to the Chief's desk and put his head in his hands. He had to breathe. *That happened before I went to kindergarten.* He didn't say any more, and neither did Rugen, who watched him and then pointedly went back to work.

Prentice sat there a little longer, trying to recover his equilibrium, and finally he got up and walked out to the kitchen. He gulped down a glass of water, then inhaled most of a bag of stale potato chips. *Why was Rugen talking as if he knew Dad?*

SOON, ANOTHER CALL CAME IN. *THANK GOD. I'VE GOTTA GET out of here.* It was another medical. It sounded like more of a hand-holding call than a real emergency, up in Forest Heights. The engine and the ambulance crawled up the mountain to help.

On the way up the hill, Prentice was back to fuming about his inability to get through to the chief. He beat himself up for his failure to get real wildfire preparedness work done right now when it mattered, when people could change the outcome. Didn't they remember all the wildfires right near Pioneersburg? They wouldn't be doomed when the next one came if they'd just listen.

Anger. That was what boiled inside him. On the outside, he looked fine and professional in his trim blue pants and blue t-shirt with the Garnet Fire emblem on it, or in his full Class A uniform. His biceps strained the sleeves of the t-shirt, and his dark-blond hair stuck straight up.

Inside, he was filled with fury at the unfairness of it all. His inability to make it better. There were fires burning all across the West right now, but they might as well have been on the moon. *What good am I doing people if I let them ignore me? I have to keep trying to get their attention.*

The crew arrived at the medical call. It was the same type of property as so many of them in Garnet, with bushes against the house and the yard over-filled with pines. As they checked out the patient, Prentice thought about the fire risks all over the property, all easily fixable before the arrival of the inevitable wildfire.

The man had indigestion as it turned out, not a heart attack. His wife thanked the crew as they got ready to go.

"Hold on!" Prentice told them, "I'd like to mention something to Mrs. Gannon."

Lt. Grimaldi gave Prentice a knowing look and said in his deep voice, "Firefighter Keene, this crew is heading back to Station #1 now."

Prentice pretended he hadn't heard him. *The road to hell is paved with good intentions.* Instead, he put on his best friendly face and approached the woman. *She ought to worry about something a lot more serious than indigestion.*

He launched into his wildfire risk reduction speech. He got so much momentum, it spilled out of urban firefighter territory into the well-practiced Tinderbox spiel he used during lot evaluations to drum up business. Mrs. Gannon was not receptive to the information, not in the least. Of course not. She wanted to be with her husband now that the paramedics had given him the all-clear.

Prentice couldn't stop. The words spilled out of his mouth as he pointed at the overcrowded pine trees only had puny branches at the top instead of all the way down the trunk. He kicked at junipers and scrub oak. He didn't care that she didn't want to hear it. He just needed to explain it.

Why won't she just listen? He followed her toward the front door, explaining things she had never asked about.

What work they should do, what was dangerous about their yard. How simple it would be to fix it…. And how to hire a company like Tinderbox to do it.

She went inside and closed the screen door. He talked right through it. She yelled, "I don't want to hear about this! Leave me alone!" She slammed the red-painted front door, and the house shook.

What's wrong with me?

Lt. Grimaldi and Owens appeared on either side of Prentice. They each grasped one of his arms at the bicep and led him back to the engine. *What did I just do?*

The drive back to Station #1 was silent.

Lt. Grimaldi walked Prentice into the chief's office himself. Rugen was getting ready to leave for the day, car keys already in his hand. Rugen looked at the lieutenant for an explanation. "This guy is out of control, Chief."

Rugen looked at Prentice but directed his question at Grimaldi and Owens. "What's goin' on?"

Owens started to explain, but Prentice interrupted her. He forced himself to focus on the chief instead of the floor. "I got carried away. I overdid it telling a resident about fire mitigation."

Owens interjected, "Unbelievable, Smokey! She called 9-1-1 for her husband. Then you started telling her about limbing pine trees. And you solicited work from her!"

"What?" Rugen lost it. His pale skin flushed with fury, but his voice was soft. "I've given ya' way too much leeway on this, Keene. That's it. No more warnings. You're suspended without pay until further notice while we review what to do with you. End… of… discussion."

Prentice started to defend himself. "I shouldn't have…"

Now the chief got loud. "No, ya' shouldn't have! I can't believe the gall of ya'. Get outta here. Right now."

"But Chief... I should finish my shift."

"Absolutely not. I do *not* want to see ya' here again until I talk to the board next week. Until then, you're not to set foot in this station." He pointed at the door. "Go!" He turned to Lt. Grimaldi, completely ignoring Prentice, and said, "See if ya' can get somebody from A Shift in here to cover for this ridiculous excuse for a firefighter until tomorrow's shift change."

Owens pushed the chief's door closed behind Prentice as he walked out.

He stood in the hallway, feeling sick. Walking briskly to the bathroom, he threw up in the toilet. His mind was blank, so much anger swirled around in it. So much heat ready to ignite. No idea what to do next. Complete and total rejection. And fury at himself, too. *I've ruined everything.*

He went down the hall to his locker, first just sitting on the metal bench without moving. Then he changed into civilian clothes. Put the gear back in the locker where it always goes. Follow the routine.

There's no routine to follow. I was supposed to be on shift until tomorrow morning. But now I'm not. Now what?

He got in his truck. His eyes burned, and his head felt full of molten lava. And grief. *I'm such an idiot.*

6

He ended up at his apartment, parked in his usual space. Mechanically, he took the keys from the ignition, walked up the stairs, and unlocked his door. Sat on the chair, took off his boots. Same routine.

Except for the choking feeling.

The next few hours were a blur of rage and more rage. Frustration at the chief. Blind fury at himself for screwing up his own plans. Fear about telling Dad what happened. *He'll be glad I'm not going to be a firefighter anymore.*

He paced the living room, and when that wasn't enough space, he walked the perimeter of the apartment building at least twenty times. The sun dipped behind the mountains. A lady sitting on her balcony stared at him with growing suspicion every time he passed by, talking to himself. *I totally know better. Why did I do that?*

Finally, he went inside to take a hot shower and heat up some food. Good move. He felt calmer. *What am I gonna do?*

He picked up his cell phone, and remembering what Jessie had said, that he didn't have to solve everything by himself, he called her cell number.

"Hey, Prentice!" She seemed happy to hear from him.

"Are you busy? I need to talk to somebody."

"Wow! How about that? I was sure I'd scared you away the other day."

"That was pretty brutal. But I've been thinking about it ever since."

Her voice had a smile in it. "I just felt I better say what was on my heart that day."

No fake conversations with this lady, for sure. "Um... Thanks," he said. "Do you think we could meet for a little bit?" No clue how to proceed.

"Oh, I wish, but I'm in D.C. this week, remember? I'll be back Friday."

"Oh, right." *Lack of oxygen to my brain. Fight or flight reflex.*

"I'm glad you called, Prentice. Maybe hitting you with both barrels like that at the lake wasn't really fair."

"No, but I needed it." He cleared his throat. "I think you might've done me a big favor."

"Awesome! Lots to talk about then. And you called at a good time. I'm just sitting around in the hotel tonight."

"Sorry it took me so long to hear what you were saying," he said. *Like, my whole life.*

"Those are not easy words to take in. It takes years, sometimes, to understand," she said. "Hey, has something happened? You don't sound like yourself."

A few days ago, he didn't even know this person, but now she'd turned into a lifeline. She was quiet, listening as he explained why he'd been suspended and kicked out of the station.

When he finished, after a pause, Jessie said, "Prentice, this might be what they call 'hitting bottom,' but that's for you to decide."

He groaned. "That sounds about right."

"But look, it can be a good thing, you know?" Her pause seemed pointed, deliberate, as if she meant him to pay careful attention. He sat up straighter. "It's like this, something I learned in my group. It's when you figure out you can't do it that you've got the best chance. So far you've kept finding the energy to keep trying. But when you bottom out and realize your life is unmanageable, when you understand you can't do it all, then your life starts to get better."

"You've thought about this a lot."

"I'm paraphrasing. Like I said, I got it from my support group." She laughed. "They literally have a 12-step program for dealing with my family. No joke."

"It's not with your church, is it?"

"No, but my church is another cornerstone. It helps me remember I'm not the center of the universe. What a relief to know that, right?"

He sighed. "I'm definitely not at the center of the universe. I'm more on the slag heap right now." By now he knew better than to think she would brush off a statement like that.

"Yeah, I can identify. I promise, sometime, I'll tell you about it. Your life has become unmanageable, as they say. The only way to go from here is up."

Maybe this isn't the end. It could be the beginning.

7

Thursday morning dawned hot, still, and hazy. Nothing moved, promising another rough work day in the heat. On the TV in the diner, a grim announcer reminded Coloradans of the recent complete devastation of the towns in California, where such a large percentage of homes and infrastructure had failed to resist the ember attacks. It was uncertain if they would rebuild at all.

Next, the weather chick sounded all sweetness and light when she promised the winds would kick up soon and make the fire danger worse. "The National Weather Service has declared another Red Flag Warning," she said, as if she were announcing the high school prom court. "Continued hot and dry for our Thursday. Another smoky but beautiful day in Pioneersburg and the surrounding area." She bubbled on about preparing for wildfire by using "a high-efficiency particulate air filter for your home." *You have to be kidding me! That's the message?*

Though he took the situation seriously, when dark thoughts about the catastrophe of his job with the fire department popped into his head, he pushed them away. *Yep, I've hit rock bottom. She was right. Time to bounce back?*

He was glad he had a client scheduled for today so he could work, just work, and avoid thinking too much about his work situation and all Jessie had said. He felt protected from the world in his steel-toed boots, thick work pants, and long sleeve shirt. At the work site in Garnet, he added Kevlar chaps, a woodsman helmet, an N95 mask, and leather work gloves to complete the armor before he revved up the chainsaw, complete with spark arrestor.

Today, for a change, he worked in Majestic Estates, another piney subdivision east of the interstate, just south of Gwilym Acres. Here too, the series of rolling hills parallel to the mountains determined the road layout. The views of the Rockies from those homes could be amazing.

Unlike in Gwilym Acres, though, a majority of people in Majestic Estates felt no need to disturb even one twig or leaf on their land, much less remove any shrubs or trees. His client, Mr. Bixby, was the exception. He'd moved into the subdivision with an understanding about the wildfire danger. A retired forest service manager, he was new to Garnet but had lived in other parts of Colorado. He'd found out about Tinderbox from the business cards Prentice left around town, and they'd hit it off the first time Prentice worked on his property two years ago.

They'd agreed that the combination of thick trees and topography would encourage a fire to race through the draws and up the slopes. Prentice worked to reduce the surrounding vegetation to demonstrate to the neighbors how well-done mitigation could help the forest. Over time, Prentice had cleared out all the scrub oak from under the pine trees, and now Mr. Bixby's land was starting to recover from the well-intentioned neglect of the previous owners.

Those people thought it wasn't natural to cut a tree or bush down. *If you won't let a fire thin out your forest naturally every decade or so, you need to do it yourself, not do nothing at all.*

Prentice also took out the puny 'lollipop' trees that were clustered too close together. Where there used to be a staggering 300 trees an acre, now it was about ten percent of that.

"It's just like growing carrots in your garden," Bixby had said to Prentice. "You have to thin them or none of them will be healthy. I'd rather choose which trees get to make it than let a fire do that for me!"

"I'm in violent agreement," Prentice had answered with a laugh.

If Bixby's neighbors would only follow his lead, besides being safer, they would have even more amazing views that included pine trees and the mountains. Unlike many neighboring homes, Bixby's house was visible from the street, since the zone around the house was maintained. He liked how Prentice described it as a "moat" that protected the house, so if flying embers landed nearby, they'd be much less likely to survive, spread spot fires, and let flames touch the house.

And it wasn't as if his yard was a barren desert. It was nothing like the rocks-only "zero-scaping" that partially-informed people installed in an effort to reduce irrigation costs and water use. It was beautiful, even now, in the dry August heat. Clusters of low-growing asters, bugleweed, and a variety of other plants demonstrated healthy xeriscaping using the right types of native vegetation. Close to the house, colorful flowers and groundcover meandered amidst selected landscaping boulders and rocks. Shrubs scattered carefully out from there were slow-growing, deciduous types, like mountain mahogany and grape holly.

Prentice worked steadily, removing volunteer pines and scrub brush up to the property line, until it was time for a break. Returning to his truck, he set the chainsaw in the shade, and leaving it to cool so he could add gas and oil, he took a bottle of water from his cooler. Mr. Bixby's porch was shaded by the deck above it, and it felt good to sit down there and breathe in the evergreen smell. As he drank, Prentice admired a resplendent gray-green Colorado Blue Spruce tree that remained near the house. It could easily be a hundred years old. He'd trimmed the bottom two rows of branches and raked out the dead needles underneath the tree last time he was here.

He was rubbing windblown dust from his eyes when Mr. Bixby hollered a greeting through the open living room window. "How's the work goin'?"

Prentice turned to look at him where he was sitting in his recliner. "Hi, sir! It's going great, just kinda windy. I'm taking my time," he replied.

"You're doin' great. Wish I could jump in and do it like I used ta.' Glad you've got your real job at the fire station so you can get a rest there," he joked.

"Sorry you mentioned that, sir. Actually, I got suspended yesterday."

"What's that? What happened, Prentice?"

"I did a stupid thing. Hope it'll get straightened out soon." *Why did I bring this up?*

"Well, that's a shame, but it'll work out. You're a smart kid."

Prentice changed the subject. "How's your hip today?"

"Onerous as usual," Bixby's voice came through the metal window screen. "Like I said, I'd rather be out there workin'."

Prentice smiled. *He'll be snoozing in the armchair in a few minutes.* He leaned back in the porch chair made of colorful old downhill skis put together into a mountain fashion statement. Mr. Bixby said he'd bought it in Ouray. Or was it Crested Butte?

His gaze roamed over nothing in particular... the trees in all directions...a glimpse of a Red-tailed Hawk coasting high above the grassland hunting for voles or mice. Maybe it saw rabbits or prairie dogs in the field, out of Prentice's view. A half mile to the south there was a pasture that was gradually being turned into a new subdivision called Prairie Flower, and the construction roused the creatures out where the birds of prey could find them.

In his head, the voice of one of his professors recited names of other raptors in High Plains County's high desert ecosystem... American Kestrel, Ferruginous Hawk, Bald Eagle, Sharp-shinned Hawk, Great Horned Owl. He watched for the hawk to reappear.

But then he saw something else that knotted his stomach and caused his heart to pound. Over the trees, above the pasture, there was smoke to the southwest. A line of thin smoke, blown upwards by the hot wind in the field. Not far away at all.

"MR. BIXBY!" HE YELLED THE OLDER MAN'S NAME AS HE STOOD up. "There's a fire in the pasture!" He banged on the screen to get his attention, saw Bixby's startled expression as he awoke.

"What?" The old man fumbled, sitting upright.

"Coming from the field, there's white smoke. Grass fire. Time to get out of here! I'll call 9-1-1," he told him through the screen, then took his phone from his pocket to dial the emergency dispatcher.

A woman answered. "High Plains County Dispatch. Please state the nature of the emergency."

"I'm in Garnet. There's a fire south of Majestic Estates. I can see a plume of white smoke coming up north of Prairie Flower subdivision."

"What is your address?"

"I'm on Columbine Way, east of Majestic Drive. But the fire's south of Sapphire Road, in the pasture between Majestic Estates and Prairie Flower."

"Do you see any flames?"

"No, but there are trees blocking my view. It's definitely smoke from a grass fire, though."

"Sir, if you can't actually see any flames, we'll need to verify the source of this smoke."

"Listen, I'm on the job! I'm Prentice Keene, with Garnet Fire. The smoke is widening out already, blowing north. It's less than half a mile from us, and coming this way. You need to evacuate Majestic Estates, *now!*" This had become a fast-moving situation, but answered all their questions before he hung up.

He pressed the red car alarm button on the back of the key fob with his thumb, and the horn started honking once every second. *That will alert the neighbors to at least look out their windows.* Tossing the keys through the open truck window, he shot back to Bixby's house, going through the front door. Mr. Bixby had just gotten the recliner to its upright position and held the phone in his hand.

"I called 9-1-1 already." Prentice told him. "You need to leave, right now! There's no time to check it out. Just go. Believe me, you'll see the smoke soon enough."

"You're reading my mind," Bixby answered. Walking heavily with his cane, he hobbled back to his office. "You need ta' get out of here too, Prentice," he hollered. "But before you go, would ya' mind helping me get my go-bag into the car? It's in the back closet by the garage door. Shut this front window for me, will ya? And make sure the front door is closed but unlocked."

"Sure!" He had the evacuation bag out of its storage spot and into Mr. Bixby's car before he reached the garage with one small file box.

"Thanks for getting' my go-bag." The old man closed the trunk and lowered himself into the driver's seat. "We c'n stop'n find out what's happenin' later. Now's the time ta' err on the side of caution! No time ta' waste!" He smiled, dipped his chin in a determined gesture, and backed out of the garage, pausing to wave once more while the garage door lowered.

"Be safe. Call me when you get... somewhere," Prentice said to the empty air.

He was gone. *What a guy! That's the way to evacuate.*

Prentice was alone now with the shriek of his truck blaring an alarm. He needed to move, but what should he do?

Ideally, he'd drive out to the station right now, even though B shift wasn't on duty. It was C Shift now, but they could use all the help they could get. Prentice knew all those firefighters. He'd trained with them. He pictured them already getting into action on the grass fire. It was seven minutes from Station #1 to the field. The key was to keep it on the ground, to stop it from torching a few trees and becoming a crown fire. If there wasn't too much fuel, the fire would lay down. It was much easier to battle one-foot flames than 150-foot flames in the treetops.

But he'd just been kicked off B shift.

Time slowed down, and thoughts filled his mind.

An ecologically appropriate fire would be smaller, less

severe, less hot. It would just clean out the understory and release nutrients back into the soil. Historically, these happened all the time and burned in small mosaic patterns, creating natural stopping points for next year's fires.

But a wind-driven crown fire careening through a packed forest would display extreme fire behavior, the uncontrollable kind. It would burn as hot as 3,000 degrees Fahrenheit and could melt Coca-Cola bottles and metal. A catastrophic fire would neutralize the soil.

I wonder how the fire started. It really didn't matter in the end. Fires were a part of nature. If this were uninhabited forest, they would've let it burn itself out. But if they didn't get the grass fire contained before it reached the denser vegetation packed with houses, the brisk, hot wind would take control of everything.

Looking around, he saw a few people from neighboring houses standing in their driveways, gawking at the smoke snaking through the pine trees, but they weren't moving. Maybe they didn't know what was going on or what to do, and the horn blaring wasn't doing much to make them move. *Fight, flight, or freeze. They're all frozen!*

The phone in Prentice's cargo pants pocket pulsed with the emergency alert. He checked the screen: *Majestic Estates subdivision immediate evacuation in progress. Wildfire south of Sapphire Road heading northeast. Life-threatening situation. All residents should evacuate. Use Majestic Drive north to State Highway 55. Press "1" to confirm receipt of this message.*

Finally! He'd registered his cell phone with High Plains County's emergency notification system. It let local officials tell the public about natural or man-made disasters. It could also target specific geographic areas.

But the message only went to people with a real land-line or those who had registered their cell phone numbers on the county's emergency alert website. It was not automatic for cell phones, and it wasn't the same system AMBER Alert issued statewide for child-abduction cases through many wireless providers. The fire department tried to explain this to residents, but still only a small percentage of people in the county had registered their cell phones.

He pressed "1", letting the system know he had received the message, ending further attempts to reach him, which would free up space to send out more messages. They couldn't all go out at once. They had to be throttled into groups based on location, with the people closest to the danger getting alerted first.

Prentice stowed his chainsaw and wiped his hands down his pants. Adrenaline was really kicking in. He felt it rushing through his legs, arms, and heart. If he were with the crew, they would work with buddies and in teams. But he had neither.

I got myself demoted to a civilian right before my first big wildfire. So what'm I going to do? He was on scene. He could smother spot fires and help folks evacuate. *It would mean going cowboy, but I have no choice. I've gotta do something.*

And if he didn't start helping right now, who would?

He had to stop and let someone know where he was and what he was doing. Grabbing his phone he typed out a text: *I called 9-1-1 for grass fire. I'm east of Majestic Drive, on Columbine Way.* But then he looked up. Who should he send it to? The chief? No way. Not his dad, for sure. This could turn into the kind of disaster that his dad used as an example for not going into the fire service in the first place.

How about Lt. Grimaldi? *He's off duty right now, but he'll get the alert.* He was the kind of man who'd never leave anyone behind, especially after what he'd gone through during the 9/11 attacks. He'd respond to Prentice despite his suspension. He sent the text.

Shifting his brain into this new reality filled with the smoke and sparks, he had to get his bearings. He'd rehearsed in his mind and studied at Red Card wildland fire training, but not like this. No more videos and classroom theories. If that grass fire sent flying embers into Majestic Estates, it was going to mean real life and death work.

He was already wearing protective equipment, leather boots, a helmet with a screen, a long-sleeved work shirt, sturdy gloves and a mask. The gear for tree cutting was similar to that of a wildland firefighter with a few exceptions.

But he was missing goggles, a heat-resistant shroud, and the fire-resistant shirt and pants that were essential uniform items for a Red Card firefighter deployed with a crew. All standard procedures he'd learned in the S-131 course and all the others from the National Wildfire Coordinating Group. He also had no aluminum fire shelter, which would've protected him up to about 500 degrees Fahrenheit. Some firefighters called that a Shake 'N Bake, though. If a hot fire flashed over him and he was away from his vehicle, it was way past being a bad day.

The relentless wind came from the south, feeding oxygen to the hungry fire. Burning embers skittered along the grass. The smoke blowing through the pine trees from the south turned from white and tan to brown as the fire, which he still couldn't see, began consuming the scattered scrub oak brush and pine trees in the pasture south of Sapphire Road. Gusts of wind already carried burning material aloft, everything from ash to sparks. Small pieces of wood that had been live twigs only a few minutes ago became glowing bits of charcoal sailing through the air.

He considered his wildland fire training. The Fire Orders and Watchouts were written in the blood of wildland firefighters who had lost their lives fighting fires. *Identify your safety zones and escape routes.*

"I'm on a dead-end road. Once I get out to Majestic Drive, I can go north or south." It wasn't great, but he felt like he had time to help before he retreated. Mr. Bixby's house on Columbine Way sat on the southeast edge of Majestic Estates, almost at the top of a ridge.

A few blocks south, Sapphire Road divided Majestic Estates from the grassy pasture now on fire. Sirens screamed along down there. They needed to set up a fire break along the road to stop the fire from spreading. The trees were so thick, Prentice couldn't see the trucks. The subdivision full of homes, brush, and trees had not been thinned by fire or humans in a hundred years.

He had his shovel to smother spot fires, and his chainsaw to rip away wooden decks. Wooden fence could act like a fuse, guiding a line of flames straight to a house unless it was cut down. But the only real hope was if the yard was pretty well cleaned up.

If the fire climbed the ladder fuels from the ground into the tree crowns, outrunning the fire wouldn't be an option. The twisted tangle of cul-de-sacs and forested hills made sure of that. Meanwhile, the fire could hopscotch over him, igniting smaller fires ahead of him that could surround him.

The world had turned upside-down so quickly.

And he had no teammates.

---

www.Tinderbox.tips -Flying Embers, Part 2:

- Tiny sparks and softball-sized coals will land on the roof or yard.
- If embers starve due to lack of fuel, spot fires cannot ignite.
- A cascade of spot fires can cause a blowup.
- A fire-adapted community has reduced its wildfire risk by removing fuels strategically.

He looked around Mr. Bixby's yard.

Small flying embers landed in a few places and started little spot fires. Some flared up as they landed on dry grass or pine needles and ignited. Just as nature intended, those small fires crept along the ground, jumped up several feet when they reached the pine tree trunks, but then dropped low to the ground again. No branches or trees caught fire in the yard as the ground fire crept along, since Prentice and Bixby had trimmed up the limbs, and the shrubs were spread apart.

The ground fires also approached Bixby's house through the grass and pine needles. About 20 feet away, they stopped at a narrow band of healthy, trimmed native grasses. Any burning brands flying past that "clean and green" zone closer to the house landed on bare dirt near the foundation. Embers landing there starved to death and went out.

You can't create defensible space like this on the fly, but Mr. Bixby's place is looking good.

Next door, and at hundreds of "next doors" surrounding him in Majestic Estates, it was a different story. The residents liked their privacy, and in the summer, scrub oak leaves were a pretty shade of green, so they didn't like the idea of cutting them back. Those ephemeral leaves blocked the view of the street and the next-door neighbor's house for a few months of the year.

Gambel oak was well-adapted to locations where wet springs and hot, dry summers created the exact conditions conducive to wildfires. Even in new subdivisions, the builders advertised the landscaping as "native scrub oak," implying it was also a safe choice, without informing newcomers to Colorado that when a fire got into dry oak brush, it would take off like a rocket. *Yes, the deer love it, but "green" is not always "good," people!*

The resinous bushes touched the cedar siding, or the wooden eaves, with bushes ranging from a few feet to thirty feet high, creating a fuel-filled home ignition zone. Completely vulnerable. *Can't do anything about those now.*

Sometimes the flames couldn't find a path to get all the way to the house. Their radiant heat wasn't enough to ignite it from a distance. They smoldered, sputtered, and starved to death.

Other embers were luckier and found fuel to eat. They landed on woody plants or bark mulch or junk stored next to the house. A bright green Astroturf made of synthetic rubber. A dry cedar shake roof. They blew inside attics through roof vents and landed on the insulation. They smoldered, and many hours later, after any firefighters who might've been there had moved on, some of them ignited into new fires.

Little fires grew and moved closer to the house along the grasses, detritus, or bushes. Sometimes those fuels led the flames right up into direct contact with the cedar siding, hugging the house with a little curtain of orange- and rust-colored fire. Convective heat ignited the splinters of wood. If there'd been a fuel-free zone, they would've stopped a few feet short of the house, and it would've been a different story. But not here.

Blizzards of glowing embers landed in juniper and arborvitae bushes and smoldered right under the picture windows. The bushes burned energetically, generating more flying embers. Plastic screens over open windows melted as soon as sparks or radiant heat reached them. The temperature differential across glass panes fractured the windows at relatively low temperatures, for a fire. The fire jumped inside the house as quickly as a thief and gobbled up the carpet, the furniture, and books, and clothing, then moved onto the floor joists and ceilings.

Even houses covered in stucco had chinks in their armor. There might be old cedar siding behind it with no flashing or unscreened vents letting the tiny sparks creep into the house.

HE YELLED A WAR CRY NO ONE COULD HEAR BUT HIM.... "What're you waiting for? Let's go to work!" Prentice got in his truck, with the horn still blaring, and drove along the cul-de-sac.

For each house he considered trying to save, he took three seconds to do structure triage. Is it a well-maintained property that could possibly be defended? Can I get up the driveway and still get back out again if those trees are on fire? Can I even see the house from the road? For most houses near Bixby's, the answer was no. *I wonder if all the work we did at Bixby's will help him, since he's surrounded by people who haven't done anything.*

These were the very same questions the firefighters would ask when and if they arrived there with crews. Garnet's fire department only had a handful of fire engines and brush trucks, but there were almost a thousand homes in Majestic Estates and thousands more north and east. The owners of the private property who had made no attempt to start the work left firefighters no choice but to move on.

The firefighters needed to focus on the properties that had a chance, where the owners had invested time to clean it up already. Those houses might even defend themselves. Drawing the line here instead of there meant saving, or losing, another half-million-dollar home. Or a whole street full of them.

In the distance, he heard the noise of the engines as they pumped limited amounts of water on the grass ahead of the main flame front, not to put it out, but to moisten the fuels in front of it and slow down its spread. They were also probably lighting backburns in strategic places to create a line of defense they could control, trying to stop the main grass fire from widening.

As he worked, Prentice pictured the crews south of him, evaluating their situation. They were two or more blocks closer to the main fire than he was. The visibility had dropped so he couldn't even see the house next door.

"I should just get out and quit messing around." But he couldn't help himself. The world wasn't saved yet.

~

PRENTICE STOPPED AT A YARD THAT WAS CLEARER THAN MANY, and the house wasn't completely defenseless. One beautiful blue spruce tree, cleared of needles underneath, gave shade to the deck. The other pines stood back from the house and away from the driveway. This place, like Bixby's, had a better chance of surviving than many of its neighbors.

On the front porch, flying embers had ignited the outdoor furniture. Prentice hopped from the truck and ran up the few steps to the deck, throwing the cushions far away from the house. They landed at the edge of the pines, where other spot fires were already burning along the ground.

He rang the bell and banged on the door, but no one answered. Good, that meant they were out.

Fifteen minutes had passed since the emergency alert. He saw a few cars pulling out of driveways to head out of the neighborhood. But not enough. *Where are the rest of the people? Why aren't they leaving!? Don't they smell the smoke?*

Waiting too long to leave could mean getting stuck on a road blocked by lines of other evacuees, abandoned cars or debris. Visibility could go from kind of smoky to inky blackness with one wind shift, even when the sun shone brightly somewhere above the thick smoke. People who got trapped in a vehicle when a flame front came through could die just from the heat. More Shake 'N Bake.

He'd assumed people would pay attention to the alert, now that it was going out on phones. He thought they'd see the smoke and get themselves out. Or they would hear his car alarm, which was still honking every second, and leave.

"What was I thinking?" Tunnel vision was a reality, even for trained firefighters. "Lives over property. I've gotta get these people out of here," he said out loud.

He stopped the spot fire work and headed back to the north end of the cul-de-sac, driving into every driveway one at a time, even the ones where the home wasn't visible from the street because of all the trees. He jumped out and rang each doorbell, banged on every door, or on the siding or a window, trying to be as loud as he could.

A sleepy man answered the door at one house, and Prentice heard the TV blaring in the background. "Get out! There's a fire!"

I can't believe these people are still here, oblivious.

Over and over again. "You have to evacuate! There's a wildfire!" When one man came to the door, Prentice felt the cold air-conditioned air flow out of the house. No wonder he hadn't smelled the smoke from inside.

At another home, he startled a tired young mom in shorts and a tank top. She had a bewildered look and held a sleeping infant. Unaware, eyes widened in disbelief. "Get out!" he told them all.

Other homes were quiet. He banged the handle of the shovel on all the doors on Columbine Way and headed to Sage Way to notify those people, maybe another eight houses.

It had been less than an hour since he first spotted the smoke, and the fire was an immense living force, growing stronger every second. Anyone who hadn't evacuated stood right in its path. The wind gusts from the southwest grew stronger and more frequent, and the air smelled scorched.

Prentice kept knocking on doors. He saw no wall of

flames, but the smoke was getting thicker every minute. Each blast of wind brought dense, black clouds of smoke full of sparks. The wind carried millions of burning firebrands across Sapphire Road, over the heads of the firefighters, into the neighborhood. Hungry little fire monsters looked for fuel to keep them alive. Like viruses searching for a compatible host in the overgrown pine forest.

Blizzards of embers swirled every which way. They blew through the air, traveling miles ahead of the fire. Collecting in smoldering piles in all the nooks and crannies of the homes in the same places the wind eddied all year and deposited leaves and needles.

Carbonized chunks of trees glowed orange in the black sky. Embers as big as kernels of corn or marbles ignited spot fires in the grass. The flames, one or two feet high, crept along the ground through the brittle fuel.

The wind was merciless and hot. The ambient air temperature was well into the 90s by now, getting closer to midday.

"I need a drink," he told himself. "Just a few more houses on this block. Then I should go."

Now that the embers had leapfrogged over the road into the residential area, they found plenty of grass, bushes, and kindling near the homes to feed them. New fires appeared all over the yards. Within minutes, homes ignited, and it didn't let up.

The flames crept across the ground but didn't stay down there. The thick vegetation and resinous leaves made a ladder for the ground fire to climb high into the tree crowns.

The sky filled with flames reaching twice as high as the bushes. Three times as high. The fire twisted forty feet into the air, intertwined with the raging wind. The unforgiving gusts blew the flames hard, sideways and upwards, swirling into neighboring thickets. Spirals of embers shot from the burning bushes.

The main fire pushed on, encouraged by the wind and all the new fuels it found to keep it alive: woodpiles, trampolines, sheds, scrap lumber, stucco houses with wooden decks, foot-high grass, rough-hewn cedar homes with dried leaves under the front steps, stands of oak.

Prentice heard more sirens in the distance. By now, mutual aid from Pioneersburg was surely arriving in full force to try to protect the buildings and check on evacuations. There was no way Garnet's firefighters and law enforcement could handle this on their own.

Evacuations.

He looked west. Flames reached above the trees a quarter mile away. His escape route was in jeopardy. The fire itself had jumped the road into Majestic Estates.

The fate of the houses, and any people left inside, would be determined by how the homeowners prepared or ignored their properties in the recent months or years.

"Time to leave!" he said to the roaring wind that blew up the slope right toward him at the far end of Sage Way. Prentice grabbed a wool blanket from the truck bed, jumped in the cab, rolled up the windows, closed the vents, and turned on the air conditioning. Not that it could stop him from being baked inside the truck if he were in the wrong place. He turned on his lights and hazard blinkers and headed toward Majestic Drive.

The smoke was so thick he couldn't see the hood of his truck. But as the wind swirled, sometimes he got a longer view. He had alerted people that would've been caught at home. But now, the narrow street was choked with all those cars and traffic in gridlock. Prentice couldn't see what blocked the way — a panicked driver, an abandoned vehicle or a tree across the road, or the shroud of smoke filled with showers of sparks causing drivers to freeze.

Sitting at the back of an unmoving line of cars, he texted Lt. Grimaldi to give a status report, even though he hadn't replied to the first one yet. *Gridlock on egress Majestic Dr. Multiple vehicles stacked up on Sage Way.* He hit send, then added a photo of the fire to the southwest. There wasn't much to see. Utter blackness and an orange glow hung around the unreadable street sign in the foreground. He stuffed the phone back in the cargo pocket on his pants leg.

He saw a movement to his right through the smoke. It was at a house on the corner of Sage and Columbine where he'd rung the bell not long ago. Nobody had answered then, but now, as he sat in his truck hoping to move forward, a man who must have been 90 years old shuffled out onto the second-story deck. *Oh my God.*

Steering to the right to free the truck of the log jam, Prentice gunned it across the grass to get to the man's driveway. As before, he left the truck running, and wrapping himself in the wool blanket, he raced up the deck steps to the second-story. "Hey, sir! We have to get you out of here, now!"

"I'm not leaving without my wife!" the old man hollered.

9

"Where is she?"

"In the kitchen, but she doesn't get around so well. She's in a wheelchair."

"What's her name?"

"Earlene."

Prentice ran into the house through the open sliding door. A frail woman in a nightgown and socks sat in a wheelchair at the kitchen table. Her backbone curved forward as if her spine were made of wax that had melted and cooled in this unnatural shape. She held a cup of coffee in her wavering hand, and she didn't look at him.

He said, "Earlene, I'm getting you out of here. Are you ready?" She glanced sideways at him but didn't respond. "I'm going to help you, okay?" Not waiting for her answer, he put the blanket over her head, ignoring her squawks and her futile attempts to bat the blanket away. "Sir," he called to the old man, "I'm going to the front door so I can go down the hill instead of the steps."

"Okay. Thanks." The man just stood there watching the chaos.

"You need to come, too," Prentice shouted, frustration edging his voice. "Can you get down to my truck? Grab your wallet and her purse and meet me there. Now!"

The sharpness of Prentice's tone galvanized the man. Prentice rolled the wife out the front door, bumping her over the threshold onto the front porch and down the two steps to the ground. It was only a short distance downhill from there to the truck. The woman yelped at being jostled. Prentice's heart thumped harder as one of their pine trees torched, and the flames shot high in the sky. It would easily spread to neighboring trees.

The man shuffled up to the truck, toting a plastic grocery bag. Prentice locked the wheelchair in place and opened the door, trying to figure how he would get the lady up without hurting her. There just wasn't time for finesse. All three of them were coughing. They had to get in the vehicle.

Pushing the shelter of her blanket aside, he bent his head to her, and taking care to speak gently but firmly, he asked, "Can you stand up?" Earlene looked at him but didn't answer. Tears ran down her cheeks. He put the blanket back over her head.

The man said, "I could go get her walker. It's in the garage." But the garage door was shut. There was no time for that. Showers of sparks landed on the blanket and blew around their heads. He could taste the heat of the fire in his throat. It burned in his nostrils.

Prentice bent his knees, leaned in, and hoisted her over his shoulder. She screamed when he heaved her up and deposited her on the floor of the truck behind the front seat. "I'm sorry," he told her. "So sorry, but the floor's the safest place for you."

"She can't take that. She has a lot of back pain," the old man said. *No kidding.*

"Yeah, I understand, and I'm real sorry, but we've gotta drive through a fire now." Prentice went around to the other side of the back seat and as gently as he could, he tugged the woman farther into the truck. It was a tight squeeze, but she was thin, and with her knees bent the door could close.

"Would it help if she were to lie flat?" Prentice asked, but the man shook his head. "Okay. Go sit on the floor on the passenger side. You can lean against each other. Hurry, if you can. We're running out of time."

While the man shuffled to the other side, Prentice popped open the tonneau cover and retrieved two N95 masks for them. Then he adjusted the wool blanket so it went over both of them, shut the back doors and got into the driver's seat. *This is exactly the wrong place to be right now.*

While the cars had moved slightly forward, it was still bottlenecked. There was no way they were going to make it out before the fire came through. Both lanes were jammed with cars trying to leave the neighborhood. Prentice watched, grim-eyed, as the wind sucked burning debris into the sky and scattered it. The inferno gathered strength and power from the surrounding forest. It could even create its own weather. There was the potential for a vortex of superheated air, a firenado, as the crown fire grew and crept ever closer to his location.

"What's your name, sir?"

"Dexter," he said. "Dexter Smith."

From the unmoving truck, he texted Grimaldi again. *2 elderly residents evac w me.* He added their names and street address, a record of their location, for the coroner and any relatives, at least.

Prentice's phone beeped with Lt. Grimaldi's reply. *When*

you get out, report to me at IC, set up at Church of Abundant Life, Contractor Boulevard.

Roger. Prentice hit send. Thanks, Grimaldi! He was stoked! Prentice was blind without his fire radio. Now he knew the location of Incident Command, the best place to go. That church was in the north end of Pioneersburg, but it was well south of Prairie Flower where the fire had started.

But he still had a lot of dangerous ground to cover, and they still weren't moving forward. Fires danced on both sides of the road and all around the houses and yards. He saw at least one house down the street was fully involved, a total loss. In other yards, the houses that were visible weren't obviously burning, but the yards were full of flames. There were fences and decks on fire.

"When you can't go forward, why not go backward?"

Jerking the steering wheel, he drove across the grass, back the way he had come. Maybe there was another way out of this neighborhood. Why not go overland? It just might work. The route had to work. He flipped on his horn alarm again. Another horn from an orange Honda SUV blared, as the driver swung the vehicle in behind Prentice, tailing him.

"We're going against the flow!" Prentice prayed to find a way out. Smoke shrouded the roadway. It was only when the wind shifted that he could see and then only for a short time and an even shorter distance. There weren't any cars in front of him, heading the wrong way like this. Even so, he crept along at a snail's pace, up the little street, then up Bixby's driveway. He shifted the gear to 4WD so the truck could make it up the slippery grade.

He appreciated how this yard he'd spent so much time in wasn't full of big flames yet. Ground fires, yes, some black patches where the fire was already exhausted. But no fire on the house itself or next to it. So far. It was cause for grim satisfaction, proof that when a property was properly landscaped, it could defend itself against the burning embers. *Good job, Mr. Bixby. I hope it works.*

"Dexter and Earlene, we're in for a rough ride."

Prentice barreled over the grass, around the house, and up the hill behind it, heading in a generally north direction, straining to pick out the path among the trees that he felt sure was there.

The woman whimpered in the back seat with every jolt.

"Stop crying, Earlene," Dexter said from under the blanket. "It's not helping anything."

She cried louder.

"Her mind's not right," he told Prentice. "It's hard to explain things to her."

Prentice tuned them out. Reaching the far edge of Bixby's property, which was familiar to him, he kept going north, up the hill toward another subdivision, unknown country named Tall Pines. Maybe it was full of doghair pine thickets and scrub oak, pure fire fuel. But hopefully there would be wide-open stands of pine he could drive through. His back and neck ached. The mask chafed his face. He resisted an urge to rip it off.

"This is risky, leaving the road." He hunched over the steering wheel, searching the near distance, eyes burning.

Dexter's grizzly voice said, "Well, things weren't much better at our house."

Prentice almost smiled. "Nope."

But now, a sudden wind shift appeared like a gift and allowed him to pick out a path through the pines. Still, it was slow going. He gripped the wheel. Ground fires were all around them. The ferocious heat in the cab sucked the energy from him. He had one water bottle up front with him, and he pushed the mask out of the way and drank half of it in a few swallows.

"How are you doing for water back there, Dexter?" he called.

"All out," the man replied.

Prentice handed what was left between the seats to the old guy.

He noticed more headlights behind him. The orange SUV was right there, along with more cars that had been stuck on Columbine and Sage. He couldn't see how many, but they were all following him. *I wish I knew what I was doing.*

"There's a house up there," he said out loud, his voice dry and cracked. Zero moisture remained in his mouth, and his eyes felt hot and dry.

He maneuvered between a pine tree and a shed, then onto the driveway of a house facing north on Tall Pines Way. The smoke was still thick, but there were fewer fires over here. Ahead, a resident with a trailer full of plastic tubs and paintings pulled onto Tall Pines Drive. Prentice followed him down the small road and took the truck out of 4WD.

The streets were filled with cars here too, but the traffic actually moved forward toward Highway 55. Behind him, other desperate evacuees from Majestic Estates followed him. "We're going east now, then south as soon as we can," Prentice said out loud to keep himself focused.

They headed toward Incident Command to get medical help for this poor couple he'd plucked out of the inferno.

HIGH PLAINS HERALD
Wildfire breaks out in Garnet, thousands evacuated
By Annie Laurie

August 22 / 12:01 p.m. MDT

Garnet, Colo. — *Construction workers reportedly sparked a wildfire in Garnet about 10 a.m., causing the urgent evacuation of over one thousand homes in the Majestic Estates neighborhood east of the interstate. Initial reports suggest many residents are still trapped now on roads in traffic gridlock as the smoke and fire overwhelmed the few egress routes so quickly.*

The Garnet Fire Department reports that they responded to the fire within minutes but were delayed reaching it because the panicked construction worker could not remember the name of the street where he was working. Additionally, this road, in a new section of Prairie Flower subdivision, was not yet entered on High Plains County dispatch's GIS maps.

Strong wind gusts pushed the fire north across the pasture, then into Majestic Estates. More than one thousand homes are in immediate danger as the fire spreads into the thick Gambel oak vegetation and climbs ladder fuels into the pine tree canopy, said Garnet Fire Chief Thomas M. Rugen.

Pioneersburg Fire Department took over Incident Command around noon after Rugen turned control over to them. "It's better to ask for assistance sooner rather than later," he said, without further comment.

Thousands more homes north and east in Gwilym Acres, Wagon Trail, Tall Pines, and Pine Shadows are also in immediate danger, and a coordinated firefighter response is under way as the resources of the Pioneersburg Fire Department have already joined the fight. Additional county, state or federal resources will likely be requested by Incident Command, due to predicted weather and fire conditions.

According to Rugen, the fire was started by workers using a propane torch to cut landscaping fabric at a home under construction in Prairie Flower Phase VI. Sparks ignited the dry grass, the workers told officials. High Plains County is currently under Stage I burn restrictions. No word yet on whether the construction company or workers will be fined or charged with arson.

Many evacuees are gathering at the High Plains High School on Contractor Boulevard in Pioneersburg, where it is rumored the American Red Cross might set up an evacuation shelter.

One evacuated resident told the Herald, "The only reason I got out was I saw the smoke coming at us through the trees. Grabbed my dog and jumped into my car. I never got a notification call, but I bet that's 'cuz it all happened so fast. I just didn't stop to think. All I've got with me is my dog and the junk that was already in my car. I hope my neighbors got out."

www.Tinderbox.tips -The Speed of Wildfires:

- Wildfire burning through grassland moves up to 30 miles in one hour.
- That's half a mile in one minute.
- Wildfire in a dense pine forest can move 7 to 14 miles an hour.
- In the trees, a quarter mile of homes could ignite in a minute.

P rentice kept glancing west at the black wall of destruction as he drove south. Although it was just noon, the world that he could see was cloaked in smoke and darkness.

He imagined the fire's progress through Majestic Estates.

Flames engulfed whole stands of Ponderosa, and the super-heated air acted as a vacuum, pulling surrounding oxygen into its power and launching it straight up into the sky. The dark vortex of smoke got wider and wider.

Inside the column, the heat lofted burning branches and

red-hot chunks of tree trunks, glowing red barbecue briquets as large as a clenched fist or even a whole loaf of bread.

All the fuel — tree branches, roof shingles, deck cushions — was pulled up into the atmosphere like floating missiles with no guidance system except the crazy wind.

People hadn't realized the urgency. Those who received the emergency notification thought they had hours to pack, when really they needed to flee right away, jump in their cars and just go. Some people never received the alert at all, either because the system failed or because they had never registered their cell phones.

Thanks for telling me where IC is set up, Grimaldi.

Prentice got far enough south of Garnet to be out of the smoke and pulled the blanket off his passengers. High Plains High School and Church of Abundant Life next to it both came into sight, on a hill on the northeast side of Pioneersburg. They had a commanding view of the city spread out on the rolling plains below them and the sharp contrast of the Rockies to the west. The church was a huge complex spread over five acres. Sunshine bathed the playground and an adjacent cemetery. Looking south, there was no sign of the fire.

"Dexter and Earlene, we're almost there. Can you see, we're back in the sun now?"

The elderly man and woman, still cramped on the floor behind his seat, cried out when the truck bounced slightly, going from the pavement into the church parking lot, and that set off more coughing. When he glanced back, he could see Dexter had his mask pulled down, stuck under his chin instead of his mouth, and he wondered how long it'd been that way. Their breathing was hoarse.

The line of cars was still following close behind him.

The shell-shocked drivers must have had no other idea what to do next when they all got clear of the fire. No family meet-up plan in case of disaster. *Or if they had one, they couldn't think straight enough to remember.*

All the cars still had their lights on, just like in a funeral procession. Not that the headlights had helped at all in the middle of the smoke. *But we made it out!*

His first stop was to find help for his two elderly passengers. A sheriff's deputy stood guard at the entrance to the parking lot. "This is for the wildland crews," he said.

Prentice expected that. "I understand that, officer, but I'm an off-duty firefighter. I have some civilians here in need of medical care, an elderly couple. Smoke inhalation. We just drove out of the fire." He gestured to Dexter and Earlene huddled behind him. "Can I take them over to the medics and get them some help?"

The officer's expression softened. "Good work, man!" He looked in the back seat, nodded, and pointed to the section of parking lot where medics were gathered. "You can take them there, pronto, but the rest of the IC is badge-only."

"Thank you. One other thing. I'm pretty sure that line of cars behind me is a bunch of civilians who thought I knew where I was going when we got out of Majestic Estates. Could you help them find the Red Cross shelter? I'm sure they'll need rest and medical help too."

"I'll take care of it." He was on his radio to call for more deputies before Prentice even put his foot on the gas.

Emergency vehicles crammed the parking lot which was normally empty on a weekday morning. The incident command system structure made it possible to coordinate disparate types of help and multiple fire, police, other agencies, and volunteers into one efficient operation during a crisis.

Prentice pulled up next to a Pioneersburg Fire Department ambulance at the west edge of the parking lot. A driver and paramedic in blue uniforms stood with a small group of other EMTs and medics next to their vehicles, all on standby. Jumping out, he hollered, "Hey, Pioneersburg, help! I have two extremely elderly people in the back here with smoke inhalation. We just escaped the fire."

Their team got right on it. Time was their enemy, and Prentice explained the little he knew about the patients. "They're a husband and wife. Earlene can't walk. She was in a wheelchair when I found them. She has extreme osteoporosis, lots of pain, and some cognitive impairment. Dexter climbed up in the truck himself so we could get away, but like his wife he must be over 90 years old too. They've been crammed in there for almost an hour now."

As he spoke, he peeled off his long sleeve shirt and appreciated the relatively cooler air. The paramedic opened the back driver's side door of Prentice's truck, and the EMT went to the passenger side door.

"Oxygen! Let's go," one of them directed. They worked together to get Earlene onto a stretcher as gently as they could, using extra padding so that her curved spine had support. Prentice heard her crying with a terribly scratchy throat, inflamed by the smoke.

Other medics helped Dexter out of the cramped cab, otherwise his legs would've collapsed when his feet touched the asphalt. They also began to manage pain, the fifth vital sign.

In less than a minute, the couple were both on the way to Pioneersburg Memorial Hospital in one ambulance.

HIGH PLAINS HERALD

Two deaths confirmed in Garnet fire

By Annie Laurie

August 22 / 4 p.m. MDT

Garnet, Colo. — *Two people have been confirmed dead in the Garnet fire, which started this morning north of the new Prairie Flower development. A sheriff's deputy discovered the man and woman in their mid-fifties in their car in Majestic Estates. Officials say it is likely they died of smoke inhalation and then fire consumed the garage and the vehicle.*

The Sheriff's Office reported that when their remains were discovered in the garage, the car doors were open as though they had been loading or grabbing last-minute possessions. All evidence from the scene indicates the couple were planning to depart very quickly, the sheriff's office reported. The car was full of burned boxes of papers, photo albums, and suitcases.

The deceased persons have yet to be formally identified using dental and other medical records. One set of human remains found in the car had a piece of surgical hardware attached to the leg bone similar to that used in ankle fracture repair surgery. Family members will be notified before the names of victims are released to the public.

A survivor from Majestic Estates said, "Our whole neighborhood was filled with smoke and suddenly, with that sun coming through the smoke, the whole neighborhood turned orange. My wife was in the driveway blowing the horn for me to get my butt out of the house."

A woman who evacuated said this, "We lost our home and our business on the same day. Ten thousand of us are now spread all over the county, the whole state. We are all zombies walking. What do we do next?"

Another evacuee told us, "It's a grieving process. It feels like the death of what we had…. It was such a beautiful community."

~

PRENTICE LEANED AGAINST THE BACK OF HIS TRUCK, WATCHING the line of cars follow a sheriff's vehicle from the church parking lot and turning in next door at High Plains High School, where Red Cross volunteers had set up an emergency evacuation shelter.

He'd just found the strength to move when a sturdy, brown-haired EMT from the second team walked over to check on him.

"Lemme take a look at you, okay?" she said. "Have a seat." The medic gave him a bottle of electrolyte drink and a disposable moist cloth.

He wiped sweat and dirt from his face. "Thanks, that's perfect."

"What were you doing up there?" she asked. "You were right in the middle of it?"

"Yeah. I was off duty, working—my side job, fire mitigation. I was in Majestic Estates when I saw the smoke and called it in. I stayed a little too long. But that's how I found those folks."

"Talk about being at the right place at the wrong time."

"I'm glad I could help 'em. They were really stuck." With fatigue, he stared at the asphalt.

"You look familiar. Aren't you Smokey? From Garnet Fire?"

Then he recognized her too. "Yeah, that name is memorable, huh? We've trained together before. What's your name again?"

"Lopez. Or Loopy, right?" She laughed. "I'm glad you got out of there in one piece."

"Thanks for your help, Lopez. Don't you hate nicknames? Thanks for the drink. I better check in with

Garnet," he said. *Even though Rugen doesn't want to talk to me.*

Lopez said, "This fire isn't stopping any time soon. But you've had enough right now."

"You think I'm going home just because I'm off-duty? You're nuts."

"Live to fight another day," she said, with a pat on his shoulder. "They'll need you tomorrow too, Smokey. They'll wanna get you back on duty for extra shifts, for sure."

"You're right," he said. *But I'm a firefighter without a fire department, not that I need to explain that to everyone.*

Returning to his truck, he climbed up in the front passenger seat and plugged in his phone to charge. Sitting with the door open, his short legs dangling toward the running board, he typed out a text to Lt. Grimaldi. If Prentice didn't check in as promised, he'd waste resources trying to find him, even though he wasn't on duty. *Thank you, Grimaldi.*

I'm at IC now. Next stop: credential, food, rest.

Hitting send, Prentice scanned the view. He'd been moving non-stop for hours, and a voice in his head agreed with Lopez that the right thing to do next was to stay still. This wasn't a voice he listened to very often. But his limbs felt too heavy, and his eyes burned.

A few stragglers who'd followed Prentice from the fire had been sent over to the medics, too. Likely, they needed treatment for smoke inhalation or other serious injuries that the Red Cross shelter wasn't equipped for. Prentice watched as four of them were assessed and loaded into the second ambulance with a paramedic in the back, and Lopez drove them away. Prentice wondered how the county's ambulance capacity of 30 "busses" would hold up as more calls for help came in.

When the orange SUV pulled up, Prentice saw the driver was a blonde woman in her mid-fifties. She looked haggard even ten yards away as she got out of her Honda and opened the passenger door for an older man to get out of the passenger side. He was gray from head to toe: his hair, his clothes, even his skin. Three medics blocked Prentice's view as they loaded the patients into an ambulance. Now a young mom appeared, calling out, "Help me, please! My baby—" She cradled a limp infant in her arms. Emergency personnel surrounded her. Prentice was relieved to see two more ambulances drive in to take the place of the others.

What an amazing system we have in this country, he thought. *I'm always grateful. Even though sometimes they can't fix everyone...* That thought remained unfinished, as he spotted a local TV news team, heading toward the ambulances, ready to document the activity.

I sure wish I could get in there and fight it, Prentice thought. *I've got my wildland qualifications.* But Garnet was never going to call him up for this incident.

"It's infuriating. I've got the training. I just need the credential." That's what he needed to be deployed to work on the fire. "I could be a single resource assigned to some other crew." He thought of the Red Card endurance field-work test that had included an arduous 3-mile hike completed in 45 minutes while wearing a 45-pound pack. "They need me!"

Jumping down from the truck, he slammed the door and headed across the parking lot to the mobile command post vehicle where he knew they'd be they scanning ID cards and printing the credential badges. A white RV with the county logo on the side had a gigantic antenna on top and a generator next to the steps at the side door. A volunteer who looked as if he were a retired military member used a hand scanner to check resources in and out.

Prentice's hands shook a bit, as he took his small nylon wallet out of one of his cargo pants pocket and removed the Incident Qualification Card. For a second, he considered stepping out of line, not taking the chance of being turned away.

"No. It's better to find out my status now rather than later." He'd have hope and a new purpose, *if* he could get a credential. *Then I'll rest and get ready, and see where they'll assign me.*

He handed his Red Card over to the volunteer in charge, and within moments, the man handed Prentice his own bright pink incident credential tag. He rejoiced inside as he took the bottle of water the man had retrieved from the fridge in the RV.

"You're parched already, son," the volunteer said. "Thank you for your service. Be careful out there."

"Thank *you*, sir." Prentice clipped the tag to the neck of his wicking t-shirt. On his arm, he carried the yellow woven work shirt he'd stripped off earlier. It was a relic, a hand-me-down wildland fire shirt he procured in college. It was breathable, and it served him well doing dusty chainsaw work.

One hurdle jumped. *I haven't done anything yet. Well, yes I have.* Jessie would remind him to give himself credit for saving the couple and alerting the people in the neighborhood. He downed the contents of the water bottle in four big swallows. It was cold on his raw throat, making him choke a little, and he spluttered. "Thanks again."

He texted Lt. Grimaldi again. *I got incident credential. Going for food and rest.*

"EIS is set up right just over there." The volunteer

pointed. "They'll fix you up." Volunteers from High Plains County, mostly more grizzly retired guys, ran Emergency Incident Support, which was essential when it came to days-long disaster, providing snacks, hydration, and safe haven for the fire crews. In an old ambulance donated by a fire district, they served coffee, cool drinks, and hot food to the crews. A brown and white Ford Winnebago from the '90s provided cooking space, a few beds, and a bathroom.

EIS helped anyone with everything and anything they could. They showed up at structure fires when requested by officials like a fire chief, or the commander in charge of a multi-day incident, which was what the current fire had become.

Gatorade sounds perfect right now. Prentice was headed wearily in that direction when the news reporter popped in front of him and stuck a microphone in his face. A cameraman behind her recorded the encounter.

"I'm Beth Garcia from Channel 8 News."

"Yeah, I've seen you."

"We've learned you rescued several people and led them from the fire zone in Garnet."

"Yeah. Listen, I've really got to get something to drink."

"We'll walk with you," she said. "Where were you? How many people did you save?"

She followed in his wake as he headed around the command truck. "I really don't have time to talk right now." He wove his way among the assortment of tables and chairs that were set up between the RV and the old ambulance. A jury-rigged canopy provided welcome shade. He apologized when he bumped a volunteer carrying a tray laden with BBQ sandwiches, lasagna, and bottled drinks.

All the adrenaline was gone. A volunteer handed him a bottle of blue sports drink and a wet towel, and he sat down in a folding chair under the tent out of the hot afternoon sun. Other men and women mirrored Prentice's exhaustion as they slumped in camp chairs.

The reporter raised the microphone.

He nudged it away. The cool drink was almost as revitalizing as the smoke-free air, but when he finished drinking, he said, "Okay." He explained why he'd been in Garnet and how he worked with property owners in an effort to reduce the risks a wildfire posed to homes and businesses. He explained how a wildfire looked at the beginning and how it behaved. "I shouldn't have still been in there myself by then. I know better. I got blinders on, trying to stop the fire. Then I saw the residents weren't evacuating either, and I decided to bang on doors as I was on my way out of the neighborhood."

Garcia asked again, "So, what about the rescue?"

"There were two elderly people who got out with me. The man couldn't get his wife out of the house. She was in a wheelchair."

"How did you find them?"

"It was a miracle, for sure. I'd already knocked on their door once and got no answer. But there he was, out on the deck, watching the fire come toward him."

"I heard you led several more on a safe route out of the subdivision, but you didn't drive on the road? You created your own emergency exit?"

"It wasn't anything," he repeated. Knees spread wide, he bent his head forward and rested his elbow on his knees, rubbing his burning eyes. He couldn't remember when he'd ever felt so tired.

The volunteer brought him a hamburger, a package of chips, and a package of Famous Amos chocolate chip cookies. Prentice opened the cookies first, gobbling a few.

The reporter pushed for more information. "How did you survive this ordeal today?

Prentice couldn't take one more question. His mind filled with images of the drive out. He couldn't help thinking about the hundreds left behind. *There were so many cars on Majestic Drive, just sitting there in front of me, waiting to go forward.* The awful realities took shape in his mind. "They weren't going anywhere. The main fire was heading that way so fast... It was turning into a crown fire."

His eyes went flat and unfocused as he pictured burned-out cars abandoned in the middle of roads, with blackened grass, forest and buildings on both sides. Sometimes the cars had skeletons inside.

The reporter straightened. "We should let you go get some rest," she said, then addressed the camera. "Ladies and gentlemen, you heard it here. This lumberjack is a hero today after leading dozens of Majestic Estates residents to safety after the wildfire trapped them in their own neighborhood..."

Prentice turned away. He didn't want to hear any more. He ate the hamburger and chips without tasting, downing the last bites with Gatorade, and then clambering into the clunky Winnebago, he shucked his boots and fell onto the bed at the back of the vehicle. He didn't care about its musty smell, and draping his old work shirt over his head, he closed his eyes and let the numbness take over.

11

P rentice rose with a jerk. *Oh God. What time is it?*

He retrieved his phone from its charger and returned to the RV. It wasn't even two o'clock. He'd only been asleep an hour. He felt refreshed, though, and he was relieved to see there was a text from Lt. Grimaldi. *Smokey, find me at IC Planning Section when you surface.*

Before he set out for the IC, Jessie's voice spoke in his head. *Where are you? Tell people what's going on. Connect, Prentice.* He hesitated to call his dad in a time like this, since that ran the risk of getting chewed out for heading into danger. On the other hand, he did want to make sure Dad was okay. A week ago, he wouldn't have thought of anyone else to call. No real close friends. His work buddies were obviously overwhelmed. But with the new way of thinking Jessie gave him to consider, a new glimmer of light shone inside him about the value of connecting with other people sometimes.

Jessie. There was little chance of getting a voice call through to her in any case. The towers would be overloaded as every family member and friend in town tried to reach everyone they could think of, whether they actually lived in Garnet or just wanted to talk about the fire.

It occurred to him that Jessie's mom ought to evacuate, though her home was miles west of the fire. She'd know the drill. "When in doubt, leave early for your safety." She'd learned the hard way in Mississippi. *I hope the dog is safe, too.*

But people still got caught by surprise, even when they knew better.

Picking up his phone, he texted Jessie. A cell tower could send 800 text messages in the same space as one voice call, so odds were much better for it to go through. He had to let her know what was happening.

He'd only texted her briefly since their phone call last night, the one that had been filled with raw honesty about his unmanageable life. This was real news, though. *Wildfire burning east side of Garnet.* He tapped out the words and hit send.

It was mid-afternoon in D.C. He expected she was still in the office, but she replied right away. *What? Are they evacuating people?*

Prentice smiled. *Are they ever! Yes. Majestic Estates. I helped.*

Y did U help? U R suspended! No FF work!

Long story. I M OK.

Be careful. Where R U?

Will do, he answered. *Command at Church of Abundant Life.*

That's my church! I'll watch news and call mom. She should get out? Due to the way cell circuits worked, it was entirely possible she'd have better luck calling her mom from D.C. than Prentice would locally.

Yes. Smoke very visible, roads jammed. Let me know if I can help Anna and dog. He wondered how he could have known

Jessie less than a week, and now he felt so... responsible? Involved?

U stay out of it. Not ur job now.

I want 2 help.

Call me soon. U have a story!?

Will try. Phone lines shaky. Text better.

TTFN, she wrote. "Tah-tah for now!" Prentice imagined her making a silly expression at him while she typed it. Not sure why. It did feel good to connect with her. So good. What a concept.

More soon. Bye.

It was so good to hear her voice again, even just through the texts. He didn't feel so lonely. Reaching out to her wasn't that hard.

Prentice was disappointed not to see a message from his dad. It had been more than three hours since the fire started, and the gray and black plume of smoke would be obvious to anyone in the city since it filled up half the sky. Bill's office was on the same road as the church where the command center was.

Prentice started to pocket his phone, but then before he could question himself, he punched in his dad's work number, not expecting it to go through. Surprisingly it did, but Bill didn't pick up. Maybe he was in a meeting. Prentice left a message saying he was safe, but he kept his location to himself. For good measure, he also tapped out a text, *Fire in Garnet. I'm safe. U should stay in office in Pioneersburg. Don't go home today.*

Outside the RV again, Prentice filled his cargo pants pockets with packets of beef jerky, a bag of M&Ms, and the bottles of water the EIS volunteers handed him. Then he headed across the parking lot to the Incident Command center set up in the great hall of Church of Abundant Life.

Inside, he scanned the sea of faces at work on computers, or on the phone, and in a few seconds, he found Lt. Grimaldi. The man towered over most of the others who were gathered in the room, and his dark face was easy to spot in this county where the majority of people were either white or Hispanic.

He talked with Chief Rugen, who was taller even than Grimaldi. The two men stood near a table full of Planning command staff. Rugen had his back to Prentice, and he thought of leaving before Rugen saw him. What would the chief do? Order him off the site?

When Grimaldi saw Prentice approaching, he pointed and got Rugen's attention, who then turned. His face was blotchy red above the neon yellow vest which read, "Group Supervisor." His expression on spotting Prentice sharpened into annoyance. "Keene! What the heck are ya' doing here! The lieutenant says you were in the fire area?"

"Yes, Chief."

Grimaldi said, "Good to see you, Smokey. Glad you checked in this morning."

Rugen cut him off, "But you're suspended!" He was a foot taller than Prentice, and he glowered down at him.

"Yes, Chief. I was nearby when the fire started. I called it in. I was acting as a civilian."

"How in blazes did ya' get an incident badge then?" asked Rugen, and Grimaldi's eyebrows lifted with the same question.

"I showed them my Red Card. I want to go back in there and help. Can you get me assigned to one of the other crews?"

A cloud of discomfort flitted over Rugen's expression for a microsecond, but he recovered his composure and regained his bravado to say, "I was in command of the fire initially, but I've turned it over to the big boys now."

The National Incident Management system created an instant chain of command where every person had a specific role to achieve based on their qualifications. For now, the incident commander was from High Plains County, not an outsider from the state or the feds.

"Well, you know the territory better than anyone, Chief. I'm glad you're on Planning." *I really want to say "I told you so, Rugen."*

The chief waved his huge hand to another corner of the great hall. "Lieutenant, would ya' escort Keene over to Operations? Maybe Pioneersburg could use him and his Red Card. I've got work to do." He turned away without another word.

As they walked to the other side of the room, Grimaldi asked in his deep but quiet voice, "Smokey, you okay for real? How the devil...?"

Prentice told him the truth. "It was awful. I've been learning about wildfires for years, but this is the first time I've worked one where the homes and forest intertwine. That neighborhood up there must be gone..." He glanced at Grimaldi for confirmation.

Grimaldi nodded grimly. "On the west side of Majestic Estates, in the grassland closer to the interstate, they've been able to set up fire breaks. But the reports are that they're about to fall back, to move the fire line all the way north to State Highway 55. No safe anchor points south of the highway. And east of there, Pine Shadows, that's severe fire behavior too. Overrun. Is that where you were?"

"Yeah. Majestic Estates. In the trees." Images of the swirling black smoke and ember blizzards flashed in his brain.

"Well, the good news is north of the highway, Gwilym Acres, and that's where the wind keeps sending it. Seems like it's going a little better on that side than it might be."

"That makes sense," said Prentice. "They've done a lot more cleanup work in there."

Grimaldi nodded to Prentice, acknowledging his mitigation efforts there. "Here we go," Grimaldi said as they approached a folding table littered with laptop computers and a cardboard sign labeled, "Operations." Prentice knew Lt. Kari O'Brien from A Shift on Garnet Fire Department.

"Hey, Smokey," she said.

"O'Brien? It's good to see you. They have you working in Ops. Good call." In a big incident like this, no one's day-to-day job descriptions and titles applied.

Grimaldi said, "O'Brien, as you know, this firefighter is not working as part of Garnet right now," O'Brien and Grimaldi exchanged a knowing glance, "but he's available as a single resource. Let's find a way to get him to work on this fire."

He patted Prentice on the back and said, "Good luck. Keep in touch, okay?"

"Thanks Lieutenant."

As Grimaldi left, O'Brien said, "I don't know what happened with you and the chief yesterday, Smokey, but I'm glad you're here. Things are crazy out there."

Was it just yesterday when I got suspended? "Yeah, I know." He explained how he'd come to be so quickly on the scene when the fire started.

O'Brien tapped on her laptop keyboard as he spoke, eventually saying, "Okay, I've found an engine strike team from Pioneersburg that could use an extra hand. There are five engines about to leave for structure protection and hot spotting in Gwilym Acres. I could send you with them if you're ready to go right now."

"Yeah! Perfect." He unclipped his pink badge so she could scan it to assign him to that crew. As the division supervisor, she could adjust tasking this way to make sure resources were sufficient and were all accounted for when they checked back in later. No matter what happened, they had to check in.

FIFTEEN MINUTES LATER, HE WAS OUTSIDE, STANDING WITH HIS new temporary unit. Captain Snyder, the company officer in charge of this unit, directed one of the three firefighters to help Prentice get the wildland gear he was missing. No bulky bunker gear for this work. Instead, they all needed lightweight helmets, goggles. And the vital VHF radio. He already wore his yellow flame-resistant work shirt, but they got him a new one.

Schnoz, Mac, and Tiny, who was the tallest of the group, all looked familiar. This strike team unit was all Pioneersburg firefighters who worked together. Prentice introduced himself with the nickname he hated, because it was what everyone in Garnet called him, and they'd all crossed paths before at trainings at the regional facility east of the city. "I'm Smokey."

"I thought I remembered you," said Mac.

"Thanks for filling in for Mouton," said Tiny.

Then there was Captain Snyder, with her strong, clear voice, a no-nonsense expression, jet black hair in a bun under her helmet, and piercing brown eyes. Mac told Prentice that back at the station, her nickname was "General." But mostly they called her Captain. *She seems familiar too, but I can't place her. I haven't trained with her like with the other guys.*

Snyder addressed her crew. "You know this, but hear me! Our mission is structure protection, but that's not as important as keeping each other safe and alive. I don't care if there's a camera crew filming a house burning down.

"You all know the Ten & Eighteen by heart. If the Watchouts indicate a trigger point, speak up on the radio, and we'll re-analyze our Lookouts, Communications, Escape Routes, and Safety Zones.

"We are not going to have a fatality or an entrapment. Got it? Now let's drive straight toward this wildfire."

Prentice was impressed with her leadership style and was glad to be under her command. But he wished he could figure out why it felt like he'd met her before.

Prentice, Captain Snyder, Mac, Tiny, and Schnoz climbed into the engine. Tiny drove them north to Garnet with the four other engines in the strike team. Snyder pulled out her copy of the purple Incident Response Pocket Guide. "Let's review the Ten Standard Fire Orders and Eighteen Watchout Situations."

"How about just call out the big ones. Popcorn style," said Mac. "No unburned fuel between you and the fire."

"Look up, down, and around," said Tiny.

"Base all actions on current and expected fire conditions," said Prentice.

"Know where your safety zone is at all times," said Schnoz. "There's more terrain and fuels to deal with in Garnet than in the city."

"Confirm radio communication frequencies," said Captain Snyder. "We just did that, but I'll verify when we check in up there at the elementary school."

"No unburned fuel between you and the main fire," said

Tiny. "But this is the wildland-urban interface. Houses and trees mixed together."

These professionals were going in with a plan. They would stay alert, keep calm, think clearly, and act decisively. Their strike team's goal was to keep the fire from gaining a threshold and taking over Gwilym Acres the way it had Majestic Estates. Stop the flying embers from starting thousands or millions of spot fires on the houses and yards. *If the house doesn't catch fire, it won't burn down.*

Schnoz mused aloud, "I hope the people in this neighborhood are not idiots. They can't expect us to save their properties if they haven't done any work of their own before now."

Mac said, "We'll be able to tell pretty quickly from the street in front of the house. Three-second triage. Yes or no. Simple as that. Is there so much vegetation I can't tell there's a house back there? Is the driveway edged with fuel that could block our way out if it's on fire? Is there a defensible space around the house?" The group agreed.

Prentice sat back in the cab and watched the dry grasslands and forests go by as they zoomed north on the interstate toward the fire. He was where he wanted to be. Working with a team, working to suppress a fire. Doing it safely. Helping people. *I'm not doing this to prove anything to Dad. I'm doing this for myself.*

He smiled inwardly at his logic, picturing Jessie, repeating it back to him, pointing out how goofy it sounded. Something like, "You're going into the middle of a wildfire to help *yourself*?"

He thought of Jessie, held her image in his mind.

They headed toward the hot zone. It felt so good to laugh.

12

Since mid-morning, other firefighters had been trying to set up defenses in Majestic Estates.

Not every home would have a fire truck parked in front to defend it, as some residents seemed to believe. The attack strategy was trying to find places to hold the line against the main fire while still keeping firefighters safe.

Meanwhile, the embers flew and started spot fires far ahead.

Dry crevices cradled the smoldering embers long enough to nurture them to life. Woodpiles, resinous bushes, dry cedar siding and pine decks. Piles of leaves and pine needles in the corners. The fire climbed from the ground to the houses. Some of them withstood the test and resisted the attack, but others smoldered and fed the flames. Multiple small fires climbed up ladders of vegetation into the tree crowns where it could find the steps. It jumped up and from tree to tree easily, they were packed so close together.

Beautiful tree-shrouded streets became too dangerous to protect. Whole streets had to be written off now. Possibly hundreds of houses were already lost, and many more were in too much danger to waste resources there. The insurance companies would tally it up soon.

Prentice thought about the hundreds of hours he'd worked so hard up here. Doing mitigation work is never a guarantee, but it hurt when he saw another house or street lost. It couldn't be as bad in Gwilym Acres as it was south of here, though. It just couldn't.

By mid-afternoon when Captain Snyder's team arrived, there was still a ripple of chaos moving north with the fire, from the frantic evacuation of residents caught completely off-guard. It had been five hours now since Prentice spotted the first smoke, but for many civilians, the fire still came upon them quickly. If they didn't get the alerts, there was no time for residents to think. They just had to react, like Prentice had this morning after he went cowboy.

He had survived. But many others delayed, slowing down to pack personal items or rounding up scared animals. Some of those people didn't make it out alive, especially in Majestic Estates, but it was possible to die in Gwilym Acres, too.

State Highway 55 ran east and west, dividing Majestic Estates from Gwilym Acres with four lanes of pavement. Last year, the county had cut trees on both sides of the highway to remove those growing directly under the power lines. Not on private property, but they went as far into the easement as they could. So there was a bit of a break in the fuel between the two neighborhoods.

To contain the disaster today, other task forces now clear-cut huge trees past the easements into the yards on both sides of the road, trying to widen the fuel break to stop the crown fire from jumping into Gwilym.

Spot fires from flying embers could either starve to

death or be stopped before they got too big, if there were enough resources. That's what Prentice's strike team was on the way to fight in Gwilym. Eighty percent of the homes lost were because of embers landing in the home ignition zone.

Crown fires pushed that fast and hard. No amount of resources could save homes here if it turned into an extreme wildfire event. The only thing that would've made a difference was whether or not fuel reduction work had been done by private property owners in their own yards in the past years.

For the most part, they had not.

On the south side of the state highway, Majestic Estates was now disappearing in ashes as the crown fire grew stronger and spread.

ONCE THE CREW TURNED NORTH ON GWILYM ROAD, PRENTICE noticed a man in a car in front of them arguing with a police officer. He read the frantic, angry gestures through the gray air. Looking over at Schnoz, he said, "I bet he's trying to get the cop to let him back in, what do you wanna bet?" Police officers and sheriff deputies had been in there for hours trying to get everyone to leave. Just leave. Stop packing up your stuff and leave with your lives. Let us do our jobs.

"They get crazy."

Most likely the man was saying, "You've got to let me in there. I was in the city and just found out about the fire! You've got to let me get to my house!"

"It's too bad for the people who weren't even home when the neighborhood got evacuated," said Prentice. "They can't get in now to save their stuff or pets. Or Grandma."

"They'll just have to wait for the all-clear," said Snyder. "And even then, they'll have to have a credential."

"It's disgusting that looters pose as residents or sheriff deputies and sneak in to steal stuff," said Tiny, pulling the engine in at the elementary school that had been bustling with little kids and teachers hours ago.

"This is where I went to elementary school," Prentice told them.

The whole crew voiced their surprise. "How about that, Smokey!" Schnoz said, "The school buses evacuated all the kiddos to Blue Mesa High School this morning." That was twenty miles north.

"Today's the day parents wish they'd updated their emergency contact information," said Mac. "Today's the day that needs to be right."

Now, heavy trucks filled the parking lot, and task force leaders had maps, radios, and laptops spread over the school cafeteria tables as they communicated with IC.

"I'll go inside to verify the plan," Captain Snyder said. "You guys wait here."

The air here on the fire's northwest side was hazy, but it didn't obscure visibility. Prentice watched a helicopter fly right over them and east along the highway, carrying a Bambi bucket holding a thousand gallons of water dipped from Two-Mile Lake.

Inside the engine cab, they shot the breeze to calm their nerves. Tiny asked the guys, "What do you call the Robin Williams movie about a hot California summer?"

"Oh wait, I know this one...." said Mac.

"I know," said Schnoz. "Mrs. *Droughtfire*." Everyone groaned, though they'd heard them all before.

"Okay," said Mac. "How quickly can a wildfire start?"

They answered at the same time. "Lightning fast."

"Yeah, it's crazy," someone added.

Mac told them, "Did you know there's both 'cold lightning' and 'hot lightning'?"

"Really?"

"When lightning starts a wildfire, it's usually from a hot lightning bolt, because they last longer," he said. "But overall, most fires are started by humans."

Schnoz said, "True story. A rancher tried to plug a wasp's nest in the ground by jamming a stake into the ground, but it created a spark in the tall grass. He tried to smother the flames by tossing a trampoline on them, but that just fed the fire."

"Woah," said Prentice. "I heard this Garnet fire was started by two construction workers. One of them was using a propane torch to cut landscape fabric in that new subdivision."

"Brilliant. And here we are," said Tiny. No one had more to say.

A minute later, an air tanker dropped bright red fire-retardant gel along the Gwilym side of the state highway. They were trying to contain the main fire by putting a protective polymer blanket of coolness over trees and houses so the fire couldn't ignite the north side as easily.

Gwilym Acres was on its way to becoming a fire-adapted community. Its residents had been working for years to make sure on the inevitable day the wildfire came, their neighborhood would be less likely to succumb to flying embers or carry a crown fire.

Snyder hopped back in the truck, and they followed the rest of the strike team north on Gwilym Road, which then curved around to the east. The engine set up as planned on

Elk Herd Path, within sight of two others, and all paying attention to the big picture of where the fire was going and what they could reasonably do to stop it from taking over these few blocks.

Residents' and firefighters' lives, first.

Property, second.

Prentice reflected that only a firefighter could look at a street surrounded by trees on fire and smoke blowing across the road and say that it was a good place to set up. It was all relative.

"We'll set up a new line if we have to," Captain Snyder said again. "Keep close to your radios."

Prentice commented, "The trees aren't crammed together like toothpicks in a box." They were healthier and stronger than what Prentice called the "Truffula Trees" in Majestic Estates. Some homes had stone or concrete walls on the downhill slopes to baffle any heat coming toward the house.

"Nice. Even if we weren't here, these houses and properties would have a chance of resisting ignition," said Mac.

"On the other hand," said Schnoz, "if the grass, bushes, and trees look like you're building a campfire waiting for a match, we'll just have to pass on by."

The team started its work. Steady and smooth; smooth is fast. Not in a rush here. Not like this morning. *None of this is like this morning. I was such an idiot.*

Captain Snyder knocked on each door to make sure the residents had evacuated. Schnoz identified small propane tanks or combustible outdoor furniture that could be moved inside the garage or thrown farther away from the house, and he used a rake to clear vegetation away from the foundation and above-ground fuel tanks. "Look at me, a big strong firefighter raking pine needles." He removed vegetation from the immediate area of the structure and closed any windows and doors he could.

When the crackle of a small fire came close, Mac was on it with a hose connected to the tender, but that water was precious.

Prentice used a chainsaw to cut vegetation that could make a big difference. With the wind and the noise from the fire and the equipment running, it was impossible to talk. But he had confirmed the use of hand signals during the ride north. They all noticed things the others had not seen, wooden fence touching a house, or a deck that smoldered and threatened to ignite.

Prentice watched Tiny as he used a backpack filled with a mix of water and fire-retardant foam, hand-pumping the spray into vulnerable chinks. The foam raised the moisture level of anything wooden, decks, woodpiles, or siding, keeping their surfaces moist for an hour longer than if they were just sprayed with water.

Snyder "swamped" the fuels Prentice cut, throwing those shrubs and little trees away from the homes and dragging the ends of bigger trees out of the 30-foot zone. She used a shovel to bury smoldering embers.

The staccato of radio static came in bursts and they all listened, alert to any warning that they had to move out. The weather conditions could change rapidly, and the spotters would send out an alarm.

Prentice and Tiny found themselves in one yard where he'd done mitigation work earlier in the year. Tiny praised the homeowner's efforts. "These guys have the right idea.

Almost nothing for us to do in this property. Let's keep going."

At the next home, Captain Snyder rang the doorbell. Prentice had started around the side of the house when he heard Snyder's voice rise in a commotion at the front door.

"Ma'am! Why are you still here? There's an evacuation order for your neighborhood! You can not be here!"

He retraced his steps, chainsaw in hand.

The lady's voice was unsteady. "I'm not ready to leave yet. I'm still packing my important things." She waved her hands in front of her as she spoke, erratically, as if she could push the captain away. Now, spying Prentice with his saw, she shouted, "Don't you dare cut down any of my trees!"

Captain Snyder beckoned at Prentice to come help, then focused on the woman again. "Ma'am, you have to go now. Is there anyone else in the residence?"

"It's just me, but I'm not ready!"

"It's not safe here anymore, ma'am. The fire is coming this way. We can't guarantee your safety if you stay here." The captain spoke with gentle authority.

Prentice left the chainsaw and walked up the front steps, close enough that he could see the shadows of fear in the woman's eyes. He guessed she was in her mid-fifties, in good physical shape, and her clothing looked expensive. She wore diamonds, a bracelet around one wrist and studs in her ears. But her blond hair was askew, and her makeup was smudged, maybe with sweat or tear stains. Her dressy khaki pants and navy silk blouse were dusty, and her hands trembled.

"You're delaying our work to save your neighborhood." Captain Snyder kept her voice low and steady. "We'll help you carry a load of your things out and escort you to your car, but you have to go. Now!" She raised her voice when the woman didn't make a move.

The woman glared but opened the door wider, and then her face fell as she got a glimpse of the fire and smoke to the south. She must have been too busy packing to notice it getting worse. *Situational awareness.* She wore fluffy bunny slippers instead of shoes, and she'd run out of time.

He and the captain paused in the entry hall, and now Prentice's heart filled with misgiving. There were at least twenty open boxes and several suitcases sitting by the door. Some boxes were overflowing with books, others contained file folders. He spotted collectible dolls, a stash of photo albums. Absolutely no way was it all coming with her, not even if she'd tried to leave earlier. It was clear the stress had robbed her of her decision-making ability.

The captain nodded at Prentice and pointed at a box of photo albums, which he picked up and carried to the front door. Looking out, he said over his shoulder, "The garage door's closed."

Snyder asked the woman to find her purse and cell phone as they headed to the garage from the inside, where they would load her car and send her away from the neighborhood.

The garage door opened, revealing a very new red hybrid Highlander in pristine condition. The interior of the vehicle was empty, totally free of a single box or suitcase. *She hasn't put anything in the car in all this time she's been packing?*

He put the photo albums in the back cargo area and, taking a second box of photo albums from Captain Snyder, he set them in the passenger seat. The captain guided the woman into her seat, placing her purse next to her.

The woman set her key fob in the nook in the dashboard. "You can't make me leave," she announced, glaring at the two firefighters. Her eyes were still flat and dull, but she seemed less defiant.

Without hesitation, Captain Snyder gently picked up the seat belt buckle and put it into the woman's left hand, letting her muscle memory take over. She buckled herself in.

"Don't cut any of my trees," she warned in a voice that was getting quieter by the minute.

"Start the car, ma'am. You need to go west on Gwilym Road to get to the interstate. That's the only way you can leave this neighborhood now."

"But I want to get to my son's house. He's east of here."

She is so panicked she can't think straight. The thought rolled through Prentice's mind.

"No. You can't go that way today. That's where the fire is heading. That road is blocked by all the firefighting equipment. Here's what you need to do. At the end of Elk Herd Path, turn right on Gwilym Road, and you can find your way to Pioneersburg from there on the interstate. There's a shelter at High Plains High School where you need to check in. Go!"

Captain Snyder gently shut the driver's side door, but then hit the door with the palm of her hand twice, loudly. Finally, the lady pushed the ignition button to start the car. Prentice and the captain stepped out of the garage as she backed out. She stopped to look at the house, then closed the garage door. And sat there without moving. Ash chunks pelted down from the sky, hitting her car, the ground and two firefighters.

Prentice gestured, pointing out the direction she needed to go. She ignored him for a long moment, but then, finally, she backed into the street and headed away.

Splat!

A fiery blob carried by the superheated air hit the driveway right where the car had just been. Since the thing couldn't cause any more damage in the middle of the pavement, Prentice and the captain left it and went back to work.

The remains of a flaming squirrel sputtered in the center of the driveway.

www.Tinderbox.tips: Our Job as Private Property Owners

- In 2018, over 58,000 wildfires were reported in
  the U.S., and halfway through 2019 it looks like
  it will be similar.
- The only thing you can control is the fuel on
  and around your house.
- Trees and plants grow. And grow.

"Smokey, you handled that well," said the captain.

"Thanks, Captain." *So did you. People first.*

She reached for her radio. "I'm just going to let the deputies on traffic control know to watch for the woman in the red Highlander and make sure she really gets out."

Prentice nodded, and the two of them joined the rest of the crew, moving from house to house, checking on conditions. It gave him a chance to think about other clients from this area.

Mr. and Mrs. Hardrath had moved to Colorado from California and had been particularly interested in what more they could do to help firefighters when the time came. He had said to Prentice, "I couldn't imagine asking you boys to come in and risk your lives to save my house if we haven't already stepped up to make it easier to do what you need to do."

That day, Prentice had said, "You and Mrs. Hardrath have really done a great job cleaning up your yard and hardening your home. Just keep maintaining what we've started here."

"Yes," said Mr. Hardrath. "We'll do that. But I've heard about how it might help to leave garden hoses out, attached to the spigots, if we have to evacuate?"

"Oh, well sure, if it doesn't take you a lot of time, that could come in handy so we don't have to use water from the engine. Did you know we can even pump water out of hot tubs or creeks to fill up the tanks, if we get a chance?"

"I'd heard that. The fire hydrants tie you down too much, right?"

Prentice had agreed. They'd save their precious resources to use in wiser ways and on streets with a better chance of creating a fire break.

He hoped their house was surviving today. It was blocks from here, so he couldn't tell yet. It would take weeks to tally the damage.

Meanwhile, at the next property, Prentice and Captain Snyder worked on pulling out a row of juniper trees along the front of a cedar-clad home. The chainsaw, whizzing along at a blistering 88 feet per second, deserved Prentice's full attention. In between cuts, he looked around to check on his surroundings and his teammates.

He hadn't fought a fire in the wildland-urban interface — the WUI — before. Not just trees but homes stood in the path of the ember blizzards. He'd studied, trained, watched videos, and talked to hotshot crews to understand better what the environment was like. This was louder, and very real. *It's really happening now!*

Almost every move he made was similar to the work he did for Tinderbox clients clearing extraneous vegetation. But it was nothing close to autopilot, this was too dangerous for that. It was familiar work done in extreme conditions.

Despite all this, he caught himself grinning while he worked. Through the smoke, through the rain of ashes and the heat and sore muscles, he was optimistic. He knew this neighborhood. He'd worked on so many properties in Gwilym Acres. The smoke obscured many houses, but he knew right where he was and multiple ways to get out of there, too.

The names of more past clients popped into his head. *Robenstein. Meyer. Brown.* It made his heart happy. *I really did some good here. I did!*

Just down the street, one of the other units was doing structure protection on a lot owned by a lady named Mrs. Keller that Prentice had worked for. She would say, "Let me hug this big tree before you cut it down," but she understood that the house needed more breathing room, as she called it. "The bark smells like butterscotch."

At the end of each of those hot days, she would say, "Would you like a glass of iced tea? Tell me how it went today." They would chat and enjoy her view of the Rockies.

She still had Ponderosas on her property now. She always said, "I love my beautiful, healthy trees. It was hard to move the bird feeder farther from the deck, but we had to do it, didn't we?"

"Yes ma'am. It's important for the branches not to overhang the roof and gutters. You've got all your trees well-spaced and limbed up now. And I'm glad you can get the bird feeder down from that branch to fill it now using the long pole with a hook." They had both chuckled over that, and she'd ask Prentice to fill it for her as long as he was there that day.

Now, chunks of gray ash pelted them, sounding like a hard rain as they worked. Embers scattered over the yards. Smaller ones, the size of a marble or a golf ball, plopped on the grass. Others were whole branches that burned as they flew through the sky. Prentice saw some on a cement patio, glowing more orange when the wind kicked up, feeding them oxygen. A lot of them landed and died, eventually turning from black to gray. Same thing happened if they hit bare earth or rock mulch. Those destructive embers starved to death.

"The air's getting thicker," said Tiny.

"Yeah," Prentice set down his saw, took off his mask, and wiped his face with his dusty sleeve. The sky was darker than it ought to be at five o'clock, no question. "This is why they call it 'eating smoke.'"

"Bet they call us out soon," said Tiny, and he nodded at Prentice when their radios went off.

"All units in Gwilym Acres. Word from planning says sustained wind of 30 mph and gusts of 40 mph or more expected in the next hour. All units head to the safety zone."

"Smokey! Tiny!" From the side yard, Captain Snyder was calling to them. They waved at her, through the haze, to confirm, picked up their gear, and headed for the truck. Mac and Schnoz met them there. He shook his head with a half-smile. *It was a joke to the Garnet guys when they called me Smokey Bear. Not so much now.*

No one spoke, climbing into the truck. While the fire blew past, they were all going back to the elementary school, the safety zone. Prentice looked around the cab at the sooty, sweaty faces of his new teammates as they chugged water and took off their top layers. Tiny drove them west with the line of other vehicles from their strike team. Within minutes, they'd arrived.

They stood blinking in the late afternoon sunlight, which could actually shine here, since the smoke was less thick. To the west, the sun was an ugly orange ball above the mountains, and the sky was an eerie, sickening shade of orange. From this vantage point removed from the battle, Prentice saw the fire more in perspective and listened to the comments around him.

"We're holding it at bay up here, it looks like. We'll see what happens as the fire burns over."

"Think they'll send us back in there?"

"Once it's black, we can go back."

"Hey Vincent, you lazy dog. I haven't seen you in forever!" someone remarked.

Prentice relaxed and looked up the gentle slope that gave those homes such a perfect view of the big mountains. Narrow plumes of smoke drifted up through the ponderosas in a few places where embers had survived and grown into fires. Long stripes of red fire-retardant gel highlighted the southern edge.

Behind him, to the west, it was grasslands sloping down toward the interstate, and on the other side, the foothills. So far, the fire hadn't even tried spreading west. The prevailing winds helped with that.

But to the southeast, the boiling gray and black smoke went up in slow motion. A few miles away, Majestic Estates was full with black and orange flames of the crown fire. They shot in the air, over a hundred feet high sometimes.

Someone behind him said, "Majestic Estates is toast. Literally."

"I heard they've pulled out from there entirely. They're lined up along Highway 55, but they had to abandon the lines they'd set up."

"There was way too much fuel. Ground fire plus ladder fuel means a crown fire turning into a freight train. Can't stop that."

"It's gonna be a moonscape down there," someone said. "But up here things are looking better."

It was hard to take his eyes away, but Prentice had work to do. The units took turns refilling water tanks at the fire hydrant. He worked with Mac and Tiny, checking equipment.

"I'll do the gas and oil on the saw when they cool off," Prentice said.

"Thanks Smokey," said Tiny.

Then they got water and snacks at one of the supply trucks sent up by EIS for all the crews. "Just time to wait now," said Captain Snyder. "Everyone take a break." The guys settled down in the grass on the shady side of the school, some sending texts to their families, others just shutting their eyes immediately.

Captain Snyder rested in the grass next to the school, leaning her back against the brick building. She pulled off her boots and wiggled her feet inside her socks.

"Hey, Smokey." She greeted him as Prentice dropped to the ground beside her. Schnoz, Tiny and Mac joined them.

"Hey, Captain." Prentice let his feet breathe, too, and unscrewed a bottle of Gatorade.

"You guys did good work today."

"Thanks," the men mumbled. Hardly anyone's eyes were open now except Captain Snyder's dark brown ones, which were open and fixed on Prentice. *Uh-oh. Where have I seen that look before?*

"So, Smokey, I've been wanting to ask—how come you're available to help us? Why in the heck are you not working with Garnet Fire Department today?"

Good question, Captain. "Yeah, well, it's my own fault. I got suspended this week."

"What for?"

I've thought about that a lot. "Being an idealist."

"I'm really asking, Smokey."

"Yeah," Mac and Tiny both chimed in without opening their eyes. Schnoz just snored.

Prentice looked at each of his crew members. It was concern mixed with natural curiosity. He sighed and ruffled his hair. "Okay. So you know how it is in Garnet. It's so frustrating to not get support on the wildfire preparedness message to residents. The higher-ups didn't believe anything was going to make a difference with regard to wildfire. Rugen is so focused on structure fires. He hasn't kept up with the research on preventing ember intrusions—"

She interrupted him from his soap box speech. "It's *Chief* Rugen. And you're not answering the question."

Prentice dropped his gaze. "You're right, Captain. Sorry. Well, I've got a business on the side."

"I heard about that," Tiny said. "You do fire mitigation, right?"

"Yeah, and I really got out of line this week with this lady about it. I was on duty—it's not like I was *trying* to solicit business, you know? I was just trying to get the homeowner to take some action."

"You mentioned your business?" The captain guessed.

"I... yeah, I did. She wasn't listening, but I couldn't seem to stop talking, and I mentioned how she could hire the mitigation work done by a business like mine. It was a rookie mistake, I know."

"I would've suspended you too, Smokey," the captain said, not unkindly.

"Yeah, she would've," said Mac, who was dozing but still listening.

"She's a straight-shooter." Tiny added, and Prentice heard the respect Tiny had for her in his voice.

"Yeah. I deserved it, I don't deny it, but my talk of the side business wasn't what made the lady so mad."

Mac rolled over and opened his eyes. "So what got her in such a bad mood?"

"It was a medical call. She hadn't asked me for any wildfire advice at all. I had just had a fight with Rugen, I mean Chief Rugen, about how the fire department ought to be doing outreach to residents about their responsibilities in wildfire preparedness. He wouldn't listen. So I totally unloaded on this resident."

"Wow. I agree with you on that, by the way," said Snyder. "Outreach is really important."

Mac asked, "You're a structure guy like we are. So what makes you so focused on wildfires?"

He told them how the big wildfires that happened around Garnet as he was growing up affected him. "I don't understand how people who lived through those can act like they never happened."

"Good question." Snyder was listening hard. "Yeah, I was here for one of those... Tom Rugen's been there since '96. I know that because, well, that doesn't matter. Anyway, he's seen them too. But he is as laser-focused on structure fires as you are on wildfires, and trust me when it comes to Rugen, the Pioneersburg department is aware of it."

"How did you end up working for the Garnet Fire Department anyway, Smokey?" Tiny, who had roused from his nap, asked Prentice.

Prentice met Tiny's eyes. "My dad lives there, and I wanted to stay close by. And honestly, I was worried about not getting a job soon enough after college. Dad was on me all the time about making my own living and being independent, so I took the first job offer I got. That was from Rugen in my own hometown."

Snyder had a funny look on her face. "And you said you went to elementary school right here, in this building?"

That was an odd question, but he answered, "Yep. I lived here since I was a little kid."

"Huh," she mused. She fiddled with a clump of dry grass until it broke into little bits and blew away. No one said anything for a while. The heat from the ground and the air enveloped them all, and the fatigue stayed put.

Prentice broke the silence. "Anyway, I've never really figured it out—why he hired me. I remember he said, 'Good, a local kid,' that day." He shifted the conversation away from himself. "How about you, Captain? How did you get into the fire business?"

She sat up a little. "I lived here in Garnet for a while too. Do you remember the Berry Fire right on the front of the mountain? That was in 1989, I think. I was in grade school."

"No. I wasn't born yet." They both laughed.

"We moved to Dayton, Ohio when I was in high school, which I really hated, by the way. My parents do everything the opposite of the way I would do it. I had to get away and be on my own."

"I hear you."

"I took the Armed Services Vocational test, and I enlisted in the Navy and served as a firefighter on a ship. My parents were horrified," she said.

Prentice laughed. "Join the club... So obviously you didn't stay in the Navy."

"No, I joined the reserves after my commitment was up. They called me up to help during Hurricane Katrina. I worked for the Norfolk Fire Department for a while, started on my degree in fire science. Got married to my awesome husband Marco."

"Oh, how did you meet him?"

She smiled and pulled her knees toward her with her hands. "It was at Virginia Beach. We literally crashed into each other when we were body surfing there one weekend. He was there on vacation from Colorado. I ended up moving out here to marry him. So I became Allie Snyder then."

"Is he a firefighter, too?"

"No, he's a consultant. He thrives on routine. It's great, because he's the stable one. He manages the girls' schedules. My hours are wacky, of course."

"Yeah. I know." He thought about what he'd heard. "So, was it the vocational test, and the wildfires, that got you into all this?"

"Not exactly." She reached back to re-do the hair bun, but she was still trying to answer the question, he could tell. She shook her head in a barely perceptible way. She didn't focus on anything while she twisted her long hair around itself and secured it. "No, when I was in high school, I had a bad experience with a house fire up the mountain. Right over there."

"Oh, no." He watched her face, but she kept staring into the grass next to her. He felt a shiver despite the heat.

"It was pretty bad. I was babysitting for some little kids,

and we were making popcorn, and it all got out of control. I felt so helpless."

Prentice tensed. "Popcorn?" was all he could say.

She turned her attention to him. "Yes...." Her brown eyes got so serious.

"What happened then?" he had to ask.

"Well," she started to answer, but stammered for the first time he'd heard all day. She stared at him. "The popcorn was in the microwave too long, and that awful burned popcorn smell was getting all through the house."

"But did that start the fire?" His hands were clenched on his knees.

She slowly shook her head no and looked at Prentice. "No, it was the pan of butter on the stove. I got distracted by the popcorn, and next thing I knew, the butter flared up and I panicked."

Prentice sat up and focused on Captain Snyder. "Captain. I have to ask you something."

"Okay." She blinked hard, looked away as if preparing for something, and then focused on Prentice again.

"Your name is Allie Snyder. But was it Allie Jackson then?"

She kept her composure, but her eyes got wide. "Yes. Allie Jackson." She took a breath. "And I know you too. You're Prentice Keene. You're the little boy I dragged out of the house."

www.Tinderbox.tips - The Fire Triangle:

- **Fire is a chemical reaction requiring three ingredients.**
- **Oxygen, fuel, heat.**
- **Remove one element, and the fire is gone.**

P rentice was almost five years old the first time Allie the babysitter showed up. It was July 1998, the day after Mommy left in a car with that other man, and right before his dumb fifth birthday. That's when Daddy took him and William to McDonald's but let them put pickles on his hamburger and got him a stupid ice cream sundae instead of a cake.

Every weekday for two weeks, as Daddy left for work, Allie showed up. Prentice didn't say much to her, but he liked to listen to her and look into her pretty brown eyes. She said she was in high school and that she had to walk up two steep gravel roads from her house farther down the mountain to get there. But when he asked her where

Mommy had gone and when she was coming back, she said she didn't know. Daddy and William wouldn't talk about Mommy either.

Allie fixed sandwiches at lunchtime, but they weren't the same as Mommy made. That first day, Prentice couldn't eat his; he felt too sick. But the next day he did eat what Allie made, because he felt bad about making her sad. She was bossy, though. She scared him a little when she put her hands on her hips and said he better eat his lunch.

But on the first day of August, Allie showed up again. Prentice knew that was weird even before William asked about it, because he could tell from his calendar it was Saturday.

"It's the weekend," William was saying to their dad. "You're supposed to stay home."

"Yes, I know," Dad answered. "But something's come up. I've got to go in." Something in how he said it warned Prentice his dad was upset, even worse than he'd been in the weeks since Mommy left.

"You said we'd work on the airplane model together!" William hit his small fist on the table.

"You'll have to work on it yourself today. You know what to do next."

Prentice wanted to be included. "Daddy... I wanna do a model plane too."

"No, you're too little, Prentice."

"This is so unfair!" William said, his arms stiff at his sides. "At least Mom would stop working and have fun," he said, arms stiff at his sides now. "You just ignore me!"

Prentice didn't know what "ignore" meant, but he could tell William didn't like it.

"Son, I can't be here like your mother used to—"

"Where did she go, anyway?" William yelled. "I want her to come home. Why can't you make her come home?"

Prentice sniffled. It made his tummy hurt to hear William so upset with Daddy. The two of them usually got along okay, when Daddy made time for it at least. "Yeah, where's Mommy?"

But Daddy didn't answer. His jaw worked like he might reply, and his face was all red, but it was a long time before he said any words, and when he spoke his tone was flat. "Today I'm going to work while you two get to stay home and play. One day you'll appreciate what hard work really means. You boys need to be more independent." He turned to Allie, who had backed into a corner, and gave her instructions for the day as if nothing happened. "There's ham for sandwiches. You can make a pitcher of lemonade, too."

"Dad," William protested. "She's made sandwiches every day. We should have something hot!"

Prentice eyed Daddy, watching as his shoulders sagged. Suddenly, he knew nothing William could say would make a difference. That was the biggest shock. Daddy loved William. But it didn't even matter. He would still leave.

"Sandwiches and chips are fine. I'll be back by five. Maybe I'll take you boys out for dinner... unless there's another outburst," he said, half to himself. With that, he hoisted the handle of his heavily-used leather briefcase and left the house.

Daddy sounded grumpy, like he always did, but he was sadder today too. William sounded more whiney than usual. *Maybe he misses Mommy too.*

William went straight up to his room, stomping loudly on each carpeted stair, as loud as he could. Allie asked Prentice if he'd eaten breakfast. "I can fix it myself," he told her, getting cereal from the low cupboard.

He played in his fort in the yard in front of the living room picture window that morning, dragging more fallen branches to it from the scrub oak and towering pine trees that filled the yard. He peeked in on Allie through the sliding door that led into the living room, but she mostly sat on the sofa, watching television or listening to really loud rock-n-roll on the stereo. At lunch time she brought his lunch right to him in the fort, which was cool. A ham and cheese sandwich with Fritos and little mandarin oranges from a can. She asked him questions about his fort and what kind of explorer he was.

By the time five o'clock rolled around, Prentice had moved into the living room with his Magic School Bus coloring book and crayons he'd gotten at Christmas. He didn't like it as much as his dinosaur coloring book, but that one was filled up.

"You're doing a good job," Allie said, glancing at his work. She began packing her things into her backpack: empty RC Cola bottles, a hairbrush and some rubber bands, a green notebook, and a book with a picture on the cover showing two people hugging. Prentice didn't like the picture. He didn't know anybody who hugged like that. It was weird.

When she was packed up, she turned up the music on the stereo and laughed when he plugged his ears. He could still hear the lady singing in a happy voice about wanting to have a little fun before she died. She mentioned a man named William who never had a day of fun in his whole life. Prentice wondered about that. *Why would she say that about someone? Or sing about it?*

"Allie, I'm hungry," Prentice told her in the brief silence before the next song started.

"Your dad will be here soon and figure out dinner." Another loud song filled the silence with drumbeats. The minutes ticked by, and Bill Keene didn't appear. Neither did William, who'd been by himself in his room all day.

When Allie went to use the wall phone in the kitchen, Prentice followed her. "Mom," he heard her say, "Mr. Keene's not here yet..... Okay, good idea. Bye." She called up the stairs to William's room. "Hey, William? I'm going to get Prentice a snack. Do you want one?"

"What? I can't hear you. The music is too loud!"

"Do you want a snack?" she shouted.

"No! Leave me alone!" William shouted back. He sounded mad. He was no fun anymore, Prentice thought. *Just like the song said. How did that lady know about William never having fun?*

Allie found his glance. "Let's you and me have a snack. I'll make some popcorn, okay?"

"Okay. Can you put butter on it? I like butter."

"It already has butter in it."

"That's what Mommy says too, but sometimes she melts more butter and puts it on top. Pleeeze?" He used his biggest smile on Allie.

She tousled his hair. "Sure, Prentice."

He watched as she tucked the flat packet of popcorn into the microwave and put butter to melt on the stove. Wandering back into the living room, he sat on the sofa. The music hurt his ears, all drums and yelling, not singing. It thumped in his chest. He went back in the kitchen and sat at the little table in the middle, leaning against the wall. Stairs behind him led to the second floor. He thought about going up and banging on William's door, but then he smelled the popcorn. "Allie?" he said, "Is it burning?"

Just then, William pounded down the stairs. "That smells horrible!" he yelled when he careened down the stairs into the kitchen. "Turn it off, why don't you!" William dropped into the chair across from Prentice.

Allie had just turned from the stove, wooden spoon in hand, to open the microwave door.

"Gah." William choked in disgust. "You're making it worse. Get it out of here."

"Whaddaya think I'm trying to do?" she cried, dropping the spoon in the sink and picking up the burned bag gingerly with a hot pad. First she threw it into the trash can by the stove, but William yelled, "No, take it outside!" and she plucked the blackened container out of the trash and carried it out to the patio.

Prentice and William saw the unattended pan of butter burst into flames, and they both screamed, "Allie! It's on fire!"

"I know, that's why I took it out—" she began, but then, spotting the fire on the stove, she screamed too. She was across the floor in an instant, grabbing the flaming pan and dropping it into the sink.

She turned on the faucet, and instantly water and grease combined into a supernova of steam that engulfed the kitchen. Prentice screamed as the searing mixture burned his skin. Allie and William were screaming too.

Above the sink, the curtains ignited.

William took off up the stairs, shouting, "I need water!"

"William, no," Allie yelled. "Don't go up there. Get out of the house!"

She was sobbing, and Prentice watched in disbelief as she ripped the burning curtains down, rod and all, and threw them into the plastic trash can by the stove. He thought her hands must be on fire. He watched her mouth move, "We have to get out!" She kept screaming the words: "We have to get out!"

He wanted to run to the door, but Allie didn't go out, even though that's what she just said. Instead, she ran up the stairs after William. Prentice heard William screaming and crying. "It hurrrrrrts!"

Prentice hurt too. His left arm and the left side of his face screamed with pain. He was glued in place, and he watched in frozen fascination as flames from the curtains rose from the trash can, feeding on the rest of the trash. Wrappers. Paper plates from lunch. He had to be brave. He had to stop it.

Going to the can, he got hold of it and dragged it toward the dining room. It fell over on the threshold and the fire crawled out of the can. It scared him so much, watching the flaming contents spill onto the carpeting.

Allie came back down the stairs without William. "He's hiding in the bathroom and won't—oh my God! What did you do?" She ran to Prentice, where he cowered in the corner of the kitchen and taking his arm, she led him out next to the garage.

Outside on the driveway, the air was cleaner, and they took huge gulps of it. Allie was crying, shaking all over. Bright red burns covered her face and arms. But she seemed to get herself under control, and putting her hands on Prentice's shoulders, she crouched down, and looked him in the eyes. "You stay right here in the driveway. Don't you dare move!" She raced back inside.

But she was back in just a few seconds, standing next to Prentice, squeezing him to her side—too hard. He wanted to ask about William, but he couldn't make his mouth work. Allie had silver trails of tears going down her cheeks. What was worse, though, was that she made no sound. The terror in her eyes. Her choked breathing.

Smoke began to billow out of all the open windows.

And the music played on the stereo in the living room. A man sang about seeing a red door and wanting to paint it black and have all the colors turn black. It was crazy music. Then Prentice saw William up on the balcony. He came, staggering but upright, appearing like a ghost through the smoke that all but obscured the upstairs balcony at the side of the house, above the picture window.

"William!" Prentice shouted.

Allie ran closer, screaming, "Jump, William!" halting below where he stood. William's eyes were wide. Allie screamed again, "I'll catch you!"

He gripped the balcony's rail, swaying, indecisive. Beneath smudges of black soot, William's face was as white as plaster. The red burns blistered his arms. Behind him, the whole house was full of crackling sounds.

Prentice saw the fear in William's eyes, even from so far away, and he crouched down even smaller on the driveway.

"*Jump!*" Allie screamed.

William shook his head, shouting, "It's too far! I'm going down the stairs!" And that quickly he was gone, lost in the smoke.

Allie darted through the kitchen door and called William's name. The fire made its own sound that got louder. He covered his ears, tried not to cry.

Prentice was still crouching right where Allie had left him when she emerged from the kitchen. "I'm going next door to call 9-1-1," she said, chest heaving. "You stay right here!" And she took off down the curved, steep driveway and was hidden by the trees.

Prentice huddled on the ground with his chin buried in his knees and his hands over the back of his neck. He'd been in the same place, in the same position when Mommy drove away a few weeks ago. He couldn't stop the tears now. They fell out of his eyes, straight onto the ground and his shoes, and the spit flowed out of his mouth.

He heard the wail of sirens from far away, and he stood up as the noise came closer.

The first fire engine pulled up the driveway soon after Allie returned from the house next door. The neighbor lady came with her, wanting to help. They all had to move to the side to make room for the pumper truck.

The firemen talked to Allie, but Prentice couldn't hear them. She was yelling and pointing at the house. A loud buzzing in his ears blocked everything out: the crazy music, the fire's roar, the voices. *Where's William? Why isn't he coming out?*

Prentice felt someone behind him. He turned his head and saw Daddy. Daddy was home. He didn't say anything to Prentice but stood with his mouth open watching the smoke.

A fireman brought a ladder from the pumper truck and leaned it up against the balcony. Another fireman, taller than all the other ones, who looked like he was wearing a spacesuit, climbed up to the balcony and went into William's room. He reappeared a half minute later, coming now out the kitchen door. The same door Prentice and Allie had used to make their exit from the burning house. The spacesuit man carried William in his arms. Prentice's throat clamped shut. His big brother was so little, and so still.

Two men in dark blue uniforms met the spaceman fire-fighter with a cot on tiny wheels, put William on it, and rolled him down the driveway to another ambulance parked at the road.

A lady and a man wearing blue uniforms approached Prentice. Squatting down to his height, they told him they were going to help him, and they put a tiny plastic mask on his face. He tried to push it away, but the lady said it would help him breathe and he should keep it on. They wrapped him in a silver blanket, then walked him to an ambulance parked down the gravel road. Allie was there already, with bandages on her arms and a mask on her face. She was like William, lying still—too still—on the cot.

From the road, Prentice saw other firefighters in space-suits aim streams of water from hoses from the truck parked in the driveway right into the windows. Another team ran a hose from the hydrant at the street and sprayed the trees and the ground around the house.

Prentice saw Daddy talking to the blue uniformed men at the ambulance where they'd taken William. He started to go toward him, but Daddy was jerking on their shirts, yelling at them. After a minute, he staggered and almost fell. The men helped him get in the ambulance. It drove away.

The lady in the blue uniform talked gently to Prentice and lifted him into the ambulance where Allie was. And then it all went black.

15

"All these years later," Allie murmured. "I think about it almost every day."

"Me too," Prentice said, just seeing the scars on her hands.

They sat, their backs against the school building, sharing a silence filled with mutual sorrow and regret. They were alone now. Tiny and Mac were snoring as hard as Schnoz now.

Prentice shifted and cleared his throat. "I never got to thank you, Allie....er, Captain Snyder. After they put us in the ambulance, I never saw you again. But you saved my life."

She shrugged and looked at the ground in front of them.

"I mean it—Allie." He used her first name deliberately. "Thank you."

"You said your dad still lives in Garnet?" Her voice was thick with emotion.

"Yeah. He had the house rebuilt. Same floor plan."

"Whoa."

"Remember all the colorful pillows we had on the sofa? That you wouldn't let me take outside to my fort?"

"Of course," she said.

"Dad didn't replace any of that stuff. No wallpaper. No flowers. Nothing decorative. Dad said mom was the one who should have done that."

"But she was gone."

"Yep. While they were rebuilding it, we lived somewhere else, a little apartment, for most of the year I was in kindergarten. He drove me to school and went to work. I don't remember we did anything else."

"And William...? Did you ever...? I don't even know how to ask..."

"He died. You know that, right?"

"Yes," Allie said. "I knew right away when I saw him."

"I didn't know it for a long time. Not for years."

She sucked in her breath. "How...?"

"I just figured he was still in the hospital and that he would come back. Kind of like with my mom. She vanished too. A man drove her away. Men drove William away. Dad brought me from the hospital, and we lived in the apartment, just without him."

"Oh God..."

"I know. But eventually when I got older and realized it was really a bad fire, I knew—I knew he wasn't coming back."

"Didn't you talk about it with anybody? At school, or....?"

"Not really," Prentice said. His voice was flat.

"Your dad didn't.... wow. How could that be?"

"I couldn't ask him. He never talked about it, or William, or Mom. Later when I got older, I realized everyone in town knew about the fire and that William had died. There was a lady in elementary school, a counselor, I guess. She wanted me to play with clay. Like that was going to help?" Prentice shot Allie a sidelong glance. "People always seemed to be whispering when I was around. I never knew what to say or how to act." Prentice was glad to cut to the heart of this with Allie. It was a relief. Allie had been there. She was the only person on earth who knew what that day had been like.

'I'm so sorry," she said, "for all you've been through— losing your brother like that—and your mom had just left."

"I didn't understand about that either. I was too little. I spent a lot of energy being mad at her, when I didn't just miss her, but I could barely remember what she looked like. She was just a dream. Same with William."

"How could you not be angry? And more..." she trailed off.

"Dad left William's room empty when he rebuilt the house. No furniture in there at all. Can you believe that? He had them paint everything plain white. There was no homey stuff. No flowery curtains over the sink..." Prentice looked at Allie with a crooked, sad smile. *She's the only person in the world that would get that about the curtains. Except William. He was there.*

She said, "I heard this term recently that might apply to him. It was, 'immobilizing indecision.' Whaddaya think of that?"

"Yeah, that sounds about right. Immobilizing indecision. Hm," he mused.

She went on. "Maybe that's why he couldn't make choices about decorating. Or talk to you about all the things that happened."

"So much happened in a short time. And, I know it was my fault the curtains even caught on fire," he confessed. "I wanted butter on the popcorn. And then I moved the trash can and went the wrong way."

"Oh, no Prentice! I was responsible! You were a little kid!"

"You weren't much older." He shook his head. "I still can't microwave popcorn. I just can't."

Allie said, "I don't think this will help you any, but I didn't get to talk about what happened either. I've always felt so guilty. I've wanted so badly to apologize."

"I never saw you again. I've always wondered..." He paused. "You disappeared after that day just like William did."

"I couldn't find you after ... didn't know where you went after the house was.... burned."

"Oh. Right. Wow. We didn't have cell phones then, hardly. No internet. Did Dad check on you in the hospital?"

"Not that I remember. He could have called my parents, I guess, but if he did, they never told me. They wouldn't talk about what happened either. And then a few weeks later, we moved to Ohio. My parents had planned that early in the summer. House on the market, pack up, drive across country, gone! It wasn't like them to be so organized. They're both artists. They'd found a hippie community they wanted us to live in near Dayton. So off we went..." She stared at the grass.

"That must have been awful to just leave like that."

"Not like closing the chapter on a book. More like ripping out all the pages you've already read."

"Wow, Allie."

"I really did hate it in Ohio, too. I figured out then that I'm a very structured person. I never fit into the freestyle life. My folks never understood it was all artsy-fartsy chaos to me."

"You would think your own parents would know you. But no," Prentice shook his head. "My dad thinks I'm the acorn that fell far from the tree and then rolled down the hill and all the way into the river. Gone forever. I know my dad wishes William was the one who had survived... They were so much alike."

"That can't be...!" Allie's eyes reflected her surprise.

"It's true. You've met Dad. He hasn't changed. Same job. Same foods. Same number of friends... zero!" They both sighed.

"That's too bad," Allie said quietly. "So do you see him much?"

"I'm all he has, whether he wants to admit it or not. I call him every few days, even though he usually barks at me."

"So do you guys talk?"

He looked at Allie and then back at the ground. "No, not much."

"I really would like to see your dad one of these days, Prentice. That would help me a lot."

Prentice shrugged, "I'll tell him."

She agreed, "It would be good to have some closure. And besides," she laughed, "you might be searching for a new job, after what you did this week. Maybe you could come work in Pioneersburg FD."

"I hadn't thought that far ahead. I've been a bit busy," he said with a half grin.

The radios crackled. "All strike teams in Gwilym Acres. You're cleared to go back in the zone." The others roused from their power naps. Prentice put his boots back on.

"I'm glad we found each other again," Allie said as she laced her boots.

"Me, too. Let's get back to work." He offered her his hand to help hoist her off the ground.

The fire flame front had passed over the area, and their new task was to re-engage with work "in the black," where the fire had gone through, to put out the embers still alive and hiding in nooks and crannies.

The crews climbed back to their trucks. One of the biggest personal hazards now was unstable trees falling on them or their equipment. And it wasn't the big flames they were fighting. Their enemy was still the smoldering embers. The invisible, destructive forces that could take down whole houses and swaths of forests if they were ignored.

"It'll be a relief to deal with a fire we know how to fight, right Captain Snyder?"

"Amen, brother," said Allie.

IT WAS JUST AFTER DARK THAT SAME THURSDAY NIGHT BEFORE the strike team drove south to Incident Command at the Church of Abundant Life. In the back of the engine, without the work to distract him, Prentice's tired brain kept filling with memories he wanted to push away. It sickened him that his dad had never communicated directly with Allie after the fire destroyed the house. How could he have walked away from a teenage girl, an injured girl, like that?

Just like when Bill Keene's wife left him, he acted like it never happened, and never confronted the facts. It was how it worked with him. Don't show your feelings. It was crazy, but his dad just took it as normal. *Because that's what we do in our family*, it was dawning on him. *We don't talk about it if it hurts.*

The quote Jessie gave him, now taped to his bathroom mirror, appeared in his mind. The flames of family dysfunction. A wave of grief overwhelmed him, tightening his throat. *Dad actually abandoned me. He was right there all the time, but he totally abandoned me. I was so little, but I had to survive on my own.*

Prentice shook his head, as if he could shake loose the heart-wrenching reality. *That can't be right. I'm just exhausted. I just need some sleep.*

Yeah, Jessie said you were exhausted too, remember that? answered a new voice in his head. It was his own voice, but it sounded different to him. Older. Reassuring. Almost fatherly, although his dad had never talked to him like that. *Maybe it's time to stop ignoring these feelings and deal with them.*

A more juvenile voice argued with the fatherly one. *It wasn't that bad!* it said. *Dad kept a roof over our heads and food on the table, as he liked to remind me all the time. I should be grateful.*

The mature voice said, *It's okay to be mad at him. It's okay to stand up for yourself.*

Prentice sat up straighter, wanting to be free of it, the voices, the tangle of his emotions., "Anybody got any more Skittles?" he asked no one in particular. "I'm starving."

He heard Captain Snyder on the radio talking with someone at Incident Command. "Oh, really? That's good news. When will that be?" She paused to wait for an answer.

Prentice wondered what good news there could be in the middle of a wildfire.

Allie talked into the radio again. "Thanks. I'll let him know."

Allie turned to him in the dark cab of the engine, and Prentice realized he was the one she'd been talking about. She said, "Our missing crew member André is coming back to work tomorrow."

His heart sank. "So..."

"So, it sounds to me like you have what's known as a Day Off. Do you think you can handle that?"

"No," he protested. "There's too much left to be done. The fire's still burning. I can't just sit around—"

"You've got no choice, Smokey," she said gently but firmly. "You did great work today. More than your share, from what you told me about your morning. But as your Temporary Commanding Officer... or something," she smiled at her own joke, then sobered. "I order you to take a break. I could try to find you another assignment, but I don't think that's what you need. Okay?"

"No. Not really." *What the heck am I going to do if I just stay home?*

Allie said, "Look, I've got a pretty good hunch you're working on a lot of stuff, Prentice." She paused. "Maybe you could take your dad to lunch." They shared a chuckle that trailed off. They both knew it was a ridiculous suggestion.

"Sure. And then we'll go shopping at the mall," Prentice joked. "But okay. I get what you're saying. That I should keep trying."

"He's not a bad man, Prentice. I don't think he wants things to be the way they are between you. He just doesn't know what to change."

"Yeah, maybe not. Thanks, Captain Snyder. Thanks Allie."

Back at the church parking lot, as they exited the truck, Prentice saluted Schnoz, Tiny, and Mac. He returned the equipment loaned to him and checked out with his Incident Command credential. He stopped by EIS for more food and something to drink. The volunteers served him as soon as he sat down in a folding chair, without asking any questions. He ate as if he'd been stranded on a desert island for months. Then they encouraged him to fill up his pockets with snacks. He walked to his truck, waved at the new shift of ambulances waiting there, and drove home.

At his apartment, unbelievably, everything looked just as he'd left it this morning. The effect was surreal. *Was that just today that I worked at Mr. Bixby's?* After a long shower, he switched on the TV in time to catch the ten o'clock news. It was no surprise that the commentator, Rachel Indigo, led with coverage of the fire.

"The little town of Garnet is in ruins tonight," she announced somberly, but her fake eyelashes and frilly red sleeveless dress didn't track with the gravity of the news she was delivering. "Multiple fire departments responded today, trying to stop the fire which began in the Prairie Flower subdivision and blew into Majestic Heights this morning.

"Sherrie Pruett, public information officer for this incident, told Channel 8 News that over 10,000 people have been evacuated east of the interstate, and possibly hundreds of homes have already been destroyed. Many more homes are still in danger, and hundreds of people are missing."

Batting her heavily made-up eyelids, the anchor said, "Let's find out more from our reporter Franklin Heiser, who's at Incident Command at the north end of Pioneersburg." Heiser had black hair and wore a black Channel 8 windbreaker. He held up his phone to read his notes, and the blue screen light illuminated his face. Behind him was the church, and command staff and local government officials moved in the background.

"Right, Rachel. While the devastation was happening in Majestic Estates this morning, crews worked to create a fire break along State Highway 55, east of the interstate, attempting to save more homes north of there that are still very much at risk.

"Wind speed and fire behavior picked up again Thursday afternoon, causing crews fighting spot fires in Gwilym Acres to retreat to safety, but more teams were back there tonight. It is too dangerous for anyone to work in Majestic Estates now. One firefighter we spoke with earlier tonight was there and has this to tell us."

The picture changed to a clip of a wildland firefighter standing in the EIS area earlier in the evening. "The official word on this has got to come from the Incident Commander, but I can tell you that what I saw at noon in Majestic Estates already looked like World War III. That tiny grass fire started small, but it found so much fuel, it grew into a roaring monster and bowled us all over with sheer force."

The weary firefighter continued. "But in other places, it was the little embers that caused the destruction, not the crown fire. In Pine Shadows, I saw destroyed houses that were surrounded by undamaged trees. The firebrands ignited the inside of the buildings hours after we left by sneaking in the cracks. We couldn't station guys at every house to watch for new flareups."

He said, "I'm so proud of the teams that slowed it down at Highway 55. I was sure it would've kept right on going and destroyed Gwilym Acres, too. Who knows, it still could. Embers were flying ahead of the fire. The wind was swirling everywhere. The retardant lines dropped by air resources helped.

"But it happened so fast, there was no time to get any air resources working in Majestic Estates."

Heiser faced the camera, "Officials say hundreds of residents are unaccounted for. All residents who are displaced should check in with the evacuation center so that the Red Cross might help them connect with family members. I'm Franklin Heiser, Channel 8 News, Pioneersburg."

Prentice was about to turn off the television when Rachel Indigo began a follow-up story that stopped him in his tracks. "Evacuating from Majestic Estates this morning was chaotic as residents of over 800 homes needed to leave the area at the same time. All the southern egress routes were blocked by the incoming wildfire and by firefighting equipment trying to contain it. Let's watch this interview from Beth Garcia earlier today."

He stared at the screen when the reporter appeared. He was there, too, of course, although it seemed like a million years ago that he'd been interviewed in the parking lot. Prentice felt weird watching himself speak. He looked like an old man, standing there, gray-faced, disheveled. He barely remembered what he'd said.

"I was doing tree-thinning in Majestic Estates today," Prentice listened to himself say. "I called in the fire about 10 a.m., then I came across this elderly couple. They couldn't evacuate. He couldn't get his wife out of the house."

"So you took charge, right? Got them to safety, and I heard from others who followed you. They said they owe you their lives."

"No. I—I didn't even know what I was doing..."

Beth Garcia faced the camera, "Ladies and gentlemen, you heard it here. This lumberjack is a hero today..."

Prentice shut off the television and let the silence envelope him. *How about that? I wonder if Dad is watching the news tonight. He's got to be proud of me now.*

16

The clock said it was after midnight in Washington, D.C., but Jessie would want to know what was going on. And he really wanted to talk with her. He connected his phone to the wall charger and put it on speaker. She picked up on the third ring with a sleepy voice, but as soon as she recognized it was him, her voice became sharp with alarm.

"Oh Prentice! Are you okay?"

"Yeah." It was gratifying, hearing her concern. "I'm home. Have you talked to your mom?"

"She's at my apartment now. She's got a key. Is her house in danger?"

"Not so far. As long as the wind keeps blowing from the west for the next few days, the fire ought to stay on the east side of the highway. But it's a good thing she's out of there. The smoke is bad; the roads are all blocked off. They had planes and helicopters flying overhead."

"I'm so glad you called me. How are you, Prentice?"

"I'm.... well, I'm fried actually. You'll never believe what happened this afternoon."

"Besides a fire burning down a quarter of our town? And you rescuing some senior citizens from the jaws of death? I saw that on the national news this evening. You forgot to mention that when you texted me."

"There was a lot going on. I just saw the story on our local news. It went national? How 'bout that..." He felt an unaccustomed flare of pride that he quashed. It made him uncomfortable.

"So what else happened?" Jessie prompted.

"Well, you know the house fire? The one when I was little?"

She paused. "You mentioned it on our hike, but it didn't seem like the right time to ask more."

"Oh, man." How could he say all this stuff over the phone?

She was still there. "What happened? Are you okay?"

He tried to pull himself together by taking a new tack. "One of the firefighters on the strike team I was working with this afternoon..."

"Hold on, are you saying you went back and fought the fire after you evacuated? I thought you were suspended."

"I wanted to help out, and they gave me an assignment at the incident command."

"Oh Prentice, you're unbelievable. You're always taking responsibility for other people."

"I'm starting to see that. Well, something really strange happened. One firefighter turned out to be the babysitter that was with me and my brother the day our house burned. I didn't recognize her at first, but she knew me even after all these years—"

"What are you talking about? What babysitter?"

Prentice said, more quietly, "Jessie, I'm sorry I woke you

up. I just wanted to hear your voice. I should let you go back to sleep."

"Just glad to know you're okay. But this sounds important, Prentice. It's okay. Really. I'm already awake, and I can listen. I want to. Let me grab my sweatshirt first, though. This hotel room is freezing."

Prentice considered quietly ending the call, but he knew that would be worse.

"Okay, I'm back. Prentice? Are you there?" Jessie asked.

He gave her the gist of their reunion. "She's got all this guilt about it, just like I do. That's what I found out today."

Jessie said, "It's a lot to take in. Wow."

"I should have waited to call you."

"No, it's okay. You needed to talk this out."

"Like you said, maybe it's time to dig up the past and really deal with it."

Jessie said, "Your dad really did a number on you. It's one thing to keep things hidden within the family, that's bad enough. But to pretend something that awful had never happened, to leave a teenager with all those questions..."

He was feeling lighter inside, just digging this stuff up and pitching it away. "No. And it's not normal to ask a five-year-old boy to just go on living life without his brother or his mom with no explanation at all." *This is so obvious now that I'm saying it.*

"You're so right! Oh, your poor dad."

Prentice huffed. "My poor dad?"

"Yes. Think about everything that's weighing on him. He must feel really guilty about all of it too. His wife, his son... It's a wonder he can even get out of bed in the morning," she said.

"Hm. I guess so."

"We have a lot to catch up on. I'm really proud of you for saying all that out loud, Prentice."

"It's not like me."

"Sorry. What I meant was, I think you're on the verge of learning some new ways of doing things. Listen, I want to talk about this some more, but I've got to be up for work in four hours. So now's not the time. But I'm going to text you a few thoughts from my support group, okay? Talk to you soon?"

"Thanks Jessie."

"G'night, Prentice."

What's happening to me? All this talking about the most horrible times of his life. It was like getting his insides ripped out.

Lying on his back, watching the night shadows flicker over the ceiling, he had a flash of memory of a time long ago with his mom, when he was almost five. It hadn't made as much sense to him then as it was starting to now.

Mom had showed him and William a black-and-white photo. It was of their father as a toddler. Little Billy Keene, dressed in a white shirt, dark suspenders, and oversized short wool pants, had been posed, sitting on a wooden stool. He had skinny, white legs and held a toy truck. Unsmiling. There'd been hints of the guardedness that was customary now. The boy looked up, mouth slightly open, as they called his name to divert his attention from the toy to the camera. He stared past the photographer to a point behind him.

"Who is that?" William had asked Mom.

"It's your Daddy. It's one of the few photos of him as a child that we have. It was taken at a department store in Boston, where they lived. His mother took him."

"Like you took us, where the man told stupid jokes trying to make us smile." William peered up at his mom.

She laughed. Prentice remembered how he'd always loved to hear her laugh. He missed that the most.

"Yes," she'd answered William.

He studied the picture intently. "It's blurry."

"He looks kinda sad," Prentice remembered saying.

"Yes, well, his father was gone an awful lot, and he, well... he didn't help very much at home. It was hard for his mother."

"Oh," said William. Prentice didn't say anything, but he peered at the photo.

"It was tricky. He couldn't bring friends home to play when he was in school, because his father was kind of mean to other people sometimes. But your dad was a little child just like you two," Mommy smiled and inclined her head to one side as she regarded the photo and then her boys.

"Hey, I'm not little!" said William. Prentice looked at his big brother and nodded in agreement at Mommy.

"That's why I wanted to show this to you. He doesn't talk about himself very much. But it's important that you know him. He's so serious now, and he works so hard. He makes mistakes, but it's not on purpose. He's a real person inside, just like you and me," Mom said.

"Daddy's a person?" Prentice said, trying to understand.

Mom nodded. "Did you know he wanted to be an astronaut, once upon a time?" she told them. "But that didn't work out."

"Why didn't he? I thought he was good at everything. He's thinks a lot. Why's he always working?" William asked.

Prentice added, "You're the only one that plays with me, Mommy."

"That's hard to say, my pumpkins," she said. "I can't get him to play with me either," she said with an unconvincing half-smile. She looked out the window at the trees and the view outside the mountain house, not at them. "I think things were hard for him when he was little. His dad had a lot of troubles..."

Little Prentice asked, "Is there a picture of his mommy and daddy?"

"No. I've never seen one."

Just a few months after that conversation, she left them. Prentice forgot about the photo and everything she said. There were too many bigger losses that happened to him in succession: his mom, and his brother.

That photo was destroyed in the fire. But he had a feeling now that his dad remembered it all too well.

Prentice's cell phone chirped as Jessie sent several texts she had copied from a website:

"The healing begins when we risk moving out of isolation. Feelings and buried memories will return. By gradually releasing the burden of unexpressed grief, we slowly move out of the past," from AdultChildren.org.

He thought about those words, and then another text came in.

"We have 'stuffed' our feelings from our traumatic childhoods and have lost the ability to feel or express our feelings because it hurts so much (Denial)," from AdultChildren.org.

Maybe it's like having surgery to take out a tumor. Once they take it out, I'll still have scars, but I'll sure feel better, he thought. *Meanwhile, how do I get the tumor out?*

It was late, but he texted his dad again. No answer yet. He was probably sound asleep on his office sofa. *He could have come to my apartment tonight, like Anna let herself in at Jessie's. I gave him a key.* He wondered why he kept asking himself questions when he already knew the answers.

Ss he switched off the kitchen light, he remembered he had a job scheduled on Friday. Tomorrow. Mr. Futey, his client, was expecting him, but he lived in Gwilym Acres, so obviously that wasn't going to happen. Prentice retrieved his phone and tapped out a text.

Mr. Futey. R U OK? Please let me know. Prentice Keene.

Despite being more tired than he'd been in his life, he brushed his teeth before he went to bed. It was a little way to spend time thinking about his mom, and the good routines of their life before she left. *I'm understanding her more now, too. A little.*

He turned off his alarm clock and fell into the sleep of an exhausted soul.

He hadn't slept so late in a long time, maybe since college, but he was still as tired as when he conked out. He sniffed the milk container to see if it was still fresh. *Nope.* He mixed up some powdered milk and poured it over a bowl of frosted wheat cereal, and then another, in front of the television.

The news show gave a status report about the fire in Garnet. The young morning anchor had just been promoted from the sports department, and he read the words from the teleprompter with the energy of a football game play-by-play. "Thousands of residents who were evacuated are now in shelters, hotels, or with friends."

He was more comfortable with enthusiastic sport-speak than reports of death, damage, and wildfire containment. "The biggest questions are still about the fate of missing people and the condition of the homes in the hardest hit areas. It's too soon to tell specifics, but it is evident that Garnet east of the interstate is devastated."

Next, a weather reporter Prentice hadn't seen before

came on the screen. Credibly, she explained to the audience that it was already over 80 degrees at 9 a.m. "So much heat in the dry air will make it that much harder to keep the fire contained as sparks continue to fly in search of tinder-dry fuels."

She continued, "We'll have very low relative humidity again today. The effects of that are emphasized at our high elevation. This will be combined with projected sustained winds of at least 45 miles per hour, with gusts into the 60 mile-per-hour range today. Those weather conditions increase the fire danger."

Prentice bent forward, thrilled to hear her present the facts without sugarcoating them.

And the facts were grim. The wind was going to make it difficult to get the fire contained. No one could control the weather or the topography. The only other variable was the fuel, and Prentice knew more than he wanted to about that. The area was a tinderbox jam-packed with bone-dry fuel after a hundred years of vigorous fire suppression. Hundreds of standing beetle-killed trees that'd burn as hot and fast as a grass fire. And now thousands of homes all tucked in there. It was a powder keg. Not just in the part of town already burning, but all around Garnet and along the Front Range.

Containing sparks. That's not my job today. But then, what is my job today? He wondered. *Nobody's expecting me to be anywhere.* His throat felt a little tight. What to do with completely free time? He considered turning on the ride-share app, but he surprised himself by dismissing that thought. *Jessie and Allie would both vote for a real day off. They're right.*

He checked his phone. Still no word from Dad. Allie's

idea about meeting up with his dad took hold. *Forget texting*, he thought. *I'll go to his office.* He won't be able to ignore me there.

To make it more fun, he decided to dress the part of the son taking his dad to lunch, though he'd never done it before. Nice but impractical khakis, leather lace-up shoes, and a polo shirt that said Central Colorado University. There was no room for his cell phone in the pocket, but he crammed his wallet in the back pocket, and he carried his phone.

He was doctoring the scrapes he'd gotten yesterday with antibiotic ointment when he suddenly stopped, and it occurred to him how lucky he was to have escaped yesterday with such minor injuries. Others had died, but all he needed was a few band-aids. He felt a rush of gratitude. He looked deep into his own hazel eyes the mirror. *But who am I so grateful to?*

Then he thought of Jessie and felt a warmth in his heart that surprised him. He remembered something she had said a few days ago. "It isn't as if God is punishing us, or abandoning us out of indifference."

He remembered replying, "I don't know. I've gotten through life just fine. I just put my head down, do what I have to do to survive all the crap thrown my way, and life goes on."

"God wants us to be healed, hopeful, and joyful," she'd replied.

Looking in the mirror again, it occurred to him that he might be living proof that a guy could have hope, even when everything around seemed crappy, like right now.

"Time to go talk to Dad," he said to his reflection.

On the radio in his hail-dented truck, the music was

perfect for the occasion. He sang along in a silly falsetto with Billy Joel's "The Stranger." Don't be afraid to try again, the words said. Everyone goes south every now and then.

"Aren't you Bill's son?"

With raised eyebrows, Prentice acknowledged the woman who had appeared at the reception desk of the Fortress Financial Building on Contractor Boulevard.

"We were about to call you," she told him.

"You were? Why?" He fingered the collar of the fancy polo shirt he'd put on in honor of his day off. He realized the khakis didn't fit his legs anymore, either; he'd put on muscle since college.

"Bill always calls in if he's not going to make it into the office. Especially with all the doctor's appointments lately. But we haven't heard from him since the day before yesterday. Is he doing all right?"

Prentice nodded at first, then shook his head as his jaw went slack. "What? He's not here?"

"No, not yesterday or today. It's almost ten o'clock. That's just not like him."

"I'm talking about Bill Keene. Maybe you're thinking of someone else. He's always at work."

"No. You're Prentice, aren't you? You look just like in the photo in his office. Well, you're older now," she said. "We wondered if he might be staying with you because of the fire up there."

He shook his head. "No, I haven't heard from him. That's why I'm here. I thought he might be staying in his office to avoid the mess in Garnet. And what about all the doctor's appointments?" Prentice couldn't follow this conversation.

"For the diabetes. It's so hard for him to walk lately. I've been worried about him." The woman's gaze was unwavering.

"Diabetes?" Suddenly, he felt so weak. "He has diabetes?"

"You didn't know?" The woman saw his confusion. "You've seen how he's lost weight. He's always exhausted...?"

Prentice got his breath back. "Yeah, I guess I've noticed he wasn't— But I didn't realize he was sick—" He broke off, at a loss. How was it he didn't know? This would explain the magnified computer screen he saw the other day when he was there doing mitigation work. And Dad drinking so much water instead of coffee. *If he has diabetes, and he hasn't showed up for work, he must be in trouble.*

"I've gotta get to Garnet," he said as he ran out the door.

Hopping into his truck, he jabbed the key at the ignition, but it wouldn't fit. That's when he completely lost it. He couldn't stop the tears, and finally he gave in to them. Frustration overwhelmed him. His head ached and he squeezed his eyes closed, trying to get it together.

His voice choked out of him into the stifling air, "Why didn't you tell me! Why didn't you tell me?" He asked, choking on the words, finally shouting them. "Why don't you trust me? You raised me, but you won't talk to me! You're a complete stranger to me!"

Sitting alone in the parking lot, the hot morning sun radiated through the truck window, heating up the cab. He yelled until he was hoarse, and his eyes burned with loss. "You don't think I can do anything right!" *Maybe I can't. Maybe Dad's right.*

Then he remembered another thing Jessie said, something like, "Your dad is an adult, chronologically at least. You're not responsible for solving everything for him. It's not your fault." *Powerless over the dysfunction. Detach with compassion.*

His next sudden intake of breath startled him back to the present, along with an inspiration. *I keep imagining that William would be dealing with Dad better than I am. But he's not here, and I am. So what can I do?*

His breathing started to return to normal. "I can't help being me," he said out loud to himself. He found a water bottle under the seat and gave himself a minute to splash his face with the warm water. He slammed the door, rolled down the window, and buckled his seat belt, getting ready to drive north.

I'm talking to Dad, but he's not even here. Sure, he wasn't responsible for fixing him, but he couldn't just ignore this whole thing now and go get himself a coffee, either. He couldn't call God on the phone and put in a special order for a rescue.

"I really can't do this by myself," he told himself. Prentice looked in the non-existent pocket in his pants for his phone but then found it in the center console. He tapped 9-1-1. Station #1 at the north side of town was about ten minutes from his dad's house on the mountain. They'd get to Dad faster than he could from the city.

Except the line to emergency dispatch was busy! There was still a fire burning on the east side, after all.

He texted his dad again. *R U OK?* and threw the phone back into the console.

Just about to put it in reverse, a text came back from Dad. Prentice knew it was him from the unique text notification tone he'd set for his dad. "Tink! Tink! Tink! Tink!" It was the sound of a hammer driving a steel drill into the rocks to build a railroad tunnel. It came from the legend of John Henry, the steel-drivin' man who worked himself to death, trying to work faster than a steam-powered rock drilling machine.

The text itself said almost nothing, but that said everything to Prentice. No complete sentences. No words at all. Just letters.

NNNNNNNNNNNNNNNNNNNN.

Prentice squinted at the row of letters, trying to make sense of what he was seeing. But there was no sense. A rock weighed down Prentice's stomach. At least Dad was alive.

He floored the gas. Stupid selfish control freak or not, his dad was most likely in big-time medical trouble. And nobody would get to him if Prentice didn't. So he had to save the world by himself after all.

～

WAITING AT THE STOPLIGHT ON CONTRACTOR BOULEVARD, Prentice searched for something sweet to calm him down. He ripped open a fun-size Snickers bar that he found under the seat and bit down on it. *I've heard of smokers desperate for a cigarette at the beach party, digging through sand for an old cigarette butt. Am I that bad?*

He felt sweat trickling down his back. His thoughts shifted, picked up speed, and swirled around as much as the wind across the Colorado plains. *He's never eaten right. I should've asked him about those waffles on the counter last week.* All kinds of stupid thoughts raced around in his head, piling blame onto himself. *No wonder he was unsteady. When did this start?*

"He needs to be responsible for himself!"

To regain control, he tried to notice his surroundings as he barreled north. To the northeast was smoke from the Garnet Fire he'd escaped and helped fight yesterday in the two subdivisions. A wide plume billowed from the forest now after dying down during the night when the air was cooler. The strike teams, task forces, and other resources were hard at work over there trying to stop it from spreading more damage and save a few more homes if possible.

And I'm on the outside looking in. He shook his head to try to stop that thought.

Ahead of him in the smoky hot blue sky, two helicopters with Bambi buckets were making wide circuits between Two-Mile Lake west of the interstate and the active fire on the east side. One at a time, they scooped up a thousand gallons of water from the lake and flew back to dump it on the edges of the fire, as directed by Operations.

They're going to handle it. They'll get it contained. It's a good thing Rugen turned over control as quickly as he did.

His brain was jumping all over the place. The fire. His dad. His job. He wished he had another candy bar.

What happened to you, Dad? Are you still trying to survive your own childhood? Why won't you talk to me? He banged the steering wheel. The traffic ahead of him on the interstate was slowing near his intended exit for State Highway 55, so he tapped the brakes and then slowed down drastically. *It must be the fire crews on the east side. Makes sense.*

How could Garnet's Fire Department be so woefully unprepared when there were great resources like Pioneersburg nearby? *Rugen. It's Rugen's fault.* He gripped the wheel tighter. *All the conversations with me, refusing to listen about the risks.* Only talking about house fires, and leaving the rest to fate.

"Get a grip, man!" he told himself. "You tried!" Jessie had said you can only control your own actions. "You can't change other people," she had said. It was starting to fall into place for him, in his own real world.

He looked east, at the sections of blackened forest a half mile from the interstate. Smoke still flowed from Majestic Estates in the buffeting wind.

It should have been a ten-minute drive to his dad's house from here. All he had to do was exit here and go west, through historic Garnet, and wind up the switchbacks for Forest Road to the top of Forest Heights. But the traffic was stopped dead, and the ramps were choked with cars.

Still watching the sky to the east, billowing smoke, he switched on the radio, hunting for news, and paused when he recognized, "Purple Haze." He was about to punch in another station when the radio announcer broke in.

"Music lovers, attention!" the DJ shouted. "I'm sorry to have to interrupt Mr. Hendrix, but we have an urgent announcement for you. There's another wildfire in Garnet. This is not, repeat, *not* the same one as yesterday. The fire-fighters are still battling the east side Garnet fire today. Get this though. The new fire is on the west side of Garnet, on the mountain."

Prentice turned his head west and got a sucker punch to his gut. A new plume of smoke rose out of the National Forest.

A whole new part of town was in jeopardy. Historic Garnet, all the homes, like Anna's house, and the small businesses were under threat. Everything in the strip mall, and the Rocky Mountain Diner on Forest Road, were in the direct line of the oncoming new fire and the blizzard storm of embers whipped up by the stiff wind. So was the Forest Heights neighborhood, with its heavy fuel load and tangle of cul-de-sacs clambering up the side of the mountain. The new column of smoke reached tall out in the national forest like a skyscraper now.

The radio was saying, "Here's Sheriff Oscar Brown with a statement."

After a few seconds' pause, a different deep voice with a subtle east Texas accent came through the speakers. "Attention, ladies and gentlemen. I regret to inform you that there is now a second wildfire burnin' in the northwest corner of High Plains County.

"Crews are still battlin' the Garnet Fire that started yesterday. It's goin' to be a long haul there, but they're beginnin' on damage assessment. That's goin' to take weeks. However, a second fire, now named the Forest Heights Fire, was spotted this mornin' on the edge of the National Forest in the mountains west of Garnet.

"New evacuation orders are in place for all homes and businesses west of the interstate. I repeat, the *west* side of the interstate. This includes historic downtown Garnet, Forest Heights and Garnet High School.

"Evacuation alerts are bein' sent to everyone signed up for county emergency notifications, and as we speak, law enforcement is knockin' on doors in those neighborhoods to make sure all residents leave immediately.

"Garnet Elementary School was already closed yesterday. Now students from Garnet High School, on the west side of town, are being bused north to Blue Mesa High School, where parents can reunite with them.

"Be aware of road closures. State Highway 55 was already

closed yesterday from the interstate east through the Garnet Fire. Today, Highway 55 is only for evacuation and first responder use. Plains Road is closed south of Garnet, since it's near the origin of the new fire.

"Residents need to follow the direction of law enforcement to minimize the traffic delays. Forest Road coming off the mountain, and Highway 55 through historic Garnet are both in near gridlock. We have reports of residents drivin' on the wrong side of the streets tryin' to get to the interstate to evacuate. The streets are over capacity with so many cars on the road at once."

Prentice sat in his truck, fighting a sense of panic. He tried to think of another route as Sheriff Brown continued, "Due to the prevailin' wind direction, we do not think this new fire is related to yesterday's fire. Initial evidence indicates that this fire could be human-caused, since no lightnin' was recorded yesterday or this mornin' in the area where the fire started.

"The resident who called in the smoke this mornin' said she's seen people campin' in the National Forest in the same general area as where the fire started, and despite the burn bans in effect, a smolderin' campfire may be to blame for this ignition.

"Resources are already on the scene, and we ask for your cooperation in avoidin' the entire west side of Garnet so they can do their jobs.

"No residents are allowed back into east Garnet at this time to Majestic Estates, Gwilym Acres, Tall Pines or Pine Shadows. It is not known when authorities will deem those areas safe for civilian re-entry, since crews are still battlin' the Garnet Fire.

"If you have evacuated, please go to the disaster assistance center set up in conjunction with the evacuation shelter at High Plains High School in Pioneersburg or the new one at Blue Mesa YMCA to let authorities know you're safe and to get a credential provin' your residence. That way, when we open up the neighborhoods later on, we'll be able to notify you directly, and deputies will know you really belong there.

"There will also be representatives from local disaster service organizations and insurance companies at the disaster assistance centers. Thank you for your cooperation. We anticipate another briefin' at twelve-hundred hours."

On cue, a turbo-charged blast of wind from the south buffeted the truck. Prentice's heart pounded in his chest. *No way,* it was all he could think. *No way.*

The interstate traffic had come to a standstill, blocking cars trying to get on the highway.

Two fires in the same town. No way.

HE THOUGHT ABOUT PICKING UP HIS CELL PHONE TO CALL DAD again, to tell him he really had to get out. Maybe the garbled text from him had been a mistake. But as he reached for it, his hands were shaking. *It's no good. Stop it. Don't get in a wreck. Even though we're not moving at all now.* To focus himself, he looked left toward Forest Heights. Through the smoke, the lick of an occasional orange flame darted into view from the thick forest, but mostly it was just more gray and white smoke rolling skyward in ever-widening billows.

He scolded himself. *How did I not see that?* Then he gave himself a break. *It's not like I have anything else on my mind today, do I?*

He saw glimpses of the backed-up lines of cars trying to get down the hill from Forest Heights and out of downtown

Garnet. The morning sun reflected back at him off car windows, stretching way up into the trees. Way back up to Dad's neighborhood.

"They're driving in both lanes. I can't go that way, even if I made it off the highway."

Down there on Highway 55, he even saw people walking around among the cars and trucks, west of the interstate overpass. A pickup truck pulling a horse trailer had gotten a flat tire and blocked one lane, further confounding the movement of traffic off the mountain.

Historic Garnet only had three possible routes from the area. Forest Road was a collector that should have taken traffic down out of the mountain subdivisions, but it was jammed up. Plains Road headed straight south, but it headed right towards the new fire.

On a normal day, State Highway 55 east would be the most obvious egress, but the east-bound route was closed by the Garnet Fire, still in progress. From what Prentice could see, the only choice for evacuees was to go north on Highway 55. Then they could keep going north into Blue Mesa County, or turn east to get to the interstate on-ramp, or continue east on Nickel Road.

Prentice wasn't trying to get out of town. He wanted to go in. The traffic moved north an inch at a time.

"Come on people. Move!"

Hot wind rocked the truck as it pushed the new fire north and sent smoke and burning brands high into the air ahead of it. Glowing embers, which must have been part of a pine tree not long ago, sailed through the air and landed on the grass, on the highway, on the hood of his truck. Through a gap in the smoke, he saw flaming branches land on Two-Mile Lake, to the northwest, extinguishing when they hit the water's surface.

He smacked both hands on the steering wheel in victory. "I know how to get up there!" he yelled aloud.

He took his foot off the brake, switched on the 4WD, and drove his truck off the interstate, onto the shoulder, and over the edge.

18

The tires kicked up sand and gravel. Then he plunged down the grassy embankment, bouncing on the seat beneath his seat belt as the tires hit uneven ground, dirt clumps and rocks on the way down.

Ahead of him was a crumbling frontage road that ran parallel to the interstate. He bumped over the dusty grass to get down there. He could have followed this little road north to Nickel Road, but that wouldn't help today since it was probably already packed with cars trying to get out of town.

No, he had another idea. He followed the frontage road another hundred yards, then clenched his teeth, veered off the frontage road to the left, and drove into a stream bed, completely dry in the drought. Now he was aimed straight at the interstate.

Heading directly west now, he followed the creek bed toward the square drainage culvert under the interstate. He'd been inside it high school, with some cross-country runners who sometimes wandered far afield instead of following the training route around Two-Mile Lake. It was light enough inside to see it was full of broken glass and other trash.

The truck's back end fishtailed slightly as he plunged into the tunnel, and the back bumper crashed into the concrete wall, but he didn't slow down. Glass and gravel churned under the tires, hit the undercarriage and sprayed behind him. "Please don't let me get a flat," he said over and over. He drove under the northbound, then southbound lanes of the interstate, and emerged on the west side. *Made it through!*

Now he was at Two-Mile Lake, closer to the mountains but also getting into the path of the smoke from the new Forest Heights fire. He was disoriented by the lack of visibility. It helped to talk to himself, to keep his purpose in mind. "I'm still on the wrong side of the railroad tracks."

He rolled up his windows and turned on the A/C, setting the air on recirculate to keep the smoke out of the cab. He kept to the south side of the lake, along the walking path, trying to find the continuation of the dry streambed. *There it is!*

The truck pushed through the weeds and brittle grass in the low drainage way. In front of him, there should be a circular opening for the concrete drainage tunnel under the railroad tracks. He careened toward it at twenty miles an hour through the bumpy streambed. He'd never been up close to the railroad tunnel, and he didn't know if the truck would fit.

Right at the opening, he took his foot off the gas for a second to make one last adjustment.

Like a cartridge shot from the barrel of a gun, he drove the truck straight into the narrow tunnel under the railroad embankment.

For a second it was almost quiet. Nothing but gravel spitting behind him in the long seconds of darkness. He could see a circle of hazy daylight, keeping him going straight ahead as he bumped over the uneven dirt of the dry creek inside the tunnel.

One big bump jarred the truck up and to the right. The roof cab scraped the curved ceiling on the right side. A terrible metallic crunching noise echoed through the tunnel. He grunted and veered to the left, trying to compensate and keep his momentum.

"I don't think I'll notice those hail dents now," he said out loud.

He exited the tunnel on the west side of the tracks. He drove through the smoke, up the grass and over a curb into the strip mall parking lot. If it hadn't been obscured, he could have seen the last Radio Shack store in existence in Colorado, the Dollar Store, and a tired little consignment shop. Usually there was a man there in the parking lot in a new VW Bug selling tamales from his car, but not today.

Cars filled the south and northbound lanes of Highway 55. Everyone from Garnet and Forest Heights was all trying to head to the interstate that way. He realized it's like they said on an airplane during a safety briefing, "Your nearest exit may be behind you." *Nobody listens to the safety briefing. They're too busy listening to podcasts.* "Why don't you drive on the grass? Go another way!"

Dark smoke blew from the south, full of sparks. It looked like dusk going on nighttime now. Not 10 a.m.

None of the drivers sitting there would make eye contact with him at the side of the road. They wouldn't let him in. *What the heck am I doing? Why am I always a fish going upstream?*

He opened the truck door and stood up on the running board, gesturing with his whole arm to the closest driver on

55. Prentice pointed across the highway toward the mountains and yelled, "I'm just trying to cross the highway!" The guy figured out he wasn't trying to cut in line and let Prentice zip across.

Blossom Street was choked with petrified drivers, and he bypassed the road entirely by driving through the postage stamp yards. He zig-zagged north through downtown.

Sparks rained down on everything. Sometimes he saw a flash of orange in a corner on a front porch. Or in the foot-high grass growing next to a house with dry wood siding. Or a rooftop or gutter full of dry leaves, anywhere something ignited from the heat of the embers and the rushing wind.

He drove right through the yard of Anna's house on Crystal Street. The bright blue shutters were barely visible through the smoke. He saw a flare-up in the evergreens. He took a second to be glad she'd grabbed her go-bag and the dog yesterday and was already settled at Jessie's apartment. *They got out early and are already safe.*

This was the really historic section of town, meaning houses were everything from quaint, colorful cottages to dilapidated cabins. The tree density and the slope of the roads got much more noticeable on the northwest side of town.

By the time he made it up to the jeep trail, the sun was getting high in the sky, at least where it wasn't blotted out by smoke. The road curved back to the south as it hugged the mountainside. The full sun hit Prentice in the side of his face in between gaps in the trees. He kept the A/C going. *What's the plan? Besides just, "rescue Dad," that is.*

He hadn't checked in with anyone this time, not even with Grimaldi or any of the other firefighters. They were all busy with the Garnet Fire. No other friends to call. His co-workers at the fire station? No, he'd gone rogue. They didn't have time to babysit him.

Who else was there to ask?

Just then, a song he'd heard a thousand times came on the radio. It was "Gloria" by U2. In his deep DJ voice, the announcer said, "Music lovers, today with another crazy fire burning, pay attention to U2 and Bono here. Hear those lyrics about trying to stand up and trying to find your feet. We're all feeling it today with these fires burning, right Lord? Woo-hoo!" *I wonder if they'll fire him for saying "Lord" on a rock music station.*

The unmistakable, poignant lead guitar by The Edge pinged to life. Bono sang, and the words spoke right to Prentice, like a shining light piercing the darkness in the middle of him. *Glooooooh-ree-ah!* It was only three minutes long, a worship song disguised for a secular radio station. He kept driving up the gravel road, toward the fire, through the smoke and the sunlight.

He sang the words over and over again at the top of his voice. About not being complete. *Glooooooh-ree-ah!* Where did those tears come from? They felt so different from the tears earlier this morning that had been so angry. These helped clean out his soul. He could feel it.

I didn't even know I had a soul.

Below him, between waves of smoke, Prentice could see hundreds of houses and cabins of Forest Heights nestled among the pine trees. All this smoke was driven by the new fire. It blew through the towering Ponderosa pines. It blew straight up in the air. It did whatever it wanted.

A few years ago, he'd built a cairn of stones on the side of the jeep road. It was to celebrate the completion of the egress trail he cut from his dad's house up the hill to the gravel road. He had to find it now to drive down to the house. "I see it!" A stack of pink and gray rocks standing next to the road. He'd made it to the top edge of dad's property.

The trail was overgrown again. He'd removed the big trees, so there was a way through, but scrub oak and chokecherry bushes had sprung up in the lane filled with sunlight he created by taking out selected trees. Plants grow. *Mitigation is a lifestyle.*

He meant to check out the rough path on foot and clear the way, then go back up for the truck and drive down to the house. He'd get Dad, whatever kind of shape he was in, drive back up the path and the gravel jeep road back down the mountain. This way he could avoid the jammed-up roads in town. And the fire, if it was getting closer.

Time to move. Dad needs my help. He put the truck in park and grabbed his phone from the truck console and sent another text to his dad.

I'm @ yr house. Coming 4 U.

HE STARTED TO PUT THE PHONE BACK IN HIS CARGO PANTS pocket, and that's when he looked down at his clothes. Fancy lace up street shoes, dress pants, and a useless short-sleeve polo shirt with his college logo on the front.

"Oh crud. I'm not dressed for this." No protection. *Total civilian move.*

He dropped the phone back in the console while he went to the back of the truck, opening the tonneau cover to survey the tools and gear. Good, there was a spare long sleeve work shirt, chaps, and work gloves. No extra boots to replace the stupid oxfords, but he had his woodsmen helmet and some more N95 masks.

Even though he was in a hurry to get down the hill to find his dad, he had to make sure the path was clear of any new tree falls before driving the truck through there. He crammed the extra mask in his pocket. Putting on the shirt, then buckling the chaps over his khaki pants, he put on the mask and helmet and set off down the trail with the saw.

Why didn't Dad just leave on his own?

"Maybe he tried to leave, but couldn't." He stopped short. "I don't even know if he's here," he said to himself. "When he tried to reply to my text, he could have been anywhere."

He made his way down the trail, muttering under his breath beneath the mask. Sweaty, frustrated, and discouraged. *I hope he's not there. I hope he's gone. Maybe he got out on his own.*

A fresh treefall blocked the path, and he revved up the saw to cut the trunk in half and push it to the side. His fancy shoes slipped on the slope full of pine needles. Carrying the chainsaw threw off his balance, and he nearly went down more than once. *Pay attention, you ridiculous excuse for a firefighter!*

It took ten minutes to get down the hill, as he stopped to cut more branches and trees that would block the way for the truck. Sweat ran down his neck, and even though he was used to wearing a mask for work all the time, today he was aware of his breath going in and out, stifled by the smoke-filled air.

What if Dad can't walk? What if he's dead? But Prentice shoved the thoughts away.

At last, he could see the side of the house above the grade of the mountainside. Glimpses of the second floor poked through the gloom. Prentice could make out Dad's office and master bedroom windows there, which were almost at ground level due to the steep slope. No light showed from either room. Prentice continued along the trail, his pulse beating in his ears, following the path toward the 30-foot "clean and green" zone around the house he'd worked on so hard over the last years. Then he could turn off the saw.

He crossed in front of the living room picture window and below the deck balcony the firefighter had climbed to save William. Then he rounded the garage, entering the house through the kitchen door on the far side. Prentice watched each window, hoping for light or movement, trying not to think why he saw nothing, no sign of life at all.

Near a cluster of three pines in the middle of the yard, he stepped on a low stump. The dress shoe slipped off the edge.

In slow motion, his left ankle twisted and then bent at a right angle toward the ground. He screamed as pain ripped through his foot and left leg. He fought to regain his balance, but the heavy saw he carried in his left hand was too much to handle with no warning.

He toppled, and his left shoulder drove into the trunk of a Ponderosa. He hit it so hard, his whole body shuddered and ricocheted from there to a second tree. His helmet protected his face and head, but he felt the bite of the butterscotch scented bark scrape the flesh from the right side of his neck. He lay crumpled on his right side for several moments, howling in pain, clutching his left leg. The ankle sent shoots like stabbing knives, no matter what he did. He lay flat with his leg up in the air.

Finally he found his breath again, in ragged gasps, and looked around. The chainsaw lay to his left side. He managed to pull off the gloves, helmet and mask, then rolled onto his right side, trying to pull the left leg closer to him, as if it would decrease the ripping pain. The motion jostled his ankle, and he yelled and rolled onto his back again. The tears flowed, dripping in his ears, and down his neck, for several minutes.

Arms stretched out. Right leg straight, left leg held awkwardly above the ground as if it were a marshmallow burning on a stick after roasting too long on the fire. A perfectly good marshmallow that was just cinders now. Ready for the trash can. *What's the use? Why don't I just give up right now?*

He looked up through the smoke and the few treetops in the yard. Closed his eyes. Breathed in and out. Coughed with the smoke. It was getting thicker. Feathery gray ashes landed on his face.

God, please help me. I just have to keep moving.

www.Tinderbox.tips - Fire Goes Faster Uphill:

- Wind currents tend to travel uphill, super-heating the fuel sources above.
- Fire doubles in speed for every 10 degrees increase in slope.
- When topography is steep, proper tree spacing and stone walls can slow a fire heading toward a house.

Very gingerly, he unbuckled the bulky Kevlar chaps that made it hard to bend his legs. As he pulled them off, the stiff edge brushed his left foot, causing another roar of pain. He rested his head on the ground again. *Think.*

Grateful for the leather gloves, he used a modified crab crawl, carrying his weight on his right foot and his butt, to haul himself across the grass to the driveway. Cursing the stupid dress shoes, the tree stump, the fire. And himself.

A section of the Incident Response Pocket Guide that

talked about "Human Factor Barriers to Situation Aware-ness" floated through his mind. It noted distraction, fatigue, stress reactions, and hazardous attitudes such as "target fixa-tion" as risk factors. *Check, check, and check.*

Then he almost laughed through his tears. "I must not be the first guy to be such an idiot," he said to the trees. "They put that in the instruction manual for wildland fire-fighters." He took a deep breath and kept crab walking. *Crabs, starfish, whatever. This rescuer needs rescuing. Give your-self a break. I want a helicopter.*

Where the garage intersected with the house, he used a three-legged stool by the kitchen door to help balance to standing. He peered in the garage window. *The car's there. Dad's here!*

He turned to the kitchen door and turned the knob, but it was locked. He reached for his keys and cursed again. "My keys are still in the truck!"

I've gotta get inside. He lifted the stool and stabbed the leg toward the window in the kitchen door, almost losing his balance when it bounced off the safety glass. It cracked under his second attempt and the next blow broke the pane entirely. He used the leg of the stool to bust through and move the sharp crumbles of glass out of the frame, then he reached in and unlocked the door from the inside.

"Dad! Are you here?" he called into a very quiet house.

Room by room, Prentice hopped on one leg, balancing on walls or furniture. It was light enough to see in the dining room which had two windows, then the living room, with its big window and the sliding door out to the yard. Calling out. No answer.

It had been years since he'd been in the house by himself. But it used to happen all the time, after he was old enough to just go straight home after school, track or cross-country practice, or tinkering at the school auto shop. Dad would show up at 6 p.m. from work. Either he, or Prentice as he got older, would cobble together some dinner. Spaghetti. Scrambled eggs, bacon, and toast. Canned soup. Hungry Man frozen dinners. Hardly a vegetable, unless it came from a restaurant in Garnet.

They would eat at the kitchen table in the glare of the fluorescent light. Never in the dining room. Exchange a few words about the day or upcoming commitments. Do the dishes. Retreat to their corners. On the weekends, they did the same, but Dad allowed meals to happen in front of the television for a treat.

No joking. No real sharing. Just coping. A man and a boy, then a young man, in a lifeboat? In a cage? In a crucible? What was there to say? Dad helped him buy the Ford hatch-back so he could drive to his college classes in Pioneersburg, and then he found the sawyer job, so he stayed away more and more. Dad continued in his same routine.

Today, there was enough dim, smoky daylight to see. Even so, every room felt filled with darkness. In the corners were all the words that had gone unsaid over the years, still hiding from the light. Piles of conversations that had not happened sat in the shadows.

Memories of statements that should never have been said by a father to a son lurked behind closed doors. So many emotions fueled and ready. Hurt feelings and misun-derstandings nestled deep into their souls, biding their time, gathering energy, just needing a breath of oxygen to make them flare up.

Prentice tried to picture Jessie's face and her warm smile. *From what she tells me, I need an emotional fire extinguisher to be in this house.*

"Dad?" he called out time after time. "Where are you?"

He sat down on the stairs and heaved himself up, one step at a time, to the second floor, balancing on his good foot and leaning on the wall. Dad's office, empty. Bathroom off the hallway, empty.

No matter what, he had to do something about his ankle. *I know!* Down the hall to his old room. He'd hardly been in there since he moved out after college. To the closet, down on his hands and one good knee, the wounded leg sticking out behind him. Reaching to the back corner.

There it was. *The walking boot!* Left over from a stress fracture during cross-country one year. The perfect solution to immobilize his ankle. He repositioned to sit on the floor, sore leg sticking straight ahead. He untied the fancy shoe and removed it, but he left the sock that stretched over his throbbing ankle. It was painful to the touch, sore just to exist.

He inserted his leg into the walking boot, but there was no way to do this without hurting. Yelling helped get the job done.

He reached up to grab the hems of a few t-shirts from hangers in the closet. *Who puts t-shirts on hangers? I do.* He packed the shirts in the gaps inside the walking boot, and he tightened the Velcro straps. *Okay, that's better.*

Next, he took off the other fancy shoe, found an old work boot, and put that on his right foot for more security. *Let's do this.*

Only one more possible place Dad could be. He headed for the master bedroom. It was decorated the same as the rest of the post-house fire house now, white walls, no curtains, plain furnishings. A brown plaid bedspread. No sign of Dad. "Where are you?" he yelled into the silence.

The master bathroom door was closed, and he pounded it. "Dad! I'm here!" He heard a faint noise, kind of a snort, or rough breath. Then quiet again. Maybe a rustling sound of something moving on the floor. Prentice tried the knob. It was unlocked, but he couldn't push the door open. Something blocked it from the other side.

"Oh, God, Dad. Can you hear me?" No answer. Prentice backed up, looking the door over.

"I can't get in. Can you move away from the door?" He pushed lamely against the door again, but it wouldn't move an inch. Normally, he could have busted it down with brute force.

He needed to go for the chainsaw.

THE WALKING BOOT PROTECTED HIS SWOLLEN ANKLE AND MADE it possible to hobble downstairs and out to the yard. He put his woodsmen's helmet back on his head and picked up the saw off the ground.

Returning back through the kitchen, he saw a tired apple in the bowl on the counter. *That'd help with his blood sugar level.* In the fridge, he found a container of orange juice, almost empty, and threw it in a plastic grocery bag with the apple.

Back upstairs, a horrible, dry moan came from his dad in the bathroom. "I'm coming," Prentice called as he hoisted himself up the stairs with the saw and the grocery bag. A hideous scream. Quiet again, then another anguished scream. "I'm coming. Almost there!"

He lowered the face shield and ear protection into place, then opened the choke on the saw halfway and revved it up. It roared as he squeezed the throttle and the engine reverberated inside the house.

With great care, he touched the saw's bottom edge to the

top of the hollow-core door, a few inches from the hinges. He held the saw as parallel to the door as he could so the tip wouldn't kick back at him, and in two cuts, he freed the top half of the door.

The wood fell into the bathroom, on top of his dad's body laying against the bottom half of the door. Dad's leg jerked when the pieces of door hit him, and he put up his left arm in an ineffectual effort to protect himself.

Prentice could see better now to cut away the rest of the door closer to the floor. Dad rested his head on the bedroom carpet, and his body stretched into the bathroom.

"Dad? What's happened to you?" Prentice noted the man was nearly unconscious, dehydrated, and his pajamas stained and smelling of urine. Dad trembled all over, and his skin appeared cold and clammy. His breath came out in rapid gasps. Bill Keene had missed work Thursday, so he might have been lying here 30 hours or longer.

"Dad?" No, he couldn't think of him as his dad. He was just another patient in the hands of a professional EMT. Prentice stepped over him, as best he could, into the small bathroom, sat down, and scooted around so he could kneel next to him and see his face. *Stay focused on your training.*

Dad's eyes opened wildly, waking from a nightmare. They landed on Prentice but didn't really see him. He kept trying to scream, obviously his body was fighting with itself, but his mouth was so dry, the pain came out as a bark. It was hideous.

"I'm a trained Emergency Medical Technician, and I'm here to help you. I think you're having a diabetic emergency." It was vital to talk to the patient as if he understood, even if he wasn't able to respond coherently. As he always did at work, Prentice talked out loud through each of his steps, both to reassure his patient and remind himself what he was doing.

"Do I have your permission to treat you?" Bill Keene could not answer, and Prentice went ahead. He'd intended to bring his first aid kit from the truck after he cleared the trail and put the chainsaw away. So much for that. At least he'd finally found him. Since dad was breathing and not obviously bleeding, and he now knew about the diabetes diagnosis, his concern was the blood sugar level.

Under dad's bathroom sink, Prentice found medical supplies and a box of disposable gloves. Behind the gloves was a home glucose monitoring kit. *Jackpot!*

"I'm checking your blood sugar first." He put on the gloves, held his dad's hand, and cleaned the tip of his finger with an alcohol wipe, very thoroughly.

He milked the finger to get a blood sample. No easy task, since Dad's pulse was rapid but ineffective, and he had very slow capillary refill when he pressed on his fingernail to check. He used the lancet to put a drop of blood on a test strip, which he then inserted in the meter. The screen had a large digital display.

In 15 seconds, he knew the answer. It could have gone either way. Diabetes was a diabolical nemesis. Sometimes the body reacted with dangerously high levels of glucose in the blood. But this time, the answer was very low blood sugar. Severely hypoglycemic. He needed sugar in his system. If he could eat, that would help, but that was not an option. Not yet.

Again, Prentice peered into the cupboard under the sink and found what he needed, an emergency glucagon injector in a red plastic kit. Starting at the left cuff, he ripped open the pajama shirt sleeve up to Dad's bicep. Then he took another alcohol wipe from the kit and swabbed his upper arm.

Methodically, he prepared the syringe by mixing the contents in the accompanying vial to activate the ingredients. He carefully swirled the syringe, not shaking it, to achieve a clear solution with no bubbles. Then he administered the dose into the muscle.

"Come on! If I don't get this to work, Dad's in trouble," he said to the quiet room.

~

PRENTICE STARTED FOR THE LANDLINE PHONE NEXT TO THE bed to call 9-1-1. *Wait a minute. Where's Dad's cell phone?* He had tried to answer Prentice's text this morning, and he must have been trapped in here then.

"Where is it?" He looked all around the bathroom and then saw it. The cell phone was in the toilet, almost out of sight down the U-bend. *Oh geez.*

Prentice hobbled over to dial 9-1-1 on the cordless landline next to his dad's bed, but the emergency dispatch number was still busy. The fires, yesterday and again today, were pushing all emergency dispatchers and responders to the limit.

He brought the handset with him and put it on the bathroom counter, then talked his patient through the rest of the head-to-toe assessment. At least the screaming had stopped. He needed to identify anything else that was unusual, in case he'd hurt himself when he fell, or if there were more medical issues. Starting with his head and face, then checking his neck, shoulders, and all the way down.

He found a nasty bruise on his right hip as a result of the fall, but no bones were broken. The assessment didn't indicate spinal or head injury, though the numbness from the diabetes damage could mask other problems. If he had the luxury of an ambulance crew and a stretcher, things would be different.

When he got down to the bare feet, he saw the ugly diabetic wounds beneath the callouses. He poked the soles with the sharp corner of a folded piece of paper. Dad didn't even grunt. Diabetic neuropathy with ulceration. *How come I didn't notice the unsteadiness? Well, I saw it the other day, I just didn't pay attention.*

He tried 9-1-1 again. No luck. *How the heck are we going to get out of here?*

Bill Keene had plenty of ways to die today, and if they waited too long, Prentice did too. He wasn't going to let that happen. Smoke was thick outside the bedroom window.

Dad stirred as his blood sugar level approached normal, at least temporarily. "Dad!! You look better." *Barely, but it's a start.*

"I've got some water here. Drink this." He poured a few drops into his dad's mouth, like a mama bird feeding her chick. His tongue moved to accept it. Prentice dribbled some more water.

Soon, Dad indicated he wanted to sit up. "Okay, Dad. Lemme help you lean against the vanity."

Bill drank a cup of water and then looked around with more comprehension. His eyes fixed on the remnants of the door. His expression puzzled at the diabetes supplies on the floor, Prentice's walking boot, and the chainsaw.

"Why'd you do that?" he said to Prentice, moving his eyes to him. "Jusss help me up."

I'm saving your life. Stay calm. Do your job. "Dad, it's me, Prentice."

His eyes looked toward him again, and finally there was

a spark of recognition, mixed with confusion, and something else. Was it embarrassment? Had he become aware of his smelly pajamas?

"Are you feeling good enough to eat something?" When Dad nodded, he sloshed a small amount of juice into the little paper cup. "This would really help you feel better." Dad slurped the juice.

Prentice bit off a piece of apple and handed it to his dad as he tried dialing 9-1-1 again. The dispatcher answered this time. "Please state your address first, then your emergency."

"I'm in Garnet, Forest Heights, with a medical emergency."

"Forest Heights? Get yourself out! The fire's heading directly that way."

"No, listen! My dad's in hypoglycemia. I need help to get him out of here. I'm injured too, sprained ankle. We're at 150 Hidden Tree Way, Garnet."

"I'm sorry. The fire is overwhelming the area. We cannot get in there with an ambulance, and we have no one to send to help you. Try to evacuate yourselves. I have to hang up now. I have more calls to take."

No one could get up here. No help was coming.

HE SAT ON THE FLOOR NEXT TO HIS DAD, WHO CHEWED SLOWLY on the apple. Time seemed to slow although it was of the essence. Prentice took a long minute to look at his father, to really see him. He thought about the photo of Billy Keene with the toy truck, the one his mother had shown him so long ago. That somber-faced little boy, holding a truck, alone on a wooden bench. *What on earth had happened in that family?*

He needed to get him on his feet, but first Prentice fed him more chunks of apple. His dad was in no hurry at all.

Prentice tried to calm the tightening knot in his stomach with Jessie's words. "Parents are just people," she'd said. "They have histories, they make mistakes, but most of them are trying their best, despite their own pasts." A few months after his mom had showed him and William the photo, all surviving artifacts of Bill Keene's childhood had been ruined by smoke and water in the house fire. *Maybe he was glad to say goodbye to those memories?*

But not his own son. His eldest son. The one he loved best.

God, I really could use your help right now. I couldn't save William, but Dad and I need to figure some things out. Don't let us die yet.

Prentice regained the present. "Dad! Are you ready to move? We've gotta get out of here."

Dad was sitting up, trying to talk, though not answering the right question. "Yes. Yes, I do. What time is it?" he asked thickly.

"Almost noon. There's another wildfire. It's coming this way. Right now! Do you feel better yet?"

Dad wrinkled his nose and squinted his eyes. "There's a wildfire?"

"Yes. A fire started yesterday morning, Thursday, east of the highway. It took out most of Majestic Estates. And now today, Friday, a second one started south of here. It's blowing this way. We have to get to your car."

Dad shook his head. "Friday?"

Prentice pointed to the bedroom windows, where even a man with bad eyesight could see the smoke and sparks were thick in the air.

"Help me up."

"We have to get you on your knees first. I can't lift you." From the floor, he guided his dad to use the vanity as a support.

"Ouch! What're you trying to do?"

"You've gotta stand up." Prentice groaned as he maneuvered himself to standing and said, "Put your hands on the counter and straighten up." *Finally!* He put his dad's arm behind his neck to support him. In a tortured three-legged walk with Prentice's injured leg in the center, they inched toward the stairs, using the walls and each other for balance.

Prentice got Dad to sit down on the top step and said, "I've gotta get your diabetic supplies. Be right back."

"Prentice!" Dad called after him, throat hoarse. "Bring pants and a shirt, will you?"

"Yeah. Sure." Prentice gathered the supplies, Dad's wallet, a hardly-used pair of sneakers, and some clothes in a bag. Together he and his dad scooched their way down the steps, dragging the gym bag behind them. Progress was painfully slow. Sweat broke out on Prentice's forehead and he swiped at it. He told his dad about the fires, trying to distract him. Trying to keep him conscious. And calm. Stress would skyrocket his blood sugar level.

Outside, he heard the gusts of fire-heated wind buffeting the trees and the house. Under his breath, he said, "I wish we could just stay here and ride it out." *I've done good work hardening the house and cleaning up the yard. It could do a good job of defending itself.*

That was madness today, though. He turned to his dad, "We've got to get you to the hospital."

"I'm fine," said his Dad. "I just need something to eat. And a shower."

"The hell you are! You're a mess! And there's a wildfire out there!"

Prentice was sick of it, sick of always worrying about making his dad feel bad or rocking the boat. Making Dad upset, or pushing him farther away than he already was. All the years of trying to discern what his dad was thinking, and what would make him fly off the handle, pushed him beyond control. The fact that his dad had concealed the diabetes added more fuel to his anger. His insistence that he was "fine" put both their lives in danger. "I could never read your mind, but I shouldn't have had to. I can't fix you, Dad!"

His dad stopped and stared, wide-eyed, but he didn't argue or defend himself. Prentice unloaded on him. "Your blood sugar is all screwed up, and you can barely walk. You never told me anything about being this sick. I had to find that out from a stranger at your office."

The pause was tense, but still Dad said nothing.

"There's a wildfire burning outside the house. And you want to stay here and take a shower? What's wrong with you!" He kept unloading. "You're always pretending everything is fine. Until you just explode. Why won't you speak up for yourself?"

Silence.

Prentice watched as his dad slumped on the step, staring at nothing. His face wore the look of the little boy in the old photo. Still Prentice kept going, years of pent-up confusion streaming out. The embers that had smoldered inside him, the hidden questions and feelings and misunderstandings exploded into words and more words. "Why can't you admit you need help? Why won't you tell me anything? Or even trust me?"

Bill took a deep breath and seemed to make a decision. He turned to face Prentice. "You're right, son. You're so right. It's not your job to fix me. But here we are." And he started to move down to the next step before Prentice knew what was happening.

Prentice was dumbfounded. *Son? He never says that.*

That single word: son—it helped Prentice stop yelling. But he couldn't stop to appreciate it. They had to keep up the momentum.

They managed to get to the kitchen table. Prentice felt lightheaded, and Dad definitely needed food in his system. More than just an apple. He looked around. Dad's kitchen was full of food forbidden to diabetics. Processed stuff with lots of added sugar and salt. Like a box of Twinkies there on the counter. They would kill him. Limping around, opening cabinets, the fridge, he found a package of beef jerky, two more old apples, and a can of roasted peanuts and added it all to the gym bag on the table.

He knelt on his good knee and used the Twinkie box to sweep a rough path through the glass on the floor. Dad noticed the broken window in the door then. His eyes asked a question of Prentice.

He ignored him. "We need to get these shoes on your feet." He took out the gym shoes and put them on the chair, explaining why he had to break the window because he didn't have his keys.

"Where's your truck?"

"Up on the jeep road. I took a bad fall, getting down here."

"Your leg—"

"We have to take your car. Neither of us is in any shape to get up the hill."

Prentice helped his dad up. Then together, they crunched their way slowly across the remaining glass out to the patio. They could barely see the garage, the smoke was so thick. Prentice helped him into the passenger side of the car. He stopped to grab a blanket from the shelf in the garage, spraying empty sunflower seed shells on the floor. The wool would protect his dad if the heat got to be too much. He couldn't be worried about the now homeless mouse.

His ankle throbbed murderously, and he hobbled back into the kitchen, grabbed a bag of frozen peas, and stuffed it into the walking boot to replace the t-shirt he'd used as padding. The design on the shirt caught his eye. It was from a Linkin Park concert he'd missed in high school. For a few months, he'd tried to dress and wear his hair in the same way as their lead singer. He'd planned to go to the concert with his friends, but at the last minute, Dad reneged, snarling at him about wasting time on a weeknight when he should be doing homework.

The band had this one great song, "Waiting for the End." The lyrics were all about trying to forget the past, things being out of your control, words left unsaid. Trading the life you had for something new. He hadn't been there or done that, but at least his friends had bought him the t-shirt.

He placed the shirt on the table, lifted Dad's car keys from the hook on the wall under the stairs, and went to the car, preparing to drive himself through another fire.

When he put the key in the ignition, it refused to turn. He couldn't start the car.

20

P rentice gritted his teeth. Dad had bought this car, a used 2010 Ford Fusion, when Prentice was in college, so Prentice had never driven it. He shot a glance at his dad.

Bill Keene appeared unperturbed, chewing on beef jerky like they had all the time in the world.

"Dad, what's the deal?" Prentice couldn't keep the edge from his voice.

"Turn the steering wheel before you turn the key," he answered, taking the stick of jerky from his mouth. "That usually does the trick."

The engine turned over and came to life. He guessed he should be glad the car had started at all. He backed out of the garage and the Ford was immediately engulfed in smoke which cleared suddenly and then returned. Ordinarily he could handle driving in smoke. The acrid smell was something he'd learned to work past when he was on the job with B Shift. But being surrounded by smoke in this precise spot on the driveway revived the old nightmares. He looked straight up at the room above the garage, the one that had been his brother's.

"This is right where I was standing when I saw the fireman carry William... carry out William's body." He didn't mean to say it out loud, but there was too much going on in his brain now. *Push it back inside.*

Dad's gaze was unfocused. He chewed the beef jerky.

He should have known better than to expect any comment from Dad. Forbidden subject. Don't touch it. But it was insane for him to pretend Prentice hadn't just mentioned William's name.

And his body. His dead body.

Just put your head down and do the next thing.

Prentice backed up and headed to the street, trying to keep his focus and keep them both alive. Small fires burned here and there in the yard. A wind gust threw a blizzard of embers in a whirlwind at the corner of the garage and under the eaves. Overall it looked okay. The little fires didn't appear to be spreading, and the house had its fuel-free zone.

The longer view wasn't so promising. He'd seen flashes of fire in the treetops in the smoke-darkened distance on their escape route. Most of Forest Heights was houses made of sticks closely surrounded by... more sticks, all those trees and bushes. So much to burn, big and small. A beautiful green tangle of fuels totally vulnerable to spot fires and then spreading the main wildfire from there.

Falling trees, set ablaze, could block the road.

Prentice drove using muscle memory, not his eyes. They wound down Hidden Tree Way, onto Forest Way, one twist at a time, down through the forest. Gravel kicked up even at this slow speed. He could barely see the edges of the street, much less the intersections. He'd driven this road hundreds, no thousands of times. But each curve today was a surprise.

The neighborhood was in a forest that hadn't burned in a hundred years, where it should have burned five times by now. Now that it was alight, accumulated burning debris was lifted high into the air with super-heated temperatures. The winds snatched it up and carried it north.

He could barely see the houses, but Prentice knew the homeowners' names for so many homes they passed. *Mrs. Gannon's house is over there somewhere. I hope they evacuated.*

Even though it was midday, the sky was like midnight. The headlight beams just illuminated the smoke without showing the way. Tongues of fire burned tall right next to the road.

In front of them, a huge tree, engulfed in flames, was falling onto the road. He sped up into the blackness. "We have to get by this tree! If it falls, we're stuck!" The tree creaked as it fell in slow motion, even louder than the roar of the wind and the flames.

With a crash that ripped through his ears, the huge trunk landed on the back corner of the car. They both cried out at the same time as the heavy timber smashed the metal frame and plastic tail light and rolled behind them onto the pavement, pushing it ahead in a burst with the force of the impact. If it had hit them any sooner, the force could have blown out the back tires or broken the window. Or totally crushed the roof. But it hadn't. The car careened forward.

Prentice gripped the wheel and made himself keep following the turns in the road. Faster now. Headlong. Couldn't see, but couldn't sit still either. He'd anticipated more cars here, but they must've gotten down off the hill somehow. Maybe there was another egress route open.

"Thank you, God," said Prentice.

"Too close," said Dad from his corner.

Just like Dad to bulldoze over the truth. *Sparing the chil-*

dren, said the quote. He couldn't just drop it again. There was no "right time" for this conversation with Dad. They might not even have another chance. "We have to face the flames head on," he said.

Bill, slumped in the passenger seat under the wool blanket, said, "What're you talking about? Just get us out of here."

The embers inside his soul showed their fiery faces and exploded out of his mouth. "Dad! Why didn't you ever tell me William was dead?"

Bill Keene took in a breath and looked at Prentice. "What?"

"You showed up at the fire, but you never checked on me. I was sitting right there on the driveway, and you walked right by. You talked to the firefighter who rescued William. And then you left in the ambulance with him."

"I saw you were all right. William wasn't. He needed me."

"They took me in the ambulance. With the babysitter. Her name was Allie. She was as white as a ghost, and I had to wear a mask. And I didn't know where you were!" His voice shook. *I have to do this.*

Dad said, "I found you at the hospital. They said you would be okay. You were sleeping. Then I took you home... er, to the apartment I'd rented, as soon as I could."

"Did you ever go see Allie? In the hospital?" He didn't pause for an answer. "I just met her again. Yesterday. She lives in Pioneersburg now. She said she never talked with you again after William... after the fire! You just pretended like it never happened!"

"Well... just a minute. I did try to find her, but her family was gone."

"How long did you wait?" Prentice yelled. "She said it was weeks before they left town."

"I visited the hospital. She was asleep."

"And you never tried again?"

"Prentice..."

"And you never actually told me what happened to William! He just vanished off the face of the earth! It was like he never existed."

Bill took a breath. "It was... not like that. I had to find a place for you and me to live. And deal with the insurance company. Start rebuilding the house."

"But what happened to William? I mean after he died?" Prentice cried out. "Was there a funeral? I never saw him again. What did you do with him?"

Dad took a breath and looked out the window at the nothingness, the smoke, the flames here and there. "He's buried in the cemetery."

"Where?"

"At Church of Abundant Life. In Pioneersburg."

"What? How come you didn't tell me?" Prentice's heart pounded even faster than the car careening down the mountain.

"I felt like you were too young to go to the cemetery."

"Why didn't you ever tell me that, Dad?" he repeated. "For so long, I kept thinking William might be okay and was going to come home. The teachers at school knew more about it than I did."

"I was trying to spare you."

"Do you go to the cemetery? Because you sure never talk about him."

"Sometimes. On Memorial Day. And the anniversary of the fire."

"You've got to be kidding me! And in twenty-two years

you've never thought to tell me any of this? It's a big secret, huh?" Prentice was on a roll now. The emotions poured out of him. Everything from his whole life. Dad couldn't get away from him. "I spent my whole life talking to counselors about it, but the one person I needed to talk to was you, and you wouldn't let me!"

"I thought you didn't want to talk about him, Prentice. You never brought it up."

"Are you totally crazy?" Prentice pounded on the dash-board. "I was a little kid, Dad!"

"Well, that's what you sound like right now, I agree," Dad said quietly. He said the most hurtful things in his quiet voice. He put more beef jerky into his mouth, working it between his jaws.

Prentice could barely breathe. How could he possibly have a conversation when it went like this? He wanted to just shut down and never open up again.

They'd descended Forest Road far enough to be out of the forest. Approaching historic downtown, the fire conditions were not as bad as up the hill. More cars here, heading toward the gridlock, but still moving now. Sometimes they passed a house fully engulfed in flames, while its neighbors were quiet and dark. No crown fire here. Just the destruction of smoldering embers taking out one building but skipping another, depending on what fuel it could devour.

Prentice could barely think. William was buried at the same church where he'd met Allie at Incident Command yesterday. *What would Allie think?*

Next to him, Dad looked pale. His blood pressure and blood sugar must be going wild, and at any time now he could go into another diabetic emergency. Could be hypo-glycemia, but since he'd had some good food to eat, the odds were higher for hyperglycemia now. Prentice couldn't do anything about it but get him to medical care.

As he'd anticipated, Highway 55 was packed with cars, and movement slowed to a standstill heading toward the interstate. But he bypassed them by leaving the paved road and driving through the yards next to the road.

"What are you doing!" his dad yelled. "Get back on the street!"

Prentice kept driving, struggling to keep the sedan going straight over the obstacles.

"Get back on the street right now!"

Prentice shifted his dad's sedan into low gear.

Bumping up and down over sidewalks and edges, he continued parallel to the line of cars. Outside her Rocky Mountain Diner, his high school classmate Elva stood with a garden hose and a grim expression on her face. He hoped the gray cat had found shelter, maybe under the dumpster. Or even inside the restaurant.

At the intersection with Plains Road, he could barely make out the scene through the smoke. A state trooper waved him away from the closed road he was trying to enter. Rolling down the window, Prentice slowed but didn't stop, shouting, "I'm a firefighter transporting a medical emergency."

"The fire is down there!" the trooper shouted.

Prentice kept going, right toward the second fire.

"You ignored a state trooper?"

Prentice frowned with a sideways glance at his dad. "I'm trying to get you to the hospital." It was quiet here, but he knew further down it would be a mess of first responders working the fire on the side of the mountain. He watched for emergency vehicles coming toward them and flaming branches landing in the road.

"What's your problem?"

"That's a good question, Dad. What's your problem?" *I'm tired of this.*

"What do you mean?"

"Okay, let's start with something easier. As long as we're here together for a while longer. Heading straight toward a closed road full of fire trucks and a major wildfire. We might as well talk about something productive."

"I don't think you're taking this seriously."

"Dad, it's my job to take this seriously."

"Obviously. You're a professional risk-taker."

"Listen! I already escaped a wildfire yesterday. Twice, not just once. The other fire a few miles east of here. I called it in yesterday morning when I was working on a job. Then I got trapped by it, and I rescued two old people who would've died."

Dad's eyebrows went up, and Prentice kept talking.

"In the afternoon, I went back into it with a strike team from Pioneersburg Fire. That's where I met Allie. She's a firefighter now in the city." He was starting to enjoy this. Speaking up for himself. Telling his own story with pride. If the end was coming, either for him or for his dad, at least he'd have said his piece.

"Well! That's something!"

"That's all you can say? 'That's something?' What about asking a question? Isn't that amazing I found Allie again after all this time? Or saying you're proud of me?" He slapped one hand on the seat next to him. "There's nothing I can do to make you proud of me. Even battling a wildfire. Or being right about all the damage prevention work I wanted everyone to do. Or rescuing you."

He took a breath. "Mom just loved me for who I am. But you don't even like me, do you?" *There, I said it.*

"What're you talking about?" Bill said. "I'm always telling people at work about your job, how proud I am of you. All your jobs. They're quite impressed with your gumption. And so am I."

It was news to Prentice. "That's the first time you've said anything about it to me. You won't even have a conversation with me about my work, or my life. You didn't want me to be a firefighter, and especially not a lumberjack."

Bill Keene tried to chuckle. It came out more like a dry cough, and Prentice reached to the bag in the back seat for a bottle of water to help him moisten his mouth.

They kept heading south, and Dad continued. "I've botched this up." He shook his head and looked at Prentice. "I thought I'd figured it out. But I've done it all backwards."

Prentice set his mouth in a grim line and said nothing.

"All this time, my biggest concern was to make sure you were independent. Not leaning on me all the time. Ready to go off and make your own way in the world."

Prentice shook his head. "Yeah, you told me that when I was five."

They were approaching the cluster of fire trucks and command vehicles on Plains Road, and he drove the sedan off the left side of the road to go around them. An officer off to the west was headed to the road to meet them, probably notified by the trooper they just avoided.

Prentice started to bypass them, then changed his mind and drove toward the officer. He turned out to be Firefighter Mike Blanch, from the Garnet department's C Shift.

"Smokey!" he said, dropping the formality right away. "What're you doing? Are you crazy?"

"Do you have any ambulances? Diabetic emergency, here." He gestured with his head at his dad, hoping they would have the equipment to start treatment sooner rather than later.

Blanch shook his head no and surveyed the smashed back end. "Go on to the hospital, but I'll call ahead and let them know you're on the way. Pioneersburg Memorial." He double-tapped the smashed back end of the car to send them along.

Prentice sped up as soon as they got south of the fire and the air cleared. They could travel at almost normal speed on the blacktop now, just watching for first responders who would not be watching for civilians on a closed road.

Dad shifted a little in his seat. "That fella one of your team? He called you Smokey?"

"Yeah. They're teasing me. It's like Smokey Bear. 'Only you can prevent forest fires.' Ironic, huh?" Dad nodded, and Prentice continued.

"Anyway, I don't understand. What did you do backwards?" *Maybe I know, but I just want him to say it.*

"My first wife left me. My second wife left me. What do I have to teach you? I'm not worthy of an ambitious kid like you. You're doing much better on your own, coming up with new ideas I hadn't thought of."

Who is this man? Where are these words coming from?

"Is that why you've never been to my apartment?"

"I want you to have your own life and not depend on me," his dad said simply. He pushed the wool blanket down and looked out the window again.

Prentice couldn't take this all in. That wasn't what he thought Bill would say. This was not the dad he knew who was always passing judgment on him. "I'm weak, Dad. I let William get killed."

"What?"

"It's my fault we had the fire. I wanted to put butter on the popcorn and…"

His dad interrupted him. "That's ridiculous. It was an accident."

Prentice pushed on, finally getting to say out loud all the words he'd had in his head, playing over and over again since he was five. "I know he was your favorite. I've never been able to live up to him. He was just like you. I'm nothing like him."

"What are you talking about? I don't blame you for all of that. You were a little boy!"

Prentice had to keep talking, now that he'd started. "Then, Allie told me yesterday that she's the one to blame. Because of the way the fire spread. And letting William run upstairs when he should have run outside. I bet that's why she became a firefighter. To make up for that. To save other people."

His dad was speechless for some time.

"It was my fault, Prentice."

"You weren't even there, Dad."

"Exactly. I wasn't there. I left you two alone with a babysitter. I couldn't be in the house without your mother there. It was too much… shame. One more wonderful wife, gone. And it was my fault. Again."

"You never told me about that. Any of that."

"When would that come up in normal conversation?" Dad said.

"When is a little kid going to start a conversation like that? That wasn't my job. I was counting on you. Who else was I going to count on? And you just acted like nothing ever happened. Sent me to school. Went to work. Rebuilt the house. We just slogged along."

"Well, you're not a kid now."

Prentice shook his head. "I just kept my head down for so long. Did the work. Stayed after school as long as I could so I didn't have to be in the house by myself. Cross-country practice. Track. Auto shop."

"I thought you liked those things."

"I did! I do! But I was also using them to avoid dealing with you."

Dad shook his head. "I should've seen that."

"You were doing the same thing with work, weren't you?" Prentice asked.

Bill Keene sighed. "Most likely. I've always worked a lot, though. Even before... all that happened."

"You can't even say it out loud, even now. Mom left us! We had a fire! William died!"

Dad nodded but said nothing.

"I've always wondered about Mom. After she left. Where did she go? Why didn't we hear from her?" Prentice glanced over and saw his eyes were very wet. His breath was rapid, and his mouth was dry as he tried to speak. *Is that the diabetes?*

"Ah..." Dad braced himself, his left arm on his own knee, squeezing it. He'd never heard this many words from his dad in his whole life.

"Your mother. Rosemary. What a wonderful lady."

"Yeah. She was. Well, I don't remember much."

"She was so artistic. Playing her guitar. Singing songs for you boys at night."

"That was great," Prentice agreed. "I remember that. 'Blowin' in the Wind.' Did you listen, too? You never came in when she was singing."

Dad didn't hear him, lost in thoughts. "Rose was such a breath of fresh air. We met in Texas, did you know that? San Angelo. Goodfellow Air Force Base. What a godforsaken country. I was just there a short time. Still trying to get over losing Suzette, trying to figure out what happened."

"I never knew your first wife's name."

"Suzette and I were about the same age. She saw me as a way to get out of Rantoul, Illinois. For me, it was all hormones."

"Hormones?" *Dad has hormones?*

Dad continued, off in his reverie. "She was a wonderful lady, too. But I chased her off with my personality, and working longer hours than I needed to. Even a steady Air Force income can't buy happiness when you're a jerk."

They were at the south end of Plains Road, almost to the interstate. "I guess not."

"You know I was just worried about your safety, after the fire. I wanted you to be strong. You're no softie, either. You have three jobs."

"Yeah...." *This is insane,* Prentice thought.

"Well, it worked. If I were praising you all the time, you would've gotten all mushy."

Prentice breathed slowly, counting the breaths. "I had no idea that was what you were doing. You didn't really lay it all out for me that way."

"Like I said, I guess I did it backwards. I should have told you about these things a long time ago. I guess getting rescued from a wildfire while I'm having a diabetic emergency ought to get my attention about being mortal." He shrugged. But his eyes were full of tears again.

"So what about Mom, then? Why didn't she come back to visit, or stay with us in the summers? Or even write to us... I mean to me?"

Dad didn't answer. At first Prentice thought he was asleep or unconscious, he couldn't tell. He had to keep going. But then he heard a sound from his dad that was new. It was sobbing. Pure pain wracking through his exhausted body and leaking out his eyes. "I never got to tell her about William's death," he said.

"What?" Prentice pulled onto the interstate and headed south. The Littlejohn Boulevard exit would get them to the hospital. Soon, very soon.

"Rose..." he tried to talk, but his voice choked up. He tried again. "Rose took her guitar and left that day. Left with her new boyfriend."

"I saw him. William and I stood on the driveway."

"He was an artist," Dad said. "They were heading for Asia. To commune with nature and sing with the natives. I was so angry at her for giving up on me, I wouldn't even say goodbye properly. I made sure I wasn't there when she left."

"I remember that, too."

"Well," Dad tried to blow his nose on a paper napkin from the glove box, but it didn't work, and he was left with snot below his nose. "They went straight to the airport and started the long trip to Asia."

"Asia?" Prentice hadn't heard this before.

"The trip took many days. Don't you remember the post-card from the Narita airport in Japan, telling you all about seeing the rice fields in around the runway?"

"No." *What is he talking about?*

Dad kept talking, undeterred. "That was just like her to be so excited about such a little thing. The card arrived before... you know, the fire. After that, I had to pick up our mail at the post office for a long time since we lived in that rented place. I must have showed you the card, before it was... lost?" He trailed off.

"No," Prentice said, afraid to say more in case his voice gave him away.

"That was a hard time for me." He looked at Prentice out of the corner of his eye. "For us, that is. She left, and then the fire, and William…" He trailed off again and regarded the mountains out the window.

Prentice glanced over at him. The snot was drying above his lip. *It makes him look like a little boy.* It didn't matter.

"So where did they go then?" Prentice finally asked. *I never pictured her in a new place. He never told me.*

"Well then, they got as far as India, a city called Kochi. They took off in a small plane heading to another city with a long name I can't even pronounce."

"India?" Prentice tried to keep up with all this new information.

"Yes. Something went wrong with the horizontal stabilizer. They crashed just after takeoff. It killed all six people on the plane and two more on the ground."

"They crashed in India? Right after she left here?"

Dad blew his nose again. "Yes, that's what I'm telling you."

"You said she died when I was in high school."

"No, son. That's just when I managed to tell you about it."

"I don't understand!"

Bill Keene said, "She died soon after she left us in 1998. That's why we never heard more. Her body's in the same cemetery, next to William's."

21

Prentice managed to get the car to Pioneersburg Memorial Hospital, but even though there was no fire in sight, the last mile was the hardest stretch of driving he'd done in the last two days.

The fire was all inside him.

His whole life, he'd been angry at his mom for leaving. And he missed her too. *I didn't want to hate her, because I loved her so much.* He'd mourned her for all the lonely years in between when he was sure she had ignored him entirely. But now Dad's news revealed that wasn't the real story.

When I was in high school and Dad told me she was dead, I couldn't find a way to ask more questions.

So, she *had* written to them. She had tried. Prentice never saw the postcard from Japan, that's for sure. *She didn't mean to disappear entirely. She didn't plan to die.*

Now that he knew about the timing, it was all different. There was an explanation for her years of silence. One more smoldering ember inside him would now starve to death. *Mom didn't forget me... The true story about what happened to Mom finally comes to light.*

Outside the emergency department, hospital staff hopped into action when the car drove up. "Are you Mr. Keene? Blanch told us you were coming."

The young lady working for valet parking took the keys from Prentice in a flash and was about to disappear with Dad's mutilated car. The medical team loaded his dad onto a gurney.

"Wait!" he called to her. "I need my dad's wallet." He retrieved the gym bag from the back seat. As she drove away, he grimaced to see the shape of the car's back end, crushed by the falling tree.

He tried to follow as they went into the ED, but he couldn't keep up with their quick pace in the walking boot. He stopped in frustration after almost tripping over his own feet. *After all I've been through, I run out of steam right in front of the hospital?*

An orderly came back for him just then with a wheelchair and took him back in the vicinity of his dad's bed, but out of the way, as the doctors and nurses began to attach tubes, monitors, and drips. He told the nurse what he knew about Dad's recent medical history and what measures he'd taken when he found him this morning. The nurse wrote notes on a tablet.

Prentice took Dad's ID and insurance card from the wallet, and an attendant checked on him. The nurse bandaged his scraped neck and x-rayed his injured leg. She replaced the mushy bag of frozen peas with a new ice pack in the walking boot. Then she asked for a contact phone number. Without thinking, he said, "You don't need my cell number. I'm staying right here with Dad."

"Mr. Keene, I know you're worried about your father, but based on what you've told us, we need to give him time to respond to treatment."

He sagged. "Can't I just wait around here?"

"You need to go home and rest." she pressed. "You're exhausted."

That's the word Jessie used. Completely and totally wrung out. *Who am I trying to kid?*

He placed a little smile on his face that he wished were the whole truth. *Why am I covering for him? It's his own fault that he's in this shape. It's his own fault he's divorced and the only person here to help him is his son who wants to wring his neck.*

"Okay. You win," he said.

The layers of betrayal went so deep. It wasn't a surprise health crisis, not to dad. He'd known about it for years, and he'd failed to take care of himself. *I could just walk out and never come back, leaving Dad to deal with his actions. Alone.*

And the secret that Mom and William were both buried at the same cemetery, not ten minutes from the house. *I didn't know about any of this. So screwed up.*

Then he said, "I don't actually have my phone, but I'll keep checking my voicemail somehow. I'll come back first thing tomorrow morning."

Prentice hobbled out to the hospital parking lot in the late afternoon sun and tried to remember where Dad's car was. *Oh, the valet.*

His first stop had to be to see Jessie.

HE SHOULD SHOWER BEFORE GOING TO SEE HER. HE SHOULD call her first, too. Give her a heads-up. But all that would take too long.

At her door, it wasn't Jessie who answered his knock. It was her mother. His heart fell. "Anna? Hi!"

Over her shorts and t-shirt, Anna wore a white apron

with an orange crab in the center. Around it, the words said, *Fisherman's Wharf of San Francisco.*

"Prentice, my goodness, what happened to you? Come in." Anna opened the door, grasping Casey's collar as the dog lunged forward in greeting. "You look as if you're ready to fall down. What happened to your leg?" As she got a better look at the rest of him, she said, "And the rest of you?"

He hobbled across the threshold. "Long story. It's my ankle."

Anna settled him at the kitchen table. "Here, put your foot up." She pulled out an adjacent chair, and Prentice lifted his leg gratefully onto it. Casey rested his jaw on Prentice's other knee, and he scratched the dog's head and soft, floppy ears.

Anna sat across from Prentice. "Go lie down, Casey," she instructed. The dog trotted to his bed, a blanket curled up in a circle in the corner.

"I'm glad you got out of Garnet early, Anna, before the second fire." Prentice said, in his practical way. "Your house is good, too. At least it was when I drove by it today. There were fires around it, though."

"There are no guarantees, are there? We'll just have to wait and find out." She sighed. "So, what were you doing anywhere near Garnet today?" She surveyed his disheveled appearance. "Jessie told me you were working the fire yesterday, but you're not dressed for that today."

He said, "No. But I got in the middle of the new fire today anyway. My dad was trapped in his house. We got out of Garnet, and I got him to the hospital."

"Oh no!" she said.

"I think he's gonna be okay," he said. "But I was really hoping to see Jessie."

"She called late this morning." Anna waved her arm

above the table that was strewn with packages of wonton wrappers, a cutting board, and a big bowl of meat and exotic vegetables that smelled delicious. "I'm making wontons. Jessie and I were supposed to do this together tonight. I bought all the ingredients this morning, but then she called from D.C. and said they wanted her to stay another week."

"Wow. That's a long time. I didn't know." *Oh. Man.*

"It was last minute," Anna said. "I'm glad I could just scoot down here and stay here at her place. So many unknowns, for me." She sighed, "but the good thing is, she'll get to spend some time with her dad this weekend. David's truck route will bring him close to D.C." Her smile sparkled in her black eyes. "Anyway, I thought she might have called you. She's been talking about you a lot."

"I don't know. My phone's... lost." *That's the short version of that.*

"Does this have to do with your escape from the forest today? Are you okay?"

He started to nod, but he had no more energy to pretend everything was fine. "Not really, Anna. I've had a rough couple of days. I was really hoping to see her."

"Oh, you poor kid," she said. Anna was going into serious mother-hen mode. "Well, why don't you call her on my phone so you can check in and tell her you're okay? She's worried about the fires and you and me too. How about that?"

That sounds excellent. Anna dialed and handed Prentice her phone. Jessie didn't pick up, so he left a message. "Hi Jessie, it's Prentice. I'm at your apartment with your mom. She and Casey are fine, but you know that. My phone's lost, but I'll get a new one tomorrow and call you. Have fun with your dad. Bye."

Anna said, "They're probably already playing miniature

golf. And I bet she'll come home with another apron with a crab on it, from Maryland this time instead of California," she joked.

"Anna, how can you be so lighthearted when you've evacuated from your house?" Prentice asked.

She smiled at him. "The scripture says, 'Do not worry.' That sounds both too simple, and too hard, at the same time, but it works for me." She went to work filling the Chinese dumplings with the mixture in the bowl, folding and sealing them while she asked him to tell his story. All the stories. With a lot of follow-up questions indicating she was really paying attention and visualizing every scene. She wanted to know about Garnet and the fires, all the neighborhoods, and how he made it through.

He told her the abbreviated version of it and what he knew about the damage east and west of the interstate, leaving out a lot of details about his dad. But he had to explain his ankle injury.

She brightened at that, oddly. "I know this sounds crazy, but I think I have something I can do to help you, Prentice."

"Really? You don't need to help me. You have enough going on." He gestured vaguely toward the dog in the corner of the small apartment.

"Yes. I want to, and I can. You are famished and exhausted. What you really need now is something to eat, and a hot shower and a good sleep, right?"

He nodded, too tired to predict her line of thought.

"With that badly sprained ankle, you're a falling risk in the shower."

"Huh?" His cheeks got hot as he realized she was picturing him taking a shower while standing on one foot, but he nodded again. "I hadn't thought that far ahead yet."

"So, what you need is a shower chair!"

"Okay...what?"

"Don't worry. I'm not sending you off to the store. But if you'll sit here and finish filling these wontons for me, I'll go over to the thrift store and see if I can find you one. Then we'll have some homemade wonton soup when I get back, and I'll send you home so you can get cleaned up and relax. Sound like a plan?"

"Okay..."

Without waiting for further questions, she brought him a bowl of warm soapy water and a dishcloth so he could wash his hands. She showed him how to fill and seal the wontons. It was obviously going to take him longer than it took her to pinch the thin dough closed over the filling on each one.

"Make sure there aren't any gaps, or else they'll spill open when we put them in the broth. Take your time. I'll be back soon."

She took off Jessie's apron, put it over his head, and squeezed his shoulders in a side-hug as she stood next to him. She walked over to ruffle Casey's ears and told him, "*You* are a *good dog!*" He raised his head to acknowledge her and closed his eyes again. She picked up her purse and left the apartment. The door closed softly.

Prentice was alone. But actually, it felt like he wasn't alone. *She trusts me!* He had to blink several times to keep his eyes clear. Some tears leaked out anyway, and he just let them go. His throat felt tight, but it was almost a good warm feeling this time.

"This is what it's like to have a mom," he said out loud. "I'm remembering so much now." He smiled to himself. *Mom didn't mean to leave all of us, just Dad. She really loved us.*

Casey got up to check out what Prentice was doing and was rewarded by a few tidbits dropping on the floor, so he remained under the table. By the time Anna got back, Prentice was almost done filling the dumplings, and he was humming. *Glooooooh-ree-ah! Glooooooh-ree-ah!*

She started singing along with him. "I really do need to turn on the radio. Not that I don't like your singing, though." They both laughed. "iGen'ers like you and Jessie don't have stereo systems, though. Just cell phones. The sound quality is not in the same league. No *bass*. It's just wrong."

"You know, if you put the cell phone in a cup, it helps amplify it some. Can't do anything about the bass, though. It's still tinny." He laughed.

She nodded, then praised his work on the wontons and added shrimp and snow peas to the broth in the pot for a few minutes. He'd never tried those two ingredients, and he considered refusing the bowl of steaming soup. However, the smell was mouth-watering, and he allowed himself to try something new. He ate two bowls full.

Anna sent him home with a fresh ice pack from Jessie's freezer, the gray plastic shower chair which she'd left out in the parking lot for him to find, and a friendly hug. His dad's car, still in one piece, made it the few miles to Prentice's apartment.

The moment he faced his own door, he remembered his set of keys was still in his truck, abandoned on the mountain.

Oh. Please no. I just want to get in my apartment.

He had Dad's key chain in his pocket. There was a chance... yes! Dad actually had put the copy of Prentice's apartment key on the ring. And Bill had added an identifier with a bright red plastic collar around the head of the key. *Fire engine red?*

His apartment felt like home today, despite its sparseness.

The shower chair allowed him to soak under the hot water and get cleaned up without slipping in the tub, but getting dressed was a struggle, even just putting on clean shorts.

He'd never been so grateful for a hot shower. Or clean shorts.

~

SATURDAY MORNING PRENTICE WOKE UP LATE AGAIN. TWELVE hours of sleep hardly made a dent in the layers of tired. His ankle throbbed in the walking boot which protected his foot from the sheet's weight.

He could hardly believe this time yesterday he'd been about to meet his dad for a spontaneous lunch. Instead, he'd ended up feeding him orange juice and a few bites of apple and rescuing him from the second wildfire in two days. *And I did not punch his lights out.*

In a groggy state, in gym shorts, a t-shirt, and the walking boot, he hobbled outside to find any neighbor who might be awake. Steve, the guy down the hall, was just leaving his apartment for a run, and he let Prentice borrow his phone to check voicemail for any news of Dad or Jessie.

One message said they'd admitted him to an inpatient ward in the hospital. There was also a cheery message from Jessie saying she'd try to answer whenever he could call, but that she and her dad were in Maryland and going hiking at Sugarloaf Mountain, so she wasn't sure about cell service.

It was a wonderful breath of fresh air to hear her voice for the second time in a day. It helped him remember more of her words over the last week about finding a higher power, playing and having fun, and finding your true self. *But why can't she just be home already?*

He put the phone in an envelope and set it against his neighbor's door with a note. "Hey Steve, thanks a ton. I owe you."

Back inside, he sat in his zero-gravity chair with his feet up, quiet for the first time in such a long time. He didn't turn on the news. There was so much to think about.

He finally knew what really happened to his mom. Bill was the one she'd left, not the boys. She'd planned to go on her adventure and come back to tell them all about it, but she ran out of time. She was only 39 when she died in the plane crash.

Out loud, he said, "Mom, I'm sorry I was angry with you all that time."

Prentice wanted to ask Dad more questions. *Who knows, there might even be more I don't know to ask about.* That worried him, but now that he had a clue about the depths, he wanted to pursue it, even if it meant learning something he didn't want to know.

He allowed himself to just sit and think.

And breathe.

Honestly, as he thought about it, he and his dad had made a breakthrough yesterday. *Is this a God thing? Will Dad tell me more, now that he started?*

Then he got ready to go out and face the day. His ankle throbbed, and his shoulder ached where he'd hit the tree. His neck was red and scratched. He was bone-tired, both in body and spirit.

First stop: the phone store. "I'm pretty sure my phone has been lost in the fire," he told the clerk, a lady about his age, with purple hair. "I can't even get up there to look for it until they let people back into Garnet." *Not to mention my truck. One thing at a time.*

He said he'd be back in a few hours to pick up the new

phone, hoping that his contact list would be intact. He did have his own backup list if something went wrong, because he followed his own advice about emergency planning. His business and personal life depended on that phone, and he sure didn't want to enter in all the names and numbers again.

Then he arrived at Pioneersburg Memorial and found his dad's room in the ICU. The shades were drawn, and Dad was asleep. A plate held the remains of scrambled eggs, bacon, and diced canned peaches on the wheeled tray extending over his bed. Wires and tubes connected him to monitors and machines.

A clock ticked. The timing and busyness of the world stopped at the door. In here, it was all about healing and resting.

Prentice sat in the soft armchair and raised the footrest for his injured leg. He hadn't seen his dad asleep very often. He looked so small. Younger. His face was relaxed, not pinched. Regular, soft breaths. Peaceful. He could see him as a man, not an authority figure or control freak. He saw him as a person with hopes and plans, not a rigid accountant stuck in his ways.

He imagined him as a younger man, as a teenager, as a little boy again. The way he was before his family and experiences shaped him. Before the responsibilities of the world pressed down on him. He didn't start out in life as a grumpy perfectionist. *How did he get that way?*

From what Prentice was piecing together, even back when he was 43 and everything hit the fan, Bill Keene was already a man who carried his thoughts close to the vest. He'd grown up in a tough situation Prentice still didn't know much about, but it had definitely had some long-term effects on his ability to get close to people.

Then, in July 1998, so much tragedy had struck within a few weeks. His wife Rosemary left him with two young boys. His oldest son was killed in a house fire that gutted their home. Days after that he found out Rosemary was dead. He became a single father, a grief-stricken dad, a homeless man, and a widower almost simultaneously. And he had no contact with his own parents to ask them for advice or help.

He had to find himself and Prentice a place to live and a way to get him to kindergarten and after-school care. He had to be dad and mom to a little boy he'd hardly spent time with before. Rose had been the creative one who made home-cooked meals. She did the art projects and put the band-aids on when needed. Bill provided the paycheck and observed from a distance. *Why was Dad so separate from us, even before she left?*

That's it, he kept himself apart. He stayed in the wings and let his wife do the nurturing. Was he afraid he'd do something wrong or didn't deserve to join in as a full-fledged family member? *That's what Jessie would call an inspiration.*

What kind of father would I be? Would I do the same thing he did, worrying I'd mess them up? All new dads are afraid at first, he was sure. Afraid of breaking something or someone. Then, most fathers started to learn the ropes and how to interact. Some of them asked their own fathers. They figured out how to be a dad, rough-house with the sons, spoil the daughters, and work out a new life with their wife in the new roles of their new team.

Some of them, like his dad, couldn't seem to make the jump from single ship to husband to father. He hung back. In his first marriage to Suzette, Bill Keene didn't even get the husband part right. Was it due to lack of communication? Unwillingness to let someone get close to him? Workaholic?

The relationships were tentative. Cool, not warm. Why was that?

Prentice contemplated the possibilities while his dad slept. He kept the shades drawn to keep out the world. He spent time thinking about long-ago days. He revisited events from his own childhood, trying to re-experience them from his dad's point of view.

As Prentice mused, his dad woke up a few times. Dad answered the medical staff members' questions about his symptoms as they bustled in and out, but he was in a fog, only focusing on them, then closing his eyes again.

Prentice stayed in the armchair in the corner, watching. He felt like a spy, seeing him in such a vulnerable position. He understood the situation on a professional level. Dad's choices had probably damaged his long-term chances of a healthy life. He would have to live with the results. He already imagined what the doctors and rehab specialists were going to suggest to his dad about changing living arrangements and long-term medical needs.

It was hard to see his dad lying there, so weak, so broken. And knowing he would have to help him fix it. That's what he'd always tried to do, even though he got rebuffed. He was the only one who could do it. It was his duty. His dad was in bad shape. As rough as it had been, he had to be there for him.

22

A nurse came in to check the readings from the little meter on the bedside table, coming from the continuous glucose monitor sensor on his dad's abdomen. He was definitely awake again and finally noticed Prentice by the window. He didn't say anything, but made eye contact with his son and dipped his chin at him.

Prentice said, "Hey, Dad." It was the closest connection he could remember having with him. He moved over next to the bed and took hold of his dad's hand. He just held it, gently, and soon Bill squeezed back. *That was a first.*

An orderly brought in lunch. Even in the ICU, it was vital to make sure he ate consistently to reduce the wild swings in blood sugar level. They still administered insulin to moderate the hyperglycemia, which otherwise could cause more damage and prolong the recovery.

Prentice stood by the tray and attempted a genial conversation, as if this situation were normal for them both. "Do you want to start with the yogurt?" *My dad has never eaten yogurt in his entire life.*

Dad took a few bites but then put down the spoon and

looked at him. Prentice waited for him to complain about the taste, but he said, "Prentice, you saved my life yesterday."

Holy Smokes. Who is this guy praising me? "Well, um, yeah. I probably did." He sniffed and spoke more clearly. "Yeah, I did."

"No doubt about it. I want to thank you."

"You're welcome." What else was there to say?

"What I can't figure out is how you knew I needed help at all."

Prentice forced a chuckle. "That wasn't easy, you're right. You kept a major secret from me." *A lot of them, actually*. He explained about meeting the coworker at Fortress Financial and a hint about the crazy drive to Forest Heights. "It would've been so much easier if I knew," he said.

"So you could keep a closer eye on me," Dad said. "That's why I didn't want to tell you. I don't need spying on."

"But that's my job!" *That didn't sound right.*

"Prentice, I can take care of myself."

"Obviously."

Dad shook his head. "No, obviously I didn't take care of it. The doctors have been very clear with me for years about what I'm supposed to be doing."

"Then why aren't you doing it?

"I've been trying to manage it myself. I read all sorts of books. It's just hard to stick with it. Diet and exercise."

Prentice was furious. "Why didn't you ask for help?"

His dad closed his eyes as if he were in pain. "I was ashamed."

Prentice wasn't expecting that. "Huh?"

Dad continued, "I was embarrassed that an educated man like myself couldn't solve it or control what I was eating."

"No kidding. You're still eating frozen waffles and Ding-Dongs."

Dad shrugged. "I have tried to cut back on the snacks." He looked like a boy caught stealing a cookie from the jar. "It's the sugar, Prentice. I get these cravings for sugary foods and it's almost like taking a drink for me."

Whoa. The way he said that hit a nerve for him. *Like the fossilized candy bar I ate yesterday.* "It's like alcohol?"

"In a way," he said. "Some people think a sugar dependence is just an annoyance or a bad habit. But it's an addiction. When I get anxious, I go straight to the cupboard for a snack. It's not a shot of vodka, but it still landed me here in the hospital."

Prentice asked, "I've never seen you actually drink. Have I?"

Dad shook his head. "No. You haven't." His focus was still off in the distance somewhere. "There's a reason for that."

"You don't have to tell me..." A prickly feeling found the back of his neck.

"Listen." He focused back on Prentice. "Yes, I should have told you about so many things a long time ago."

"I know."

"Well, I guess the short version is, when I was a boy, Father drank a lot. I didn't understand it then at all. I'm sure it was because of whatever happened to him in World War II. Mother raised me on her own, for all practical purposes. It was mostly just me and her in Boston."

"Hm. You've never told me about her."

"My father was gone so much. There are a lot of bars in Brighton. He didn't have steady work. Mother did her best. It was the '50s. She couldn't tell anyone how bad it was. I don't think she had family in Boston, and it was all about keeping up appearances." Bill's face was thoughtful. "Even at home, she wore a housedress, never slacks. She wore high heeled shoes when she mowed the grass. She got a job as soon as I was old enough to go to school, to cover expenses."

"What did she do?"

"Oh, she was a secretary, of course. It was at the Brighton Five Cents Savings Bank. She was proud of that. She dressed up every day for work. Every week she washed her hair and curled it with a metal iron."

"That sounds like torture," said Prentice.

"All the women wore those shiny black shoes with the high heels and pointy toes. They made her feet so sore, and she got horrible bunions. I saw them a few times."

Prentice shook his head.

Bill kept talking. "She wore a pair of more comfortable shoes when she sat at her desk. One day, she told me, a manager called her into his office in a hurry, and she ran in to see him without changing into those high heels. He actually made her go back and put them on before he'd tell her what he needed from her."

"That's crazy." *I can't believe he's telling me all this.*

"That's the way it was."

"Yeah, I guess so. It's hard to picture it all."

"She cooked on the weekend, and during the week when she got home from the bank, she warmed a late supper for us on the stove."

"Huh." *I had no idea.*

Bill continued his reverie. "I rode the yellow street cars everywhere as a kid. There were loads of us boys roaming around after school. We'd collect cans and bottles and turn them in for a few coins. Or sweep or shovel snow in front of the shops. They'd pay me for that. Later I got a regular job at the Home Supply Hardware store."

Prentice was entranced. "How old were you then?"

"That was much later, maybe seventh grade. Sometimes I'd go to Rourke's Drugstore on the corner and buy a few pieces of candy. I've craved sweets from the beginning. I always felt guilty when I did that, though. Mostly I turned over all my earnings to Mother."

He looked into the distance, into his past, talking out loud to himself. "She was always yelling. She pointed her finger at me a lot." He pulled his lips tight over his teeth. "I got myself off to college. After I graduated with my finance degree and went into the Air Force, which is a good, steady job, by the way, she said, 'Why didn't you become a doctor instead?'" Bill's eyes wandered around the hospital room. "She carried a lot of weight on her shoulders."

Who are you, and what have you done with my dad? "What about your father?"

"Hm. This is hard to say. He was rather unpredictable. Once I made a mistake of bringing a buddy of mine home after school, to shoot marbles or some such silliness. Right inside the front door, there was Father, passed out on the sofa."

"Oh wow."

"All of a sudden, my friend had to be somewhere else. I followed him out to the front yard, but he was already down the block. Before I knew what was happening, I threw up, right in the bushes. I think they were lilac bushes. I remember the smell. Or, the smells." He frowned a little.

Bill continued, "I felt terrible. I felt like I'd betrayed Father by letting my friend find him like that. As if it were my fault, think of that."

"No way." *As if it were your fault. Hm.* "Why're you telling me all this, Dad? I mean, after never telling me any of this, my whole life, why tell me now?"

Dad half smiled and took a bite of the chicken tenders on his plate. Finally, he said, "Father's example showed me that if you talked too much, if you shared things, it meant you weren't tough enough. And it was disloyal to the family to share private information."

"I can identify with that," said Prentice.

Dad smirked at him and kept going. "I just learned it was safer not to talk. Not to have feelings or to react to how life was at our house. There wasn't anything I could do about it. Mother couldn't either. We just coped with each circumstance that came along. In our own ways... so much yelling."

"That kind of sounds familiar. Except you don't yell," Prenticed dared to add. "Your mother must have had a hard time swinging all that in the 1950s, too." *This is blowing my mind. He was a lonely boy raised by his overwhelmed mother.*

Dad shook his head and ate some more lunch. Prentice wondered if he'd forgotten about his question about why Dad was opening up so much.

"Yesterday, I almost died, Prentice. Right before I passed out in the house, I knew I was in trouble, but I couldn't help myself. I thought that was it. Then you showed up with that chainsaw..." he chuckled lamely, "the one I was so against you buying. You saved my life. I have owed you an explanation for a long time now, and I almost never got a chance to tell you any of this."

"Wow, Dad. Well, I'm glad you did."

He turned brusque again. "How about getting out of here and letting me get some rest? Don't you have someplace you ought to be?"

Ah, that's more like the Dad I know.

~

243

THE SATURDAY AFTERNOON SUNSHINE WAS BRIGHT AND HOT after so long in the dark, air-conditioned hospital room. In front of the building, Prentice stretched his sore leg on a sunny bench to get his bearings. *I need to talk to Jessie.* She was the only person that could help him make sense of all this.

"That's ironic. Me wanting to talk to somebody," he said to the crows hopping across the grass.

He drove to the cell phone store, and right there in the store, he plugged the new phone into the outlet to call Jessie while the battery charged. The call went to voicemail again. It was mid-afternoon in D.C. and she and her dad were probably still hiking, or telling stories and catching up. Jessie didn't always see him even when he was in town, since she lived in the city.

He allowed himself to just sit there and appreciate the air-conditioning while he looked at the Front Range through the big glass windows. He wondered about her dad, David, the long-haul trucker who married an artistic Chinese-American lady with smiling deep black eyes, and was still married to her after all these years. David let his domineering mother-in-law come live with them and they named their daughter after this Tiger Grandma, Jessie. They'd even come through Hurricane Katrina all right as a family.

He couldn't help comparing David DeGroot, sight unseen and in full imagined perfection, to his reserved, emotionally scarred dad. *That's not really fair,* he told himself. *You have no idea what he's like.*

He laughed a little, thinking of what Jessie would probably say. Something about not knowing the half of it. Her stories of Tiger Grandma confused him. What was she like? Why did Anna let her mom take over and run everything, as

Jessie said? There was more to that story. Maybe like there was turning out to be lots more to his own story than he'd known about.

His own story. Back to reality. He unplugged the phone, went back to Dad's car, opened the windows, and a wave of responsibility washed over him. The car was drivable, but he was missing a tail light – the whole back corner of the car was imploded – so that was a mechanical violation. Who knew how long the abused tires would hold out? He really ought to help Dad get an insurance claim started on the damage to the car from their escape and get a rental car. *Really ought to. But do I have to right now? Right this minute?*

"No, I need to take care of myself first," he told himself, using that new fatherly voice.

He went to the grocery store, hobbled inside, and got a cart like he always did. *Hold on!* It would be fun to ride, so he swapped it for a motorized shopping cart with a seat and a tiny basket. He was injured, after all. *Jessie will laugh.*

He took a selfie of himself in the seat, sticking his wounded leg out to the side, just to be silly. *This is not like me.* He texted her the photo. *Maybe being silly is okay. I need a fresh start.*

"Good idea," he said to himself. "Okay. Time to shop. I better get a handle on this sugar thing." Addiction, even, the way Dad talked about it? *I don't know how to start.*

He spent more time in the produce section than he had in a long time, wandering around, but not sure how to cook most of what was there.

I need a cookbook first, he reasoned as he glided through the store on the battery-powered cart. *That's a way of asking for help.* He parked out of the way in the vitamin aisle, and on his phone, he found a recipe for stir-fry that called for a bag of frozen vegetables to get started. *No time like the present.*

At home the rest of the afternoon, he tried to keep himself busy, but he still wouldn't let himself call Dad's insurance company. He puttered around at his apartment doing some cleaning, but then his sore leg told him to take a break. He sat in the gravity chair with his feet up high, thinking about his mom. His dad. And even William, who never knew about all the history Dad told him today.

He thought about this week's fire, both fires! What was going to happen now for Garnet? He had all kinds of questions and ideas. On his laptop, he worked on his Tinderbox.tips website and added some of his photos showing recent fire damage, without identifying the addresses. Maybe no one was reading his website, but it was a good place for him to collect information to help him think.

He even took a little nap and woke up refreshed.

The stir-fry he made for dinner was edible. *I might do that again. It was better than opening a box of frozen pre-cooked mystery something.*

After dinner, his phone rang. It was Jessie.

"Hi. You're really there," he said. "I mean, it's good to talk to you in person."

She asked a million questions, starting with the second fire and ending with his joy-ride in the motorized shopping cart. "I loved that photo you sent."

"What about your dad?" he asked. "It's so cool you can hang out with him."

Jessie agreed. "He's been gone so much, it's good to spend time together."

"It must've been hard to have him on the road so much when you were younger," said Prentice.

She said, "I hope he's okay. He seems a little off right now, but I can't figure it out."

"What do you mean?"

She sighed, "I'm sure it's nothing. He's probably tired from all the miles on the road."

After a long time, the conversation wrapped up with warmth, happiness, and even expectation. He said, "I can't wait to see you. I miss you so much."

I feel like I've known her my whole life.

"THAT'S QUITE AN ACCOMPLISHMENT, SON," WERE BILL Keene's words as he greeted Prentice Sunday morning at the hospital. He'd just watched the news report, including the interview with Prentice in the church parking lot.

Prentice's vision suddenly got all blurry and his eyes smarted. "Thanks, Dad."

The screen changed to show reporter Franklin Heiser on location, on the shoulder of the interstate running through Garnet. This was as close as he could get to the action, since the town was still full of dangerous areas.

"In the distance behind me, you see the Rocky Mountain Diner in historic Garnet." Prentice noticed a gray blur that he knew to be the stray cat prowling along the side of the restaurant, avoiding the first responders in the parking lot. "This building survived Friday's wildfire, but many others on the west side of town did not," said Heiser.

Next was a montage of images of firefighters at work, aerial views of familiar neighborhoods, devastated now, and lines of evacuating cars scrolled by on the screen, as the reporter summarized. "Beginning with the Garnet Fire on

Thursday, and the Forest Heights Fire on Friday, Garnet has been pummeled with disasters.

"Neither fire is 100% contained yet, and there are hot spots within the boundaries of both fires. Because of the complexity of the two incidents and the involvement of so many homes and neighborhoods, fire crews from across the county and state are here now.

"Access to most of Garnet on both sides of the interstate is still restricted to first responders as they work to contain both fires and minimize damage to homes."

The video showed greener neighborhoods with standing houses. "Sources with the Pioneersburg Fire Department told Channel 8 News that preliminary indications are some neighborhoods fared better than others. Gwilym Acres, which has been actively encouraging residents to reduce the amount of vegetative fuels on their private property over the last years seems to have had less damage than those like Majestic Estates, where very little wildfire risk mitigation was done.

"Channel 8 will bring you more information about these and other efforts as soon as we hear the news. This is Franklin Heiser, between the two fires in Garnet."

Prentice shut off the television. "Did you hear that?"

"Which part. The fires are still burning?"

"No. They're actually talking on television about Gwilym Acres. That's where I've done the bulk of my work. It's making a difference, Dad. Pioneersburg FD noticed and talked to the news crews about it!" Prentice stood up, wanting to move, but the boot hampered him. He opted to rake his hands back and forth through his hair, making it stand straight up on top of his head. "Don't you see? It's information everyone can use, you know? After the fire, the people who aren't burned out might actually take action when they wouldn't before."

Hope mixed with rising excitement filled Prentice's chest. He caught his dad's eye. "I've been wishing they would do this for years. Garnet FD never would. Don't you see? They're going to be searching for knowledge, and everything they need to know is on my website. I've got lots of references that'll link them to other sources, too. It's what I want, why I started the company—to help people get the information they need. This means companies like Tinderbox.tips will gain credibility."

"The best kind of advertising is free," said Bill, meeting his eye.

Prentice took a breath. "I wonder who turned the news people around and got them to speak the truth. I'll call Allie, for sure. She'll know who it was. And..." he frowned. "Well, the other person I really need to talk to is Chief Rugen."

www.Tinderbox.tips: After the Fire – Hydrophobic Soil

- Catastrophic fires can destroy the organic material on the soil surface.
- Hydrophobic soil repels water, increasing surface runoff and erosion.
- Place fallen logs across slopes to slow runoff and intercept sediment.
- Use seeding, straw bale check dams, silt fences, and other practices that control erosion and reduce runoff.

Three girls played in a treehouse and chased around the yard. Prentice sat in the shade with Allie Snyder and her husband Marco on the back deck of their Pioneersburg home while he explained what happened since he left her and the crew at Incident Command.

"That's amazing, Prentice," said Allie. "You got in there and rescued your dad just in time."

"The really unbelievable part is how he opened up to me. I learned so much."

"Communication is a wonderful thing," Allie said.

"Right. So I don't know how it happened... maybe you had something to do with it? The news channels finally see themselves as an education outlet, and they're sharing information about wildfire risk work."

She smiled, and her brown eyes flashed. "I've been trying for years, and now I've got interviews scheduled with them. I'm glad they're finally on board."

"Can I help you out?

"Yes. I'd love your help. It'll be recorded so the station will have a lot of material ready to use, lots of short clips over the next few weeks after the fires."

The next morning, Prentice was on a cloud. He met Allie at the Channel 8 studio, wearing his old yellow long-sleeve work shirt and cargo pants, as befitting a wildland firefighter and sawyer. When Allie saw him, her look said, "What's that?" She wore her Pioneersburg uniform of white shirt emblazoned with insignia, and navy pants.

"I didn't think my Garnet Fire uniform would be right, especially since I still haven't talked to Chief Rugen."

As they'd arranged, Beth Garcia focused on Prentice first. She asked more about his escape from Majestic Estates, his mitigation mission. "And what about the sales pitch that got you suspended from the fire department?"

"Beth, I do have a side business, with a website called Tinderbox.tips. My goal has always been to get the word out to more residents that they're the only ones who can do the work on their private property before a fire. Or even during a wildfire, in most cases."

"Doesn't the fire district you work for teach people about wildfire risk?"

"Well, they try. They could do more." He plastered the smile on his face as he thought of Rugen. "But it's hard to get people's attention, too, and I do get kinda laser-focused. I overdid it while I was on duty one day and gave information no one was asking for."

"So the chief suspended you?"

"Yes, but it was the right thing for him to do."

"And what about the people you talked to that day? Did their house survive the fires?"

He sighed. "I don't know."

Garcia kept asking questions to draw out all the nuances of preparing for wildfires.

"There's a great analogy from Dr. Jack Cohen about how wildfire actually spreads just like a virus. The flying embers are the insidious germs, incubating and smoldering in weak spots on your property," he explained.

"If the virus has nothing to eat, it will die. But if it gains energy, it will spread like... well, you know," he smiled his crooked smile. He had a glimmer of a thought that he was doing a good job with the camera. His blond hair stuck up all over, just like it was supposed to. Maybe people were going to pay attention to what he had to say.

"The key to wildfire behavior is three things: fuel, weather, and topography. You can only control the fuels. Spending time and money on cleaning up before a fire will pay for itself if it protects your house. But get this, if your house doesn't ignite, it won't burn down. It's that straightforward."

Garcia asked, "Aren't you worried that talking about this so soon after the fire will be like rubbing salt in the wounds of people whose homes were gone?"

He shook his head. "I'm really sorry for all the homes that are destroyed. But there are many, many more that did not burn, and they're still at risk for the next fire." Garcia nodded for him to go on.

"If we can get those residents' attention and have them channel all their nervous energy into clearing out some fuels now, it will help them and all their neighbors. There's still so much material out there that can burn, even tomorrow or next week. The critical piece is that each property owner needs to do what they can, in their home's defensible space, to be ready."

Prentice was on a roll. "Beth, everyone's thinking about wildfire, but there's another topic that we should get to, and that's flooding. It's important to get this information out there right now after these fires." He motioned to Allie.

Garcia flashed a smile and said, "Please welcome Captain Allie Snyder from the Pioneersburg Fire Department, ladies and gentlemen."

Allie explained some more. "We've had the wildfire disasters this week, and people might think this is all they have to deal with. Not so. There's another disaster brewing now, and that's the flash flooding we should expect next spring."

She described how the heat from a high-severity fire can kill all the vegetation and bake the soil to the point that water cannot be absorbed into the earth. "After that kind of fire, the ground becomes just like concrete. This causes excessive run-off when it rains on the land that's been burned. Even areas that have never had flooding before are exposed to a new risk."

"Oh, since it can't soak up the rain, that makes it more vulnerable to erosion," Garcia said.

Allie said, "Yes. Even a light drizzle falling on a burn scar can cause flash flooding, with mud and debris flows cutting deep channels into the ground where there used to be just a little depression." A monitor next to them displayed images of damage in other communities.

"It can turn into flash floods that wash cars off the road, rip gulleys across roads, and blow out bridge supports. The streams scour out the channels with an enormous volume of water, full of sediment, that was part of the ground up the hill a few minutes ago."

Prentice added, "The mud and debris flows can happen for up to five years after a wildfire. It'll start this next spring, for sure. We have years of damage that can happen before the grass starts to grow back to slow the rainwater's speed."

Allie said, "After the fire, the rain becomes a torrent on the ground, because none of it sinks in like it used to. I've seen water flowing right into basement window wells in areas where rainwater used to stay hundreds of feet from their house in a little stream. If they'd known the risk, they could have put sandbags around the house. It survived the wildfire, but not the flooding."

"So what should people do now?" Garcia shook her head.

"We have to act this fall and winter. Right now is the crucial time. The city and town public works engineers need to re-evaluate the infrastructure," Allie said. "They need to check the size of culverts going under the roads. Odds are, they have the capacity for only 10% of the volume they need to handle when spring comes. This is going to cost money, but if municipalities spend money immediately, this fall and winter, to beef up the drainage, it will save the cost hundreds of times over by reducing flood damage to roads and homes in the future."

As she explained, Prentice kept his eyes on her. *She used to make sandwiches for me. She tried to save William.* It was a miracle he'd found her again.

Allie continued. "Anything you can do to slow down the water in the spring is good. I'm talking to private land owners too, even if they didn't get burned out. If you're downhill from a burn scar, watch out."

Garcia nodded encouragingly for her to continue. "You need to put sandbags around vulnerable points. There are different kinds of mulch, from straw bales to hydro-mulching on the bare ground." Allie counted off the ideas on her fingers. "Plant grass seed and keep it there long enough so it can sprout and begin to rebuild the soil, though that takes time. It costs money but it will reduce the amount of damage downstream, which will be extraordinarily more expensive."

Prentice jumped in again. "And on private property, as people are having the burned trees cut down, don't haul them off right away. You can ask the sawyer crews to use the bigger tree trunks to slow down the water rushing down the hillsides by turning them into log erosion barriers. It's a way to make terraces to intercept water running down a slope, and trap sediment. You lay them in a bricklayer pattern and secure them with big stakes." He demonstrated with a stacking motion with his hands. "It helps for a few years after the fire."

He went on. "You could limb them and get rid of the slash...Oh!" he looked at Allie as he had another idea. "The city or county ought to be making sure there's a place for all the branches and little trees to be hauled off," he turned back to Garcia.

"We anticipate there'll be volunteer groups wanting to help, too. They can help position the logs after a sawyer team has cut the burned trees. They can also drag slash to low piles along the roadside," Allie said.

Prentice interjected. "We call that 'gift wrapping,' since

it's a gift to the chipper operators. It's a lot more work to pick up tangled up slash and get it in the chipper."

Allie laughed. "I hadn't heard that one before. Gift wrapping." She turned back to Garcia. "Also, flood insurance. I would recommend that everyone in Garnet, whether they're in a burn scar area or not, check into flood insurance. More people are going to need it sooner than they think."

"People need to make flash flood evacuation plans," Prentice added. "On days next year when it starts raining on top of a burn scar, you need to think about going somewhere safe before it gets dangerous. You might only have a few minutes' warning, but signing up for the county's notifications is a good idea no matter what."

Prentice and Allie spent longer in the studio than anyone anticipated. "You've given us enough information here for weeks of daily segments about the fire. We'll probably run them morning and evening to get the most exposure," said Garcia.

"That sounds great," said Allie.

"We'll come back any time," Prentice replied.

THEY WENT OUT FOR LUNCH AFTER THE INTERVIEW TO celebrate. Allie chose a casual restaurant with a shaded patio. The August noon sun was withering. The view of the Front Range would've been relaxing, but both of them kept looking north at the smoke coming from both fires still alive in Garnet.

On the patio, patrons could be seated with their dogs, and Allie asked the couple next to them if she could pet their little white Bichon terrier. Then she settled down to talk some more with Prentice. "I could tell you were nervous at the beginning," she said without preamble, "But you did a great job. I think that went really well. It's going to help people. If you're up for it, I have some more ideas about getting the word out right now. People are really listening."

"I'm really worn out," he said with another half-smile. "I can talk to people when I have to, when it's important. But at this moment, I am toast." He laughed. *Why do I laugh when I'm completely serious?*

"I understand. You were like that when you were little, too." She laughed. "You used to fall asleep after lunch every day, head on the table. I didn't even have to tell you to take a nap. Or sometimes you made it out to your fort and slept in there."

"I forgot about that."

"Have you told your dad that we ran into each other, that we've talked?"

"Yeah. We had a big, er, discussion. It was pretty heated."

"I'm sorry it was such an ordeal. I didn't mean for it to be a tasker, but I don't want to miss this chance to talk to him. As an adult, you know? I think it would really help me."

"He's still pretty wobbly. But I hope he's coming around. And he owes it to you."

"MR. BIXBY? THIS IS PRENTICE KEENE."

"Well, I be darned. It's good ta' hear from you. Last time I saw you was in my rearview mirror as we all high-tailed it out of my neighborhood." *Hm. That's what you did, anyway. I stuck around and almost got killed.*

"I'm so glad you answered your phone. First of all, how are you? Where are you?"

The older man laughed. "That's the miracle of the

modern era. You can call someone and you don't even know where they are. Actually, I'm sitting at my sister's house in Blue Mesa. How're you doin', Prentice? Where are you?"

"Home. I've been with my dad at the hospital."

"Oh? I'm sorry to hear. What's up?"

Prentice briefly explain his dad's condition, and finished by saying, "He's going to have to make some changes, but he should be okay."

"Good ta' hear."

"Listen, the reason I'm calling– do you have a minute?"

"Sure do. I've got a lot o' time on my hands right now. Say, I saw you on TV, that interview about the fire mitigation. Impressive."

"Really, I'm glad, because that's why I wanted to talk to you. Yes, sir. A lot has happened since I saw you a week ago. I'm glad to know you've got a good place to stay, too."

"I'm getting pretty spoiled here. She's cooking up a storm, all her favorite comfort foods. Anyway, what can I do for you?" Mr. Bixby was always right to the point. *He must've been a good guy to work for when he was in the forest service. You never have to guess what he's thinking.*

Prentice asked, "You heard they're letting people back into some neighborhoods in Garnet?"

"Yah. I hope to get up there soon to see what's become of my house. I'm not optimistic. I know we did a lot of work at my place, but not so much the others around there ..."

"How about we drive up there and check it out? Do you have your resident credential so they know you belong in the neighborhood?"

"Sure do. Got it the other day at the disaster action center."

"Great. I'll come pick you up. I want to check out my

dad's house, too, if it's okay, if we can even get there. I've got a credential for Forest Heights. I'm driving his car—"

"Where's your truck?"

"That's partly why I was hoping you'd come with me. My truck's up near my Dad's house, and if I'm able drive it, I hoped you wouldn't mind following me in Dad's car."

"Sure, I can do that. When do we leave?"

"How about first thing in the morning? Let me have your sister's address."

www.Tinderbox.tips - Radiant Heat:

- Window glass cracks at 180 degrees.
- Fahrenheit 451 is the temperature to ignite a sheet of paper or dry wood.
- Tempered window glass will break at 630 degrees Fahrenheit.
- The air in a wildfire can reach 1,500 to 2,000 degrees Fahrenheit.

"I guess you missed out on some action on accounta' your leg, huh?"

"Well, some of it." Prentice glanced from the road to Mr. Bixby in the passenger seat. They were going south on Emerald Road, with Gwilym Acres on the west side and Wagon Trail on the east. He slowed down to see which departments and fire vehicles were still there, a week later, as firefighters continued to do mop-up in Gwilym Acres. This was the dirty, tedious work of detecting smokes and hot spots in what appeared to be a "cold" area so the fire wouldn't reignite. *Starve those smoldering embers.*

"They held the line against the east flank of the Garnet Fire here at Emerald Road. That'll look odd on the fire map later, that ruler-straight line where the fire stopped," said Bixby, looking at the five-acre estate lots. "Just a few spot fires got across. Easier to stop on pasture land full of fire-fighters."

Prentice said, "The Garnet fire started in that pasture."

Bixby said, "That seems like years ago, Prentice. And it definitely didn't stop at the road down there. After we parted ways, what happened to you?"

He explained about trying to evacuate neighbors and getting stuck on the clogged roads.

"I knew I'd be glad I left when I did," said Mr. Bixby. "Why didn't you high-tail it out of there too, instead of staying there to do all that?"

"Stupid...human...tunnel vision," he said to Bixby. "I understand more than I did before the fire."

"That's what training is for, Prentice. The best experience is someone else's!"

He conceded with a shrug. "Gwilym Acres, here, is where I worked with the Pioneersburg Fire Department team on hot spots. It seems like a lot of houses survived here."

Mr. Bixby said, "I've spent my lifetime working in forests, and I've seen healthy ones and mismanaged ones. But I've never had to head into a burn scar to check the status of my own house."

"I know that a good number of these homes up here were able to defend themselves," said Prentice.

"The 0-to-30-foot zones are well maintained up here in

Gwilym, and the tree canopy was thinned. You had a lot to do with that, Prentice."

"Sure, I did a lot of work here. I wasn't the only one. Their manager, Marlene, really did a good job of getting people's attention. They had whole streets of residents doing slash chipping days together, so everyone knew they were doing their part and it was adding up all around the neighborhood. They had entire blocks where all the properties had done at least some mitigation to reduce ladder fuel."

"You've gotta cut a few trees to save more trees. It's good stewardship. That's great to have everyone on the same page," said Bixby.

"Yep. Some of them had potluck dinners together afterwards. Good bonding time for the neighbors."

"They've done all this cleanup, and they still have plenty of beautiful Ponderosas and firs all through there, too. Even now. See how many of them are just burned a little at the bottom of the trunk, but they're still mostly green? They're going to make it." Mr. Bixby nodded and looked intently out his window at the forest.

They kept going south toward Majestic Estates. By the time they crossed State Highway 55, they got into the worst of the dark burn scar.

Prentice reminded him, "You were trying to get that same kind of momentum going on your street. Your property was really in good shape!"

"It's never easy being the first one. I didn't mind that. I really needed a retirement project, and I was hoping ta' show how nice it can look ta' reduce the risk but still have a good number of healthy trees. But we ran outta time with the neighborhood."

Prentice started to try to reassure him that his house

might have made it, but he bit his tongue. Most of Bixby's neighbors had never cleared out a stick of dead wood or thinned out the tangles of new trees sprouting in doghair thickets, even though only one out of every twenty trees could grow to healthy maturity.

"I used to try to explain it using the same carrot analogy you did," Prentice said. "When you grow carrots in your garden, you have to thin them."

Bixby chuckled. "Lemme guess. They'd never grown carrots either, so they didn't have a clue what you were talkin' about. 'Green Acres' mentality."

"Right. And yet, they wanted it to be, quote, 'natural.' But there's nothing as natural as a wildfire cleaning out a forest."

"It ain't natural to keep every tree seedling that sprouts and hide your houses in the middle of the mess, either," said Bixby.

The farther south they went, the fewer trees or houses had survived, and the blacker and more uniform the burn scar got. The ground, the bushes, the treetops, and all the houses. Piles of gray ashes. Carbonized trees, bushes, deck chairs and cushions, welcome mats, structural timbers, campers, and roofs.

"There's sure more bare space between the houses now," said Prentice. When homeowners did their own clean-up work, they could be selective about which bushes and trees to keep. They could clean the gutters and sweep the deck. They could design their own checkerboard pattern of vegetation so a fire would not be drawn to the house.

But if they decided not to clean up anything for the sake of privacy, the fire had to make the decisions for them. It burned all the fuel it could find and was indiscriminate about it. It only stopped when it starved.

Fuel, oxygen, heat. Take away one side of the fire triangle, and it collapses.

∾

"THANK YOU, MR. BIXBY," SAID THE GARNET POLICE OFFICER, checking his resident credentials. "We're letting residents in today because the wind has died. There's less chance of trees falling, but you need to understand there's still risk. I can let you in to see your property on Columbine Way, but don't go anywhere else, all right?"

The men nodded.

"There are first responders working in the area. Therefore, some streets are blocked off. Please follow their directions if conditions change." She was now reading from a script. Prentice understood. He did the same thing in similar situations to be sure no information was missed.

"Also, we need to advise you that at this time, even if your house survived, no one is allowed to move back into their home. Electricity and natural gas have been turned off to the neighborhood. The homeowners' association has determined that no camping will be allowed."

She handed Mr. Bixby a sheet of paper with a list of instructions and rules from the HOA. "This will tell you more. For now, do you have any questions?"

Mr. Bixby shook his head, looking past Prentice at the officer outside the window, then shifting his focus north into the wasteland. "No, I just want ta' see what's left."

"I understand, sir." She handed him a clipboard where she'd written his name and address taken from the credential. He signed in with his name and the time, 9:45 a.m. "We need to talk with you again when you exit the neighborhood so you can sign out."

Bixby's property was only three blocks from the checkpoint. Not one house on those blocks remained. None of the Ponderosas in this area was still green. Instead, there were now thousands of tall, blackened sticks standing in a charred landscape of rolling hills, pointing high into the cloudless blue sky. The seared branches had no needles.

At the curb, they identified his plastic mailbox melted sideways with the adhesive metal numbers still barely visible. Bixby said, "Let's just stay in the car."

They drove toward where the house was supposed to be. The brick chimney stood alone in the center like a watchtower over a gray prison yard. The foundation was visible, but the cement was crumbly after being exposed to such intense heat.

Twisted metal bits stuck up amidst charred ruins. The remains of the melted composite deck sagged over the front door. Prentice said, "I don't think your cool ski chairs made it, sir."

"Nah. Not much did."

"I'll take some photos for you to send to the insurance company, Mr. Bixby."

"Thanks, son."

The two men were back at the checkpoint inside of twenty minutes.

As they left the area, it was quiet for a long time. Finally, Mr. Bixby said, "Well, that's a darn shame."

PRENTICE DROVE WEST INTO DOWNTOWN GARNET.

The Rocky Mountain Diner parking lot was full of command vehicles and trucks as authorities began to assess the damage.

"Let's go north through town," he said. "I want to check on my friend Anna's house." Mr. Bixby didn't argue.

He went north on Crystal Street, taking the same route he had almost a week ago. "You can see where I drove through the yards here."

"I see some ruts through that garden there," said Bixby.

Prentice said, "Some houses made it." Here, blizzards of sparks had landed in thousands of scouting parties, looking for something to eat. They survived, grew, and burned things down where they found fine, dry kindling. But it was more like in Gwilym Acres, where many homes and trees survived.

Mr. Bixby finally found his voice. "It's not hit or miss. It's not just luck when a house survives."

"No. The fire makes sense," Prentice said, remembering the neglected state of some of these houses last time he saw them. "A little maintenance could have gone a long way."

One house would be intact. A house next door, with a bad roof or other chinks in its armor, would have succumbed to the flying embers and burned from the inside out, leaving green trees with scorch marks around the empty foundation.

They got to Anna and David DeGroot's house, and Prentice turned into the driveway. "This is the home of my friend's parents." The house was still there, but it was badly damaged. The metal flower sculptures still stood in front of the porch, but they were sooty instead of colorful.

"What do you think did the damage here?" he asked Mr. Bixby, who was regaining his composure and looking around.

"Ah," he said, looking closely from the car and analyzing the evidence. "I'm sure you'll have your own theory, but let's take a look-see."

With him, Prentice observed that the junipers along the front of the house were scorched into inky black skeletons, and the front windows above them were broken. The blue paint on the shutters was blistered and coated with soot near the top corners where the smoke had billowed out. It was unnaturally dark inside.

Bixby said, "Well, it seems to me, those 'kerosene on a stick' junipers under the windows made a landing pad for the flying embers. The tall grass in the yard didn't help either. See how it burned right up ta' the house? The heat from the juniper fire cracked the windows. More embers blew in the broken windows, and the fire consumed the house from the inside out."

Prentice agreed with a nod.

Mr. Bixby continued. "By then, though, looks like the firefighters got here and were checking for spot fires. You can see where the water pooled on the ground. They kept it from burning down, but it's probably still gotta be gutted."

"I think so too." Prentice got out and took pictures from a few different directions so he could show Anna and Jessie when they asked.

"Well, let's go see about my truck, and Dad's house." He avoided the direct route up Forest Road because it was still full of equipment and responders. Instead, he retraced the route he took on Friday, following the jeep road up the mountain. He had to go slowly because Dad's sedan wasn't ready for the challenge.

"Prentice, you said you came up this way during the fire?" Mr. Bixby asked.

"Yeah, more of my adventures. I found out Friday

morning that Dad had missed two days of work for no good reason, and that's just not like him."

"Except there was a possible reason," Bixby said.

"Diabetes, yep. I couldn't get 9-1-1 to check on him because of the Forest Heights fire. So I thought of this way to get there."

"I s'pose the main roads were probably clogged with people evacuatin.'"

"They were. I went overland in several places. And then I twisted my ankle, so I could barely get me and Dad out in this car. I'm surprised it's still moving."

"Well, the title of that story should be 'How I Saved My Father's Life and Escaped from my Second Wildfire in Two Days,' not 'How I Hurt My Ankle,' Prentice. Ya' need ta' give yourself more credit."

"I keep hearing that lately."

The fire had pre-heated the air above it on the steep topography, resulting in terrible damage to the forest, and the homes hidden in it, going all the way up the mountain to the jeep road. The road cut acted as a small fire break, and in some places the burn scar stopped at the road. But in other stretches, the trees were black all the way from the bottom to the top of the slope above the road, as far as they could see.

"We should be almost there. I had the A/C turned on when I drove up here, so I know I left the windows closed. Maybe that stopped the sparks from getting in the cab," he said hopefully. "Maybe I still have a truck."

As soon as they came around the bend and saw Prentice's pickup truck, even from a distance they could tell it was a wreck. "Never mind," said Prentice. They parked behind it and Prentice got out to look more closely.

A tree limb stuck straight through the front windshield,

and the puncture hole through the glass was a jagged circle around the branch. The safety glass was cracked in a crazed pattern out from the hole, and the glass crumbled away at the edges, leaving big gaps.

By then, Mr. Bixby had hoisted himself out of the car and said, "You got a chink in the armor there, Prentice. The sparks got in and ignited the upholstery an' all."

With a grimace, Prentice opened the driver's side door that he'd left unlocked last week to find a burned-out mess. The seats and carpet were melted, as were his phone and the rest of the plastic console. The metal seat springs stuck out like skeletons. His keys were surrounded by blobs of melted plastic. Catching his breath, he leaned back against the truck to look at the sky instead of at his ruined truck.

Mr. Bixby said, "I'll take photos of the truck and the VIN number for you, son. That'll help with your insurance claim." He walked with his cane up to the passenger side. "Hey, when did you scrape the roof like this?"

"That was from driving through the culvert under the railroad tracks."

"Well, you don't do anything halfway. I'll see if the papers in the glove box are intact, by any chance. How about you look in the back and see about your tools?"

"Good idea." *Never know, they might be useable.* He opened the tonneau cover and loaded the saws and the rest of his gear into the trunk of Dad's car. They seemed okay, and he could check their condition later.

Shutting the trunk, he found Mr. Bixby's glance. "I wonder if my dad's house did any better?"

"I'm not really up for a hike down there, Prentice. But you're not either."

"Right. I didn't think about this part. I can't see the house from here, though. Do you mind waiting for me for a few minutes?"

"Sure. Go ahead. Here, take my cane. It'll help you keep your balance." He sat down in the car again to wait.

Prentice didn't like it, but he accepted the offer and made his way down the trail, which had burned in places. There was a house down there, but what shape was it in? He surveyed the yard to see evidence of spot fires. None of them had spread very far or reached the house. He began talking to himself. "It's actually still standing."

He didn't remember leaving the garage door open, but doing so had resulted in the destruction of some lawn chairs which were now melted into the corner where storms of embers had blown in.

He peered through the broken kitchen window and opened the door. "Scorched linoleum, but the flames didn't make it to the carpet." He sniffed for evidence too. "The power's been out, and everything in there is spoiled," he said, not bothering to open the refrigerator.

"Smoke damage for sure, but it's still standing." He took the time to snap a series of photos and grab some file folders from Dad's office to help with insurance claims.

Back up at the car, he told Mr. Bixby the good news.

"There are no guarantees, I know," Bixby pressed on when Prentice started to object. "We did the same at my house, and it didn't work out. But at least we tried. I feel much sorrier for the folks who acted like nothing would ever happen, no wildfire would come along. The ones who didn't so much as trim a branch or rake out a pile of leaves. They're the ones who complain that luck wasn't with them. But that's not true. They didn't deserve to make it, in my opinion."

It was harsh, but it made sense. Prentice blew out his

cheeks, switched on the ignition. *Would I dare say that next time I'm on TV?* "Thanks for coming with me today. I hope I didn't wear you out. We can get you back to your sister's now."

"Hold up." Mr. Bixby flattened a palm at Prentice. "As long as we're here, don't you have one more person you need to check in with? I get the feeling you're avoiding talking to the chief."

Oh man.

Mr. Bixby sensed the delay, adding, "You said he was workin' at incident command, but they should be scalin' back, so by now it's likely he's back at the fire department. I'll go with you, if you' like." He waited for a reply, but none came, so he added, "I don't have anywhere else to be now, do I?"

Prentice saw the layers of wisdom in Bixby. "You know, I think I'll take you up on that. I could use some moral support."

Prentice parked close to the fire station so Mr. Bixby wouldn't have to walk as far with his cane. Bypassing the security door, they went in through the open vehicle bay doors, where Prentice waved at his crewmates on shift, but he kept walking.

Mr. Bixby said, "I'll head down to make a pit stop."

"I'll be down the hall with the chief. I shouldn't be long. Meet me in the kitchen?"

"No worries, Prentice. Take your time. I've got some thinkin' to do."

Prentice's mouth was dry when he found Rugen at his desk, frowning at his computer. Hunched the way he was, over the screen, made him seem smaller. Older. He had dark circles under his brown eyes. Prentice knocked softly on the door to get his attention, and the chief looked up.

It surprised Prentice when the man seemed to brighten and said, without missing a beat, "Oh good. I needed to talk to you, Keene."

"Umm. Okay."

"Have a seat." The chief gestured to a chair in front of his desk. "What happened to your leg?" he asked as Prentice settled onto the wooden chair.

Prentice gave him the short version. "It'll be good as new in a few weeks, they said."

"Good. That's good." The chief looked away, then back, like he had something on his mind, Prentice thought, but he didn't ask. Better to wait, let the chief go first.

"So, everyone's out working their tails off. Going house to house ... missing people. Doing mop-up. The big boys are leaving soon."

Prentice tried to jump on this moving merry-go-round with the fire chief. "But the mutual aid departments are still helping?"

"Yah. They got some good training experience out of this one."

Training experience? Pioneersburg? Are you kidding me? What about our department that never trains for this? "How are our guys all doing? Were there any injuries?"

"I'll save the details for another day. We didn't get off scot-free, for sure. Some vehicle damage too. Might need to make some repairs. I'm knee-deep in paperwork here. So many forms to fill out, hours and money to track."

"I can only imagine."

"The Office of Emergency Management is activating their plans about long-term recovery, beyond the disaster relief and recovery already in motion. The volunteer agencies have jumped in, with the shelters and all. Ash-sifting to find valuables. Civilians are crawling out of the woodwork, wanting to help." He raised his hands in a helpless gesture. "Some of it makes no sense. They're trying to donate old furniture to people who just had their houses burn down and are currently living in a high school gymnasium, for Pete's sake! And some out-of-state organization just tried to deliver an 18-wheeler full of lettuce to one shelter! They got 'em re-directed to the regional food bank."

"That's ridiculous," Prentice said.

"It's all ridiculous," Rugen said, looking back at the computer, shoulders sagging even more. *He looks as tired as I feel.* "It's more horrible than anyone could have imagined. All the homes lost. All the people..."

"Well, it didn't have to be this bad, either, Chief. I tried to tell you. I've been trying to tell everyone."

"Are ya' saying this was someone's fault?" The chief stared hard at Prentice, who was barely taller than the chief even when he was standing and the chief was sitting down.

"No, not at all."

"Well, what did ya' mean then? If ya' have something to say, why don't ya' just say it?"

"Why wouldn't you talk to people about wildfires, chief? We're surrounded by risks! But the only public education you were willing to do was about smoke detectors, over-loaded electrical outlets, and dryer lint."

"One house fire is one too many," said Rugen. "We've gotta teach people how to keep themselves safe."

"Yes, I agree! But we just lost hundreds or maybe thousands of homes in these wildfires. And too many people."

"I've always wondered why ya' don't take house fires more seriously, Keene."

"Oh my God, of course I take 'em seriously. My brother died in a house fire! Right in this very town!"

"Whaddaya think I am, stupid? Ya' think I don't know that? Why do ya' think I'm so obsessed with stopping those fires?

"I have no idea."

"Give me a break."

"What're you talking about, Chief?"

Rugen shook his head slowly. "Ya really don't know... I was the one who carried your brother out the day your house burned."

Prentice missed a beat.

"You... what?"

"Yah. I was new in the department, but I was ready, all suited up with the breathing apparatus, and I was the one to go in."

"You were?" he said, numb all over.

"I climbed up the ladder to the deck, through the sliding door. The kid must have left it open, so I didn't have to break it. I found the kid laying in the hallway. Picked him up and carried him down the stairs and right to the ambulance."

"It was William?"

"Ya' have any other brothers?"

Prentice shook his head, staring at Rugen. He reached behind for the chair he knew must be there somewhere and sat down hard.

Rugen looked at Prentice. "Ya' had no idea?"

Prentice kept shaking his head. "No. How could I? I was just a kid."

"Well, I thought for sure your dad woulda' mentioned it. At some point."

"How could I not see it!? *You* were the tall firefighter in the space suit?"

"Like ya' said, it was almost twenty years ago," Rugen said in the quietest voice Prentice could ever remember him using.

"My dad knew? I mean, you met him?"

"Well, sure. This is a really small town, if ya' haven't noticed. He's hated me for years. I don't know if he ever forgave me."

"For what?" Prentice asked.

"He walked up to the burning house and found me there in the driveway, holding his dead son. Of course he hated me."

"It wasn't your fault, Chief. You got him out of the house, into the ambulance... I'm the one who—"

"Get a grip. You were just a little squirt!"

Prentice looked away. "That's what Allie said."

"Allie Jackson. She was your babysitter, I remember. Now she's Captain Allie Snyder."

"Did you know I worked on her crew last week, where you got me assigned? We had a chance to talk...a lot."

"How 'bout that. Well, our chief at the time talked to her parents as part of the investigation."

"There was an investigation?"

"Ya' know there had to be."

"Now, sure, but not then. Nobody told me anything."

"You were only, what, five? It wasn't the right time. But there never is a right time, is there..." Rugen put his elbows on the desk and ran his hands through his greasy salt and pepper hair, pushing it back behind his ears. He hadn't had time for details like a haircut. Prentice wondered if the man had even been home since the fires had started. "I was sure ya' knew it was me."

Prentice shook his head. "No. I had no idea."

"I've thought about that fire every day of my life for the last twenty-plus years. And how to stop it from happening to anyone again."

"Structure fires..." Prentice said. The fixation all made so much more sense now. "Was he... was he already dead? When you found him?"

Rugen nodded. "I'm pretty sure he was. That smoke was toxic, acrid stuff. A coupla' whiffs of it and he woulda'... well, yeah. I think so. But they had to try to save him."

Prentice stared at the floor and shook his head slowly. "I never put two and two together."

Rugen said, "Well... how about that."

"Hey." He looked at the chief. "So you knew all about this when you hired me? Out of college? It was the first job I applied for, and I got it. Did you just feel sorry for me? The shrimpy kid whose family fell apart?"

"Oh no, nothing like that."

"Well, what then? It wasn't like I was the most experienced candidate or anything."

"No, but ya' were just as qualified as any other applicant. So much energy. Don't think I gave you a free pass. But your dad contacted me around the time of your interview..."

"My dad? Talked to you?"

"Sure did. He called me and said not to say anything to you about it, but that it would mean an awful lot to him if he could keep an eye on you. If you could get a job close to home. Like I owed him a favor."

"What? He didn't even want me to work as a firefighter."

"I'm well aware of that. He made that very clear to me, too. When ya' were in college and going into forestry. But he couldn't change your mind."

"He never told me any of this. But he never told me William had... that William was dead, either. I found out from a lady at school."

Chief Rugen let that sink in. "Prentice, we're a sorry mess, aren't we?"

"Yeah, we are." Prentice's breath was regular again. The darkness that narrowed his vision was clearing.

Rugen said, "Come back to the kitchen. Let me buy ya' a root beer."

∿

PRENTICE SAT WITH THE CHIEF AND MR. BIXBY AT THE TABLE, propped his useless ankle up on a chair, and made the introductions. "Chief Rugen, this is Mr. Eddie Bixby. He's a retired U. S. Forester and one of my mitigation clients. He lives in... er, I should say, his house was in Majestic Estates."

Mr. Bixby clinked a root beer bottle with Prentice's. "You're right, Prentice. I'm not living there now, am I? I'm a property owner, but not a homeowner. That's for darn sure." He turned to Rugen, never one to beat around the bush. "Prentice said he got suspended right before the Garnet fire."

"That's right. He was soliciting work for his business while he was on duty here. That's not permissible."

Prentice spoke up. "Hey, I'm sitting right here. I know that was stupid. I was mad. I was trying to..." A picture of Jessie popped into his mind as he said, "I was trying to save the world all by myself." *That's what it was.*

Rugen didn't notice. He was busy processing some things himself. "I didn't see the forest for the trees, as they say. Like Prentice said, as I worked my way up and became the chief, I thought I had to stop every possible structure fire. I couldn't deal with wildfires too. They're just too big to consider."

Mr. Bixby said, "Yessir, and they've gotten bigger as time goes by, Chief. It's not just your imagination." He went into professor mode. "That U.S. Forest Service wildfire suppression policy from the early 1900s really put us all behind the eight-ball. It encouraged so much fuel to accumulate that woulda' been cleared out by little fires if they'd been allowed more regular-like. And Smokey Bear can't stop all the lighting strikes, anyhow."

The three of them looked out the window, considering

the truths that needed to be dealt with. Prentice readjusted his foot in the walking boot on the chair.

Rugen glanced at it and asked, "So, your father's in the hospital now?"

"Yeah, it's going to be a few days for sure. I'll handle it."

Rugen pursed his lips. "Or maybe you can let him and the doctors handle it," he said quietly.

Prentice ignored it. "So anyway, Chief, I'm actually here with some questions for you, if you're up for that. I have some ideas about what to do next for public service announcements after these fires."

Rugen said, "Yah. I saw you and Captain Snyder on television the other day talking about the flooding potential for next spring. Lotta energy. As always."

"There's just so much information that people should know. It's hard to bring it up when the fires are not even out yet. It feels like kicking people in the teeth, talking about needing to do more fire mitigation, and now the flood mitigation."

Rugen was shaking his head. "I know flooding is the next danger, the next disaster waiting to happen. I just don't know what to do about it, and I sure as heck don't have time to figure it out."

"I bet you don't. But as you can see, I'm gonna be off my feet for a while. Maybe I can help. I've already started updating my website. But," he cleared his throat, "it's very important that you as the fire chief help with the messaging. You, and the mayor, and all the other leaders in town. The police chief. Everyone. Supporting what the experts say. I'm no expert, though."

"You've got an earnestness about you though, Smokey," said Rugen, with a thoughtful expression.

Mr. Bixby piped up. "Prentice, I'm glad you've brought

this up. And Chief, I b'lieve I can be of some assistance in this area." They both turned to Mr. Bixby. "As Prentice said, I worked for the U.S. Forest Service my whole career. My specialty, however, was in hydrology."

"Oh!" both Rugen and Prentice said at the same time.

"Yep. I've worked quite a bit with forest management and the relationship of vegetation with erosion. Just like Prentice said on TV, it's terribly damaging to the watershed when you get a bunch of sediment washing off the mountain and into the streams. People, and some of our local governments, I might add, could take action on some things this fall and winter that would sure help come spring runoff time. If they would spend money now, it'll pay for itself in a year. I promise you that."

The chief nodded. "Bixby, I've got to get ya' involved in this recovery effort. If you have time, that is. Are ya' game for some consulting work? And spending time with the powers that be to figure out what needs to be done?"

"That'd be the cat's pajamas, Chief Rugen," the old man said with a gentle smile. "I'm glad to be able to live at my sister's place, but it would suit both of us better if I had somewhere else to be during the day, if you know what I mean."

Rugen's face had grown less pale and lined in the last few minutes. Optimism? "And Keene, you're gonna be the new face of the Garnet Fire Department."

Prentice suppressed a grin and looked first at Mr. Bixby and then Rugen.

"So does this mean I'm not suspended anymore?"

~

FRIDAY MORNING DAWNED JUST AS PARCHED AS SO MANY OTHER days this month. Nothing unusual, if a drought and two wildfires can be considered usual. *Yes, they can.*

Prentice was up early, more like his old self. No slug time. His routine was taking new shape as every hour and day went by. Best of all Jessie was getting back today from her trip to D.C. He sent her a text.

Hi Jessie! Is UR plane on time?

So far. C U tonight?

Yes! 5:30 @ your place?

;) SYL

"Thank God for her," he said out loud.

Meanwhile, today he would go up to Garnet again. Rugen had him doing paperwork and phone calls related to the fires. He was charged with assisting the lieutenants and coordinating with local emergency management officials about fire recovery efforts, while Mr. Bixby helped plan flood mitigation. Prentice and Allie planned more interviews and prepared information for the public. He added information to the Tinderbox.tips website constantly.

At lunch time, he and Mr. Bixby put their heads together over their sandwiches. "I'm working on Tinderbox in the evenings, and I have some ideas to run past you."

"Tell me about 'em," Bixby said, leaning forward.

"I can't do the physical work, but if I could just get a handle on the organization part, I could hire some more guys to work when they aren't on shift here. Even hire college kids."

"That's a great idea. Strike while the iron's hot... Or, maybe that's not the best analogy..."

"I know how to run a saw and a chipper, but what if I don't know how to manage people?"

Mr. Bixby smiled. "What if you do? Then you'll be the boss. What if you succeed?"

So many ideas, so much to do. He added more tasks to the lists every day.

Prentice worked his tail off for eight hours, left himself a list of what needed to be done in Garnet next time he was at the station, and clocked out at 4 p.m. In the parking lot, he looked for his own truck. Then was reminded, again, that it was gone. *Dad's going to need his car back soon.* That brought on a fresh wave of questions as he chugged home in the blue Ford Focus.

I still haven't gotten his car fixed. Where's Dad even going to live when he leaves the hospital? Is he going to rent an apartment? He won't want to stay with me, I'm sure. But where will he go? Is he going to rehab first?

The habitual responsibility rolled over him in waves. *How is he going to manage? When will he go back to work? How am I going to solve all of this on top of what I'm trying to do about the fire?*

"Hold on, Prentice!" he said out loud to himself. "This is not your job. Those are not your decisions."

They're not? No, they're not. He's going to have to figure it out. Of course, he will. I'll help him if he asks. But that's different than me assuming I have to fix everything.

But I do need to decide what I'm going to do about a new truck for myself. He smiled. *Well, a newer truck.* "Maybe I'll get a 2017 this time," he told himself. "Big spender."

"**J**essie, it's me, Prentice." He took a breath, leaned on his right foot to release the weight from his left foot in the walking boot, and knocked on her door. Casey's booming bark made him smile. *Maybe I should have bought her some flowers. Too late now.*

The door flew open and Jessie stood in front of him with a big smile on her face and in her eyes. Her long hair was loose around her shoulders, still damp from a shower, and she was barefoot. She wore a light sundress with little blue and yellow flowers all over it. Even when she was standing still, the fabric did nice things around her, reminding him how much he'd missed actually seeing her instead of just talking on the phone.

"I thought you'd never get here," she said.

"I thought you'd never get back from D.C.!"

"Come in!" She started to step to one side, but he tipped his chin at her while still looking straight into her entrancing eyes. Then he reached out slowly and wrapped his arms around her in a hug that felt like the most natural and wonderful way of reconnecting he could think of. She smelled like coconuts and just like... herself. *Mmmm!*

She definitely hugged him back, saying into the crook of his neck, "I'm so glad to be home. This is just what I needed." They stood there, so close together, long enough for Prentice to feel safe and happy again. *She still likes me!* It was comfortable. It was warm. She was more perfect than he remembered.

Casey didn't want to be ignored, and he leaned against their legs. Prentice started to lose his balance, and when he tried to fix it, he stepped on Jessie's bare toes with the rubber and aluminum walking boot. "Owww!" She took a step back, noticing his foot. "Oh no! Mom told me about your foot, but I forgot. Come here and sit down."

"Is your mom here?" Prentice asked. *What an idiot. Now you sound like a high school kid.*

"Yes, she's here. But she's in the other room, being discreet. She left the dog out here to chaperone." They both laughed.

"That's good. I mean, it's good that she's here so I can say hi. And thank her! For the shower chair. Did she tell you about that? And the wontons?"

Jessie nodded, and leading him to the sofa, they sat together close enough that Prentice could feel her warmth. He put his arm around her shoulders, holding her gaze. Soaking up the goodness. *She's amazing.*

He leaned in closer, closed his eyes, and brought his cheek next to hers, staying just that close for a few breaths. It was totally mesmerizing and wonderful.

Then he gently touched his nose to hers and kissed her lightly on the lips once, waiting to see what happened next. Jessie kissed him back as if that were the best idea ever. Which it was. *Perfect.*

"I missed you so much, Jessie."

"You too, Prentice." She held his other hand in her lap.

He settled back so he could see her better but didn't let go of her hand. *Wow.*

They heard a door open down the hall, and Anna peered around the corner. "Is it safe to come out now?" she teased. "Hi, Prentice."

He turned toward her. "Hi Anna. How're you doing? Thanks for helping me out last week with everything." She sat down across from them. "I'm glad you can stay with Jessie. But are you okay? Have you talked to any of your neighbors from Garnet yet?"

"You look loads better than last time I saw you," she smiled, seeing their hands intertwined. "I've talked to a couple of people. And David will be home soon. I mean, he'll be here at Jessie's too, so we can figure out what we need to do. Oh, and I saw you on Channel 8 this week a few times. Nice job!"

"Thanks!"

They all regarded each other for a minute. Jessie took a deep breath and said, "I could see a lot of the fire damage when we flew into Pioneersburg. We came in right over Garnet and I saw both burn scars. Still smoking..." She looked at her mom, then back at Prentice, who gripped her hand a little tighter. "Have you, um, have you seen any of it up close?"

He had been preparing for this. *I hoped it wouldn't be tonight already.* "Yes. I have." He paused. "I went by your house again, Anna."

Her her eyebrows went up and her eyes went wide.

"I took some pictures. Do you want to see them?"

Anna and Jessie both nodded. "I've been trying not to get my hopes up," Anna said.

"There really is a lot of damage. But it's not totally destroyed, not like some houses." He got his phone out and shared what he'd seen on the drive with Mr. Bixby. He gave them time to scan all the photos and try to comprehend the story they told.

"There might be some things in there you could salvage. When you want to schedule that with the fire department, I can help you arrange it. They'll meet you there, give you personal protective equipment, and guide you around. It's hazardous now. Sharp edges everywhere."

He didn't bother to mention the junipers or the tall grass, though. Too late for this round.

Anna said, "Okay." She sighed. "Okay, maybe let's do that when David is here. He keeps missing all the excitement."

Jessie nodded. "He wasn't with us for Katrina, either, was he mom?" Anna shook her head.

Prentice said, "That'll help with your insurance claim, too." They both nodded again. "You might want to find out when your insurance company is doing on-site evaluations. With two big fires like this and so many houses... I saw one company setting up their mobile trailer in Garnet today by the diner, presumably to help with all the questions and claims." *Oh, I really did not want to talk about this right now.*

Anna said, "I've been here hiding out, pretending I'm just here visiting Jessie and not homeless. But I better get working on that. Jessie has a flash drive here with all our documents on it. We learned a lot from the hurricane, didn't we?"

Jessie told her mom she'd help her print out documents, then asked Prentice, "Do they know how many homes... I mean, do they know all the numbers yet?"

He shook his head. "They're getting there. It's not good."

Nobody spoke.

"I'm so sorry," Prentice said, finally.

Jessie piped up, "It's not like it's your fault, is it? You were the one who warned everyone this was going to happen and were just trying to keep it from being this bad."

"Yeah," he inclined his head to the side.

"And there were people who listened, right?"

"Yes. It could have been a lot worse in some places than it was." Casey reappeared near his knee hoping for an ear scratch. *Sure thing.*

"See? So you've gotta give yourself more credit!"

"I'm starting to get used to the idea." He did the half-grin and tilted his head sideways the other way. "Especially after all the television interviews. Do you want my autograph?"

Jessie reached out and scrunched Prentice's dark blond hair, which was already standing up on top.

Anna smiled at her daughter. "Are you two staying here for dinner? Or going somewhere so you can... ah, talk?" All three of them laughed out loud. Prentice raised his eyebrows at Jessie.

She said, "Let's go out. We could get some burgers and go sit at the park."

He agreed. "That sounds great. We can't walk much, but we have a lot to talk about." They all exchanged silly smiles.

They got their food in the drive-through lane, and Jessie put the bags on the floor under her feet. Instead of going to the nearby city park, Prentice asked if she'd go with him to Church of Abundant Life. Specifically, the cemetery.

"That's a good picnic spot..." she joked.

"No, it's just, there's something I need to see there. I'm not even sure where it is, what I'm looking for. And I don't want to go there by myself. It's about William. And my mom, Rose."

"Oh gee. I see. Sure, I'll help you."

He let go of the wheel with one hand to take hold of hers for a few seconds. "You're the best friend I've ever had, Jessie."

"Asking for help is the way forward."

"You're also the best kisser in the en-tire universe, Jessie DeGroot."

"That's what friends are for?" they both laughed.

AFTER THEY ATE DINNER ON A BENCH NEAR THE ENTRANCE, Jessie helped Prentice find what he needed to see. The head-stones said, "Rosemary Elwyn Keene, 1958 – 1998," and "William Shannon Keene, Jr., 1991 - 1998." He took plenty of time to just sit there and ask God a lot of questions.

Then, he and Jessie talked on the lawn at the edge of the cemetery with the astounding view of the city and the mountains until the sun disappeared and the shadows cooled. For a while, they kept each other warm, but eventually reason won out and Prentice drove her home. It was excruciating to say goodbye, but at least it was with the promise of seeing each other soon.

In the morning, she drove to Prentice's apartment. "When we set up this date last week, or two weeks ago I guess, we were planning to go bike riding today," she said. "Part of your well-rounded childhood education was supposed to be learning to ride a bike, since you didn't get much practice when you were an actual child."

He shook his head with mock sadness. "Too many hills. And no bike."

"You're not starting today either, with your foot like that." They sat on the floor in his apartment next to the zero-gravity chair, which was the only chair in the living room or dining room.

They brainstormed about other dates they could go on. Interrupted with more kissing. That was just fine. And delicious.

Eventually Jessie said, "I can't sit here any longer. My butt's falling asleep, Prentice!"

"Right! Sorry about that. Mine too, actually. I'm not a very good host." They laughed again. "It's the first time I've brought a woman to my apartment. I never ran into this problem before."

"You're really a gentleman. Well, what now? Seems like I keep coming up with ideas and I never give you a chance."

"I'm not complaining. But you know, I can't believe I'm saying this, but would you go shopping with me?" Prentice said, with a gleam in his eye.

"Seriously? Right now?"

"Yes. Truck shopping. My truck is toast. I can't keep driving my dad's car." He gave her a quizzical look to see what the answer was.

"That would be fun. Spending other people's money."

"And just so you can plan your day, I've got to be at Channel 8 studios again by three o'clock. They're interviewing me and Allie again. This time I'm wearing my Garnet uniform, since I'm officially un-suspended now. Wanna come along?"

"I wish I could, but my mom needs some company today too. She acts like she's fine, but she's really in limbo at my place. I think I'd better spend some time with her."

"That's awesome how you two like to be around each other."

Jessie grinned. "It hasn't always been this way. She and I have butted heads a lot, but it's good now. You know what, I think I'll text her and see if she wants to go to a wine-and-painting place this afternoon, just for fun." She sent the message while Prentice responded to that idea.

"That sounds... awful!" Prentice laughed. "You two will enjoy it, I bet. But for this morning, I'm glad we can be together, Jessie."

Prentice was a no-nonsense vehicle buyer. He'd been trained by the best. His dad had also trained him to buy only "American-made" cars.

Because of that, he drove straight to the Toyota dealer. Prentice knew the Tacomas and Tundras were mostly made in the U.S., but it would bug his dad to no end that he didn't buy a Ford.

"You know, I haven't even read the Consumer Reports..." he started to say.

"You're scaring me with your spontaneity, Mr. Keene," she laughed. "This was your idea. Trust yourself."

"I'd better be careful. You really are good at spending other people's money."

She was a good sport about how long the process actually took. While he browsed around, she pulled weeds at the edge of the parking lot for entertainment, which he teased her about. After an hour of wandering around and two test drives, he started on the paperwork to buy an electric blue 2017 Toyota Tacoma Double Cab pickup with a gray interior. It had a few scratches, but it would be just right.

They didn't drive it off the lot, because Prentice ordered a locking cover on the cargo bed to be installed, so he could load his tools in there as soon as possible. "I'll come get it on Monday." *That way Jessie and I will still be in the same car a while longer, too.*

"I'm in the mood to spend even more money," he

announced when they got back in dad's car. "Are you up for one more stop?"

"Sure, but first let's get lunch. And I'm buying," she said. "Did you remember I never even paid you for the second ride you gave me, the day we met?"

"Nope. You didn't?"

"No. I'll make it up to you."

This time they went to a nicer restaurant, where the hostess seated them in a booth, brought them menus and glasses of ice water, and returned to tell about the day's special and take their orders. Pretty classy. They sat next to each other, and Prentice put his foot up on the seat on the other side.

"I like sitting in a booth. It's just quieter. Easier to really talk," Jessie volunteered.

"It is."

When the waitress brought their salads, Jessie took Prentice's hand and bowed her head for a quick prayer. Nothing fancy or memorized, but simple words of gratitude for the day, the meal, and "getting to spend time with this sweet, caring man again. Amen."

Prentice said "Amen," too, and really meant it.

He asked about what her mom and dad's plans might be to deal with the fire damage, and what she'd been doing for her job in D.C. She asked him more questions about the fire fights and the new need to tell people about potential flood damage to prepare for.

They were starting on dessert, carrot cake with cream cheese frosting for him, chocolate pudding for her, when she asked about his dad. He told her the facts about the diabetes and damage. She already knew about William, but he didn't know how to explain the whole series of betrayals in communication.

He felt his throat start to tighten up again. It was the kind of reaction he was used to covering up. No one should have to panic so much when talking about a parent, he started to think. It was his normal reaction, just a habit. *Hold on a minute here.*

"Jessie, there's more to it."

She nodded. "Uh-huh.... I wondered about that. But it's not my job to point it out every time you have veins popping out in your forehead. You're an adult. You'll tell me when you're ready."

He nodded. "Got me." He held his fork but neglected to get more cake. "He... Well, there's so much. I keep finding out more about his story. Like you said, he's a flawed human."

"Yeah."

"He told me about his childhood some last week. I don't know why he finally told me so much. About his father and mother. What a mess!"

"Uh-huh..."

"It's amazing he ever got married at all, much less twice! He had no role models to follow. No one supported him. He was really on his own."

She nodded. "I saw in your apartment you had that quote about facing the flames up on your refrigerator. I'm glad it's helping you see things clearly. That's a good start."

"This is not what people are supposed to talk about on dates. I'm sorry."

"What else is there besides our families and our pasts? It's who we are."

"I don't want to be like him."

"You're definitely like him, but not in the ways you think."

"You haven't even met him yet. How do you know?"

"I just have this feeling. I'd like to meet him sometime, though."

"He's going to a rehabilitation facility soon. They're trying to get him well enough to go home. But he doesn't have a home to go to. What am I supposed to do about that?"

"That's a good question. What did he ask you to do?"

"Huh? Well, nothing."

"Uh-huh. Maybe you could be there to help him, but wait until he asks you," she said.

"Why hasn't he already? Doesn't he trust me to do anything?"

"Maybe you're asking the wrong questions. You're even more confident, at least about your job, as far as I can tell. Compared to when I met you."

"Yeah, I feel like that too," said Prentice.

"But when it comes to your dad, I don't know. Are you still trying to fix him? Save him? Win his respect and admiration?" It was a high-handed sentence, but she said it so sincerely he knew she wasn't teasing.

Jessie paid the check as promised and they went out to the car. It helped a lot that she stopped to give him another really warm hug next to the car before they got in. "Thank you for being you," he told her.

"It's all I can do. Thanks for not running away from me. Sometimes I'm too much for guys. This is too much talking for them. And feelings! Even though so many people are hurting and should let it out and deal with it."

"You are a really fun date."

"I know. So where are we going shopping now? I still have time before meeting Mom." she asked as they got into the car.

"I would like to buy a sofa for my apartment so you'll be

willing to come back again sometime and be treated like an honored guest."

"Bonus points! Let's go."

THEY BROWSED AROUND A BIG DEPARTMENT STORE THAT SOLD American-made furniture, and they stopped several times to sit on sofas to test the comfort level and if Prentice would fit on it if he stretched out to his full 5-foot-6. This involved a few more nice warm kisses, and at one point a saleslady asked them if they needed any help with anything.

"No, we're doing fine," Prentice said with a big smile. "Actually, no kidding, I think this is the one to buy." It was an apartment-sized sofa in a Sixties style that Prentice liked. He said he'd be back to pick it up on Monday when he got his truck, then changed his mind. "No, would you deliver it instead? I can't haul it inside myself."

"I hoped you didn't want me to try to help you carry it. I'm glad you asked for help. You're learning some things."

They sat on his new sofa for a long time in the showroom. "It's mine now. They can't shoo us away."

"There's a nice view of the mall parking lot from here."

"Yeah." He changed gears to a more serious topic. "The way I see it now, there's more to me than just the fact that I had a hard childhood. Losing my mom and my brother and my house."

"Okay, go on."

"It's that my dad abandoned me. That's it. I just realized it."

"I'm not disagreeing with you. I want to help you think through this. Your dad took care of you, got the house rebuilt, bought you a car and sent you to college." She was nodding to keep Prentice talking. "So how did he abandon you?"

"He left me in the lurch! He didn't tell me what was going on. He didn't talk to me or ask me questions about what I was doing or how it was going for me. He fed me, but he wasn't there for me."

"Yeah..."

"So it took him almost dying last week for him to tell me why he did it. Get this. He stayed far away so that I wouldn't lean on him all the time and would just go off and do my own thing! Can you believe it?"

"Yes."

"Really?"

"Prentice, like I said, you have to get all the way down there to the bottom so you can push off and start heading toward the surface again."

"You're a real riot," he said with a smile.

"Yes, remember my support group?"

"Yeah," he grinned at her. "It's still just inconceivable to me that so many other people have the same kinds of questions and problems that they could make it into a world-renowned organization. And also that I have never heard of it until I met you. All the counselors I had to meet with in school..."

"Now you're open to so many more possibilities than you were before."

"You know, when you say it that way, it makes a lot of sense."

"Remember the day we were kayaking, and I told you there were two words that I thought of to describe you then?"

"Yeah. The first one was 'exhausted.' I didn't like hearing that."

"Mm-hm... Would you like to know what the second word was?"

"Yeah. Hit me. I've hit bottom already," he smiled.

"Okay. It was 'permission.' It seemed like you needed to get permission from other people to admit you're okay. You spend a lot of energy trying to please your dad, don't you?"

The linoleum floor of the department store absorbed all his attention. "Sure. Maybe all my energy, if you put it that way."

Jessie said, "You know God loves you, and you are worthy just as you are right now...."

"I don't even know how to process what you just said."

"It's okay. It's still true, no matter what you think." She snuggled her head onto his shoulder and looked out the department store window again. Prentice put his arm around her shoulder and breathed deep, even, breaths of calm.

An elderly couple slowed down to stare at them sitting on the sofa so companionably. Prentice and Jessie waved at them, just for fun. The couple waved back, reddened, and kept walking through the store, talking to each other in whispers.

27

After a proper farewell in the parking lot at Prentice's apartment, Jessie headed home. "Who's that?" Steve asked, with a nod to Jessie's car leaving the lot. His neighbor was heading inside about the same time, and he caught Prentice on his way in to the apartment.

Prentice smiled. "That's Jessie. She's the lovely young lady I heard from when you let me borrow your phone. Thanks again, Steve!" He got a salute and a smile in return.

Inside, Prentice put on his navy blue pants and short sleeve duty uniform shirt with the embroidered Garnet Fire Department patch, American flag patch, his engraved name badge, and several significant colorful small pins.

He tried to put his sore foot into the sturdy black station boot, since it would've offered good support, but he still couldn't quite get it on over his swollen ankle. *It was worth a try.* A purposeful tousle of his hair gave the professional-but-approachable appearance he hoped for.

Allie met him at the television station, and the two of them continued to present a united front for the public so they might learn what action each homeowner should be taking now. The Pioneersburg and Garnet Fire Departments were going to be coaching people from the same playbook and sharing ideas and resources.

They talked about the burn scars, what residents could do, what services were available to them, and the volunteer efforts under way to help with property cleanup and preparing for the coming floods. In places, grass would start sprouting next year, but it literally couldn't hold back the tide for years.

They showed video of the forested neighborhoods that were still at extreme risk for the next fire, which could happen as soon as today. They asked people to get to work and take responsibility for their own land, since no one else could do that for them.

Allie pointed out there were many local businesses that specialized in this kind of work, and that residents could also get free advice any time from their fire department. Prentice was careful not to mention his own website or business by name this time since he was in uniform.

"Super job, Prentice," said Allie as they left the building. "I bet it's gonna do a lot of good."

"Are you taking a day off to be here again? Or did they realize they better pay you for all this great publicity you're creating for them?"

She shrugged. "It's all good. We're working it out with my schedule. How are things shaping up for you? How's your ankle?"

"It's going to be another few weeks like this, but you know, I think it's a good thing I got injured. Rugen... I mean, Chief Rugen needs a lot of help, and this way I'm learning about administrative things I wouldn't have otherwise if I were just back at work."

"What about your business?"

"Wow! I have some ideas I'm working on, nights and weekends. Mr. Bixby's helping me, and so is Jessie. I'm hiring people and trying to figure out how that works, how to connect them with the clients, payroll, all that. Right now, I'm making a huge mess. I have no idea what I'm actually doing. That really stresses me out."

"The way you said that made me think of you when you were little. As messy as your coloring was, you always wanted to put all the crayons back in the box in just the right order."

He frowned. "I haven't changed a bit, have I?"

"You have! Oh my gosh, just look at you, Prentice. You just have a much bigger box of crayons now. It's more like several cases of crayons. Maybe you need to hire someone to help you sort them all!" She crinkled her smiling eyes at him. "Need some referrals?"

His frown went away. "I'm so good at keeping my head down and doing what's next, I completely forgot there are ways to solve all these things. I could hire an organizer to help me keep track of my life."

"Yes," said Allie. "There are people who would love for you to hire them to push buttons on a computer or write contracts while you go out and rev up the chainsaw and show your pretty face on television. You do have your photo on your website, don't you?"

"I am such an idiot," said Prentice. But he smiled when he said it.

Saturday after the interview, Prentice visited the hospital again. It had been just over a week since they admitted Dad. A week since the fires... He was out of the medical intensive care unit and now in a step-down care unit where the staff kept a very close eye on an array of numbers as well as the wounds on his feet.

Dad had just finished dinner, which was a small piece of baked salmon, half a baked potato, spinach salad, and a cup of skim milk. Prentice could tell what they'd served, because Dad had only eaten a little of each and then pushed the tray off to the side.

"They're trying to starve me to death here," he grumbled when he saw Prentice come in. "How about you get them to bring in some steak, French fries, and chocolate cake?"

"Nope." Prentice didn't even try to joke about it. "You can't eat that way anymore."

"What're you talking about? That's good American food."

"Well, too bad. Then you'll starve." Prentice stood at the foot of the bed, with most his weight on his good foot. His shoulders squared and facing his dad. "If you're still hungry, why don't you eat what they gave you." It was not a question.

"This is exactly why I didn't tell you, years ago. I knew you'd take their side."

Prentice moved to the armchair in the corner. "You're welcome, sunshine," he retorted. *I sure wouldn't have let you eat yourself to death.* "Listen, Dad. They're talking about sending you to a rehab next. Right?"

"I don't think it's necessary." He frowned at his hands. "My feet are just a little numb, and my blood sugar's off. I can handle it."

"Those things could kill you," Prentice didn't bother softening the edge in his voice.

"I can take care of myself at home," Dad said.

Prentice got up again and approached the bed. Locking

his eyes with his dad's was uncomfortable, but he said, "You're forgetting something–two things." His voice shook. "You did not take care of them at home. And I doubt you have a home to go to now, not one you can live in anyway."

Dad closed his eyes and sank back into the pillow.

"I haven't brought it up before. I was waiting until you felt better. But you've got to tell me what insurance company to call, what to do about the house, and your car, and all that."

Dad shook his head, keeping his eyes closed. "Nuts."

"I went to see the house on Monday."

Dad opened his eyes, meeting Prentice's glance. "Was it–?"

"It didn't burn down, but you can't live there now. I took some pictures." He got out his phone, and after enlarging the photos, handed it to his dad.

Dad took his time, scrolling through the assortment slowly.

Watching him, Prentice smiled a little and waited for the good news to sink in.

Dad exhaled. "I can't believe it didn't burn down."

"No. No, it didn't. A lot of the other houses in the neighborhood are gone. But not ours. I mean yours."

"Why didn't it? That doesn't follow. There was burning stuff coming out of the sky. I saw it. It was right on top of us."

"There was nothing to feed it. It's because of all that work we did, Dad. It was never a guarantee, but it sure helped."

"All the work you did, you mean."

"Yeah, okay, but you agreed to it."

"It took a lot of convincing. I'm grateful now you didn't give up."

"Thanks, Dad. It sure means a lot to hear you say that."

"I just can't ever seem to get the words out, about a lot of things. I can't believe it, but I have to believe I have a house that survived a wildfire."

"There's probably smoke damage, and they've shut off utilities to the neighborhood, so everything in the fridge and freezer will have to be thrown out. Actually, you'll have to get rid of all of it because of the smell. But the main problem is the rest of the neighborhood."

"What does that look like? It was hard to tell in your photos."

"From the little I saw, and what I've heard at the station, your neighbors are pretty much burned out. Even if they do rebuild, it will take months even for the quickest ones to come back. The utilities are off for the duration. And now, you've got flash flooding to worry about.

"You mean because of the burn scar."

"Yeah. So, I was thinking, I could go up to the house again and get more of your important documents from your office. Your account numbers and everything. Winterize what we can. And really, we should get all the furniture and everything moved out of the house so they can clean it, get rid of the smoke. Then they could put it in storage while we get the house fixed up."

"Hold on now. Slow down. You're ahead of me on some of those things. Well, a lot of these things. But I can make those calls myself. I'm fully capable of doing it."

"But...."

"I have a brain, and I'll do it. It's my house. It's not your job, Prentice."

"I just thought you'd want my help."

"There's no need for you to take over the whole process. I'm fully competent."

"Seriously?" Prentice made himself speak rather than

holding back as he'd done in the past. "This is really hard for me to believe. You're lying in a hospital bed after almost dying because you didn't take care of yourself, and now you're telling me to back off?"

"Yes."

"But I... Never mind. You know what? You're right." He heard Jessie's voice in his head. "You're an adult, obviously, and I should just let you handle it."

"Thank you. I'd appreciate that."

Prentice felt like he and Dad had come to an understanding. "I've just always felt kind of, responsible for you."

"You did?" asked his dad.

"Yeah. I never was aware of it until lately. But today's a great example, huh? I just met this lady named Jessie, who is a knockout by the way, and super smart. She's in IT," he said, parenthetically. "She's been showing me different ways to ... stop trying to save the whole world... by myself," Prentice said.

"That explains a lot," Dad said simply. "I never saw it that way. You took on a lot then, but I didn't realize it." He pondered for a moment. "A lady friend, you say?"

"She's great. You can meet her soon." Prentice hadn't planned this at all, and he wanted desperately to change the conversation to a new subject. "Well, would you consider hiring Tinderbox to help do flood mitigation on your property? Your house is in a vulnerable position, and I have some ideas."

"Yes!" Dad sat up straighter. "That's a great idea! That's taking initiative, being a self-starter, Prentice."

"What?"

"You've got skills, something to offer, expertise that people ought to pay you for. Take a stand. Like you're doing now. Like you did the other day, talking about promoting your website."

Prentice gulped. "Umm, I thought that's what I've been doing. That's great." he said, hesitantly. *Was he just talking about making sure I get paid what I'm worth? Is that it?*

He found his stride again. "So great. You can pay me, then." He smiled at his dad. "Then I really want to take some photos of the property after we do that to add to my website. Just like we did for the fire mitigation. You've got a real story to tell there. You have got before and after from when we did all the vegetation management, and now we can add, 'survived the wildfire.'"

"Yes, you do," said Dad. "Those pictures are worth a million bucks to me, truth be told."

IT WAS LATE SEPTEMBER NOW, AND IN THE TYPICAL WEATHER pattern of Colorado, it was a blazing hot day, and dust blew across the parking lot in a stiff wind. Prentice met Allie in the foyer of the rehabilitation hospital on the far east side of Pioneersburg. The mountains were barely visible off to the west because of all the dust.

"Hi Allie. I'm glad we can do this."

"Me too. I've waited a long time." She was in civilian clothes, jeans and a spiffy t-shirt with a cartoon flower on it. She wore her hair in a bun on the back of her neck, just as she did for fighting fires.

"Dad ordered lunch for all three of us. His treat. I think he's nervous."

"So am I, really. I feel like I'm a teenager again. Like last time I saw him. Let's go."

Prentice showed Allie where to sign in and they went

back to the sunny dining room. On this sultry late morning, it felt more like a greenhouse. The facility residents tended to feel chilly more than the average population did, so it was fine for all but the few outsiders.

Allie walked right up to Bill Keene and stuck out her hand. "Hi Mr. Keene. I'm Allie. I'm 36 years old, but I'm still not sure what to call you." She was always so direct. *That's why she's easy to work with.*

His dad shook her hand again and motioned for her and Prentice to sit down at the table with him. There were paper placemats covered in daisies, yellow paper napkins, and real silverware.

He started to make light of it. "The reason I've called you all together here is... No. Well, it wasn't my idea at all, I'm ashamed to say. This is Prentice's idea."

Prentice said, "No Dad, this was a request from Allie. This has gone on way too long. And it was such a miracle that I ran into her again. Yes, I'll say it that way. It was a miracle. So now here she is so both of you can say what you need to say to each other."

His dad didn't say anything, and surprisingly, neither did Captain Allie Snyder of the Pioneersburg Fire Department. *Come on. You're all adults.*

"Oh, for Pete's sake... How about this, say something to each other before you *die*, Dad."

Bill Keene's face was a mask, more like his old self. Allie's intense brown eyes shone and she spoke up. "Mr. Keene, it's been a long time since we last saw each other." She faltered again.

Rough place to start. *Last time we saw each other was when your house was on fire and your son was dead,* thought Prentice. He took the baton. "You know Allie and I had a good long talk the other day, and what I found out is that we're all blaming ourselves for what happened. It was a huge disaster, a tragedy in all our lives and we've never talked about it to each other. That's not good for any of us."

"Right," said Allie. "Thanks, Prentice. Yes. It was a horrible day. The most horrible day of my life." She shifted her focus to Prentice's dad. "I'm so sorry I was careless, but it was an accident, a horrible accident. All these years later and I've never stopped thinking about it. It's shaped my life, my whole career. I've so wanted to speak to you, to ask your forgiveness, so I can move on."

Dad didn't answer. He looked at the placemat.

Prentice swallowed.

The silence grew sharper, more difficult. Prentice finally broke it. "Allie, I've already told you, but I want to spell it out again. I never blamed you, so there's nothing to forgive. What I remember is how we were all screaming, because of the burns, when the water hit the butter–"

"Enough!"

Startled at Dad's outburst, Prentice and Allie stared at him.

"I had no idea until Prentice and I talked the other day, that either of you blamed yourselves. I'm the guilty one for leaving three kids alone all day, putting such an enormous responsibility on a teenage girl." Dad stopped, fighting for composure. When he began again, his voice slipped and caught. "I'm the one who should apologize and ask forgiveness from both of you."

No one spoke. Prentice could barely breathe. He watched the tears track his father's cheeks in wonder. It was Allie who finally moved, who found a tissue and handed it to his dad.

He mopped his face, blew his nose. "Allie, I need you to know, I did try to find you. I wanted to talk to you that day in the hospital, but by the time I'd checked on Prentice and came to your room, you were asleep. I should have called your parents. They couldn't contact me, not really, since I was at a hotel then. I was so just so overwhelmed—" The breath he drew in was ragged. "Next I heard you'd moved away with your family. I couldn't find you. I should have done more."

Prentice said, "I've always felt like I was supposed to take William's place as the oldest son. He was the perfect kid."

Allie attempted to lighten the mood a little. "Actually, Prentice, I always felt like William was kind of a stick-in-the mud."

Dad looked horrified, and Prentice felt like someone kicked him in the gut. *How can she be making fun of William?* Then he saw his dad start to grin at Allie. *What?*

"You're quite a young woman, Allie. Very perceptive." He turned to Prentice. "Have you noticed that we never talk about William at all? Nothing good. Nothing bad about him. We don't say anything about him. What I just realized was that it's as if he never existed. That's... that can't be right."

"Yeah. That's true." *This is unreal.*

"Maybe we need to stop pretending. It won't make us miss him less. But maybe we can remember him better."

Prentice stared at his dad with wide eyes. "Okay.... Wow. That is huge.'"

Dad said, "I'm sorry it's taken me so long to see this."

Allie ventured back into the conversation. "William was a smart kid. We all know that. I bet he would've become an engineer or a scientist."

Prentice and Dad agreed. She continued, "But he was so serious all the time, working on his projects or reading a book. I liked spending more time with you. You were so cute in your home-built forts. You were always so dirty!"

Prentice said, "I thought he acted serious because he understood more about when mom left? But no, he was already like that, wasn't he?"

"I'm afraid he was very much like me," said Dad, with a contemplative look on his face. "Rosemary told me all the time, how William wasn't her child at all, just mine. It was her way of teasing me, but I didn't really see the humor in it." He gazed into the distance. "And yes, we both agreed Prentice seemed to be more like Rose in many ways. Good ways. He has the same smile, the same way of seeing things. Idealistic. And always listening to music."

Allie said, "It must have been so hard for you when she left."

"I didn't know that," Prentice said. "I didn't know I reminded you of her."

"Oh, quite a bit. Every time I look at you, I think of Rose. She had the same energy. Such enthusiasm. Although you do take after me in other ways. Folding your underwear and socks, that sort of thing." Dad laughed then. "Very methodical. And you're such a hard worker. You never take a break."

Prentice said, "If I took a break, you'd give me a hard time."

"I was just hoping you'd be able to take care of yourself. In case I couldn't be there for you, or if something happened to me. You know."

"Wow." Prentice was sitting with his chin in his hands, shaking his head, looking at Dad.

"This feels better. It feels like, it feels like the memory is out in the open now, where we can understand what happened," Allie said.

A staff member finally arrived with lunch for the three of them. She apologized for the delay, something about the broiler. She served them all open-face tuna melts, raw carrots and celery, and hummus dip.

"I'm trying to learn some new tricks. Not just with my diet. I'm grateful for your initiative in coming to find me, Allie. I'd like to ask you what you're doing now. Prentice said you live in Pioneersburg. And you have a family?"

She smiled at Prentice and then leaned in to tell his dad about the life she'd built. It dawned on Prentice that Allie was almost the same age now as his mom had been the last time he saw her.

www.Tinderbox.tips - What's the Wildland-Urban
Interface?

- It's not a location. It's a set of conditions.
- The key to your home's survival is reducing its
  "structure ignition potential."
- Each home can reduce its vulnerability at the
  micro-level.
- It doesn't always take money, just knowledge
  about how to keep the fire 100 feet away from
  your house.

Prentice sat in the middle of what used to be the
empty dining room in his apartment. Now, it was
Tinderbox central, complete with a new desk and a
computer with a big monitor. It was a Tuesday evening in
late October. In the last eight weeks, Jessie had shared her
organizational skills to make the space practical and
ergonomically sound with two lamps and a good desk chair.

She'd also helped him set up a secure cloud-based business model. *What a lady!*

The dusk had not yet deepened into twilight, and he took a short break on the sofa, looking out the living room window at the aspens, golden islands sprinkled among the evergreens on the mountains in the distance. Haze from a faraway wildfire had made the sunset stunning, and he managed to appreciate its ironic beauty without shaking his fist at the sky and railing at the universe.

He sighed with gratitude. *I'm finding my true self.*

He'd framed the quote from Jessie, and it hung on the wall next to the front door:

> **Family dysfunction rolls down**
> **from generation to generation,**
> **like a fire in the woods,**
> **taking down everything in its path**
> **until one person in one generation**
> **has the courage to turn and face the flames.**
> **That person brings peace to their ancestors**
> **and spares the children that follow.**
> ***Terry Real***

"There are a lotta people out there who have wisdom to share with me," he said to the mountains. "I'm glad I can hear 'em now."

He went back to work for a bit longer, reading a message his assistant Janet had posted for him while he was working in Garnet at the fire station today. Janet worked from her own home during the day, doing bookkeeping, answering calls, and coordinating the work days for clients. They shared schedules and messages using a collaboration platform Jessie had helped organize, minimizing the need for email and urgent text messages.

"I guess I'm going to have to hire another coupl'a guys," he said to himself. "Word's getting out." That was an understatement. It boggled his mind to see himself becoming a leader, a manager. He'd quit doing the ride-share gig altogether, he was so busy.

His website now included a section about the aftereffects of wildfire and how to reduce the amount of damage the floods would cause. He posted some instructions for the web designer who did contract work for him. She was a college student at Great Northern University, the younger sister of a friend of Jessie's. He'd never met her in person, but she did great work.

A knock on the door made him smile and turn away from the computer. "Hi Jessie!" He opened the door, looking forward to a warm hug and more kisses. "I'm really glad you're here."

"You always say that."

"Well, I'm working on saying things out loud instead of just thinking 'em. You look real nice, too."

She wore dark corduroys, suede boots, and a sweater decorated with cream-colored aspen leaves. It was a warm shade of brown that matched her eyes. It was worth it to pay attention to that kind of detail, since it made her happy when he noticed.

"Okay, be quiet now," she laughed. They sat on the sofa together and appreciated being very close together without talking at all for several minutes. The cool autumn air from outside didn't hurt a bit either. *Delicious and wonderful.*

Finally, he said, "I promised you dinner." He went to the kitchen, rummaging around for a few minutes. Jessie followed him and watched him arrange everything to make two hearty salads piled high on dinner plates. "It's a late dinner, but you'll like it." They took their plates back to the sofa. The view out the window was now a silhouette of the Front Range.

"How many starfish have you saved today, Prentice?" she asked.

"I've quit counting," he said. "They're all important. I'm glad to help the ones I can, but some of them are going to have to get back to the ocean on their own."

The End

A NOTE FROM THE AUTHOR

Why did I write this novel? Wildfires happen. Anyone living near a "natural area" needs to be aware of the potential and how to prepare for it today. These fires have happened within my sight:

• The burn scar from the 1989 Berry Fire up the front of Mt. Herman made me ask questions when we moved to Monument, Colorado.

• Then, half a mile south of my house, came the unnamed grass fire in October 2001. We watched it burn toward us across the Higby Ranch, but we just sat there, not knowing we should do anything. The fire jumped the road into our subdivision, but that day the firefighters stopped it. (This was the inspiration for my short story, "Just a Little Grass Fire," which describes the beginning of the fire in *To Starve an Ember*.)

• The 2002 Hayman Fire burned 137,760 acres, blew embers onto our deck, made the sky over the Front Range glow orange at night, and was the biggest fire on record in Colorado. So much damage due to the fire and subsequent erosion due to flash flooding.

- In 2008, a tire fire burned 9,000 acres at Fort Carson.
- The Waldo Canyon Fire hit in June 2012, burning 18,247 acres, 346 homes, and killing two people. Over 800,000 people in El Paso and Teller County could see it, and at night pops of flames appeared on the distant mountain as each beautiful home caught fire. Over 32,000 people had to evacuate in a very short time when it blew up that Tuesday afternoon. I joined the Woodmoor Firewise Committee. Larry Adkins and I asked the Office of Emergency Management to bring a four-day Community Emergency Response Training to our church so we could form a CERT team.
- The Black Forest Fire in June 2013 created a 14,280 acre burn scar ten minutes' drive from my house. It destroyed 509 structures and killed two people. Our Tri-Lakes United Methodist Church Emergency Preparedness Group learned from groups like Byron Spinney's Hope Restored disaster recovery ministry, Sunrise United Methodist Church's Colorado Rebuilds, and the grassroots Black Forest Together. I learned to run a chainsaw and a chipper and give a very serious safety briefing for other volunteers. We worked for six years cutting and chipping the burned trees before the remaining ones were too rotten for volunteers to fell safely.
- April 2018 brought the Mile Marker 117 Fire in southern El Paso County. It was a grass fire started by a spark from a truck on I-25. It burned 42,795 acres and 23 homes.
- In January 2020, I thought, "After all the fires around us, and all the PowerPoint presentations for residents about doing their part to be ready for wildfires, many are still not listening. Maybe if I put this information in the form of a novel...."

• Summer 2020 brought the three biggest fires recorded in the history of Colorado, all bigger than the record-setting Hayman Fire: Pine Gulch Fire, East Troublesome Fire, and Cameron Peak Fire.

How can we pretend fire isn't going to affect us?

Share this novel with friends, family, and your local fire district. I hope it can be a tool to save lives and property.

Write a review of *To Starve an Ember* on your favorite review platform, such as BookBub.com, Goodreads.com, or Amazon.com, so it will get noticed.

See LisaHatfieldWriter.com to sign up for my newsletter and get your free remote home ignition zone evaluation tool. It will help you see your home through the eyes of a wildland firefighter.

RESOURCES

Adult Children of Alcoholics®/ Dysfunctional Families World Service Organization. "Am I An Adult Child?" https:// adultchildren.org/newcomer/am-i-an-adult-child/

American Diabetes Association. www.diabetes.org/diabetes.

Boise Mobile Equipment. "Reading Smoke Signals: How Skilled Firefighters Use Smoke to Determine Characteristics of a Fire." www.bmefire.com/reading-smoke-signals-how-skilled-firefighters-use-smoke-to-determine-the-characteristics-of-a-fire/.

Brooks, Randy. "After the Fires: Hydrophobic Soils." Land Conservation Assistance Network. www.landcan.org/article/ After-the-Fires-Hydrophobic-Soils/9.

Burr, Sally, and Gail Ross. *The Role of Wildland Fire in Our Forests.* Colorado State Forest Service. https://csfs.colostate. edu/media/sites/22/2015/07/FireEcology-Role-of-Wildland-Fire6x6bk-www.pdf.

Cohen, Dr. Jack. "If Your Home Doesn't Ignite, It Can't Burn." National Fire Protection Association. https://youtu.be/RqKFDDBGd5o.

Cohen, Dr. Jack. "Your Home Can Survive a Wildfire." National Fire Protection Association. YouTube video. https://youtu.be/vL_syp1ZScM.

Colorado State Forest Service, "Colorado's 'Are You Fire-Wise?' Program." https://static.colostate.edu/client-files/csfs/pdfs/wholenotebook.pdf

Colorado State Forest Service. "Colorado Forest Atlas." https://csfs.colostate.edu/wildfire-mitigation/colorado-forest-atlas/

Colorado State Forest Service. "Colorado Wildfire Risk Assessment Portal (CO-WRAP)." https://csfs.colostate.edu/wildfire-mitigation/cowrap/.

Colorado State Forest Service. "Colorado Wildfire Risk Public Viewer." https://co-pub.coloradoforestatlas.org/#/.

Colorado State Forest Service. "Colorado's Wildland-Urban Interface." https://csfs.colostate.edu/wildfire-mitigation/colorados-wildland-urban-interface/.

Colorado State University Extension. "Fire-Resistant Landscaping – 6.303." https://extension.colostate.edu/topic-areas/natural-resources/fire-resistant-landscaping-6-303/

Colorado State University Extension. "Firewise Plant Materials, Fact Sheet No. 6.305 Natural Resources

Series|Forestry." https://extension.colostate.edu/topic-areas/natural-resources/firewise-plant-materials-6-305/.

Cooper, Drea, Director. "Fire in Paradise." Netflix documentary on the Camp Fire. ZCDC Production. www.netflix.com/title/81050Emergency Incident Support (EIS). https://epceis.com/.

DeBecker, Gavin. *The Gift of Fear*.

FEMA and CSFD. "Wildfire Mitigation: After the Waldo Canyon Fire." https://coloradosprings.gov/fire-department/page/wildfire-mitigation-0.

Fire Adapted Colorado and Wildfire Adapted Partnership, *Building Your FAC Ambassador Approach Workshop,* Jackson, Wyoming, October 8-9, 2019.

"Fire Incident Complexity." https://gacc.nifc.gov/swcc/management_admin/Agency_Administrator/AA_Guidelines/pdf_files/ch5.pdf.

Glasser M.D, William. *Control Theory: A New Explanation of How We Control Our Lives.*

Gollner, Michael, quoted in, "Embers, Firenados, and Modeling Wildfires," Wildfire Today. www.WildfireToday.com.

Hallock, Zeb, "Starfish Walking on the Beach," https://youtu.be/Lbg-tQ6FJgQ.

Headwaters Economics. "Federal wildfire policy and the legacy of suppression." https://headwaterseconomics.org/natural-hazards/federal-wildfire-policy/.

Hoey, Shauna L. *Fire of Hope: Finding Treasure in the Rubble*. (Waldo Canyon Fire).

IDGA Wildfire Management Summit. "Wildfire Situational Awareness." https://wildlandfirefighter.com/2020/06/25/wildfire-situational-awareness/.

International Association of Fire Chiefs. "Wildland Urban Interface Chief's Guide." www.iafc.org/docs/default-source/pdf/iafc-wui-guide-print-version.pdf?sfvrsn=c0d5820d_2.

Keisling, Phil. "Why We Need to Get the 'Fire' out of 'Fire Department.'" https://www.governing.com/columns/smart-mgmt/col-fire-departments-rethink-delivery-emergency-medical-services.html.

Larkspur Colorado Fire Protection District. "Wildfire Mitigation and Prevention." www.larkspurfire.org/wildfire-mitigation, 13-minute video on Black Forest Fire.

Los Angeles Times. "Want to Fireproof Your Home? It Takes a Village." www.latimes.com.

Milne, Murray. "Designing Your Home to Survive Wildfires." Research Professor of Architecture, UCLA. www.energy-design-tools.aud.ucla.edu/FIRES.html.

National Fire Protection Association. *NFPA Assessing Structure Ignition Potential from Wildfire (ASIP) Training.* Huerfano County, Colorado, Jan. 23-24, 2020.

National Fire Protection Association. "Preparing Homes for Wildfire." https://www.nfpa.org/Public-Education/Fire-causes-and-risks/Wildfire/Preparing-homes-for-wildfire.

National Interagency Fire Center. Wildland Fire Summaries page. www.nifc.gov/fire-information/statistics.

National Park Service. "Wildland fire incident qualifications." www.nps.gov/subjects/fire/wildland-fire-incident-qualifications.htm.

National Public Radio. "Megafires: The New Normal In The Southwest: How The Smokey Bear Effect Led To Raging Wildfires." www.npr.org/159373691.

National Volunteer Fire Council. *Wildland Fire Assessment Program Toolkit* and associated *WFAP Checklist.* www.nvfc.org/wp-content/uploads/2016/02/WFAP-home-assessment-checklist.pdf.

National Wildfire Coordinating Group. "How to Become a Wildland Firefighter." www.nwcg.gov/how-to-become-a-wildland-firefighter.

National Wildfire Coordinating Group. "Incident Response Pocket Guide." www.nwcg.gov/sites/default/files/publications/pms461.pdf

National Wildfire Coordinating Group. "Wildland/Urban Interface Watch Outs." www.nwcg.gov/committee/6mfs/wildlandurban-interface-watch-outs.

National Wildland/Urban Interface Fire Protection Program. "Using water effectively in wildland/urban interface." www.youtube.com/watch?v=KKT-KH3QMxo.

Pikes Peak Regional Office of Emergency Management, *Community Emergency Response Team Training*. Monument, Colorado, November 2012.

Quinn-Davidson, Leyna. "Renewing - and Radicalizing - Our Relationship with Fire." Fire Adapted Communities Learning Network. Fireadaptednetwork.org/renewing-and-radicalizing-our-relationship-with-fire/ .

Real, Terry. "Multi-generational Trauma: Healing the Past to Heal the Present." https://terryreal.com/trauma/.

Rowett, Jr., Anthony. "The Importance of Preassigned Responsibilities." Fire Engineering. www.fireengineering.com/2017/01/20/286997/the-importance-of-preassigned-responsibilities/.

South Metro Fire District, Centennial, CO. "Chatridge 2 Fire – Community Incident Review." www.youtube.com/watch?v=TNWXR4SQsPc&feature=youtu.be.

South Metro Fire District Denver. "A Day in the Life of a Firefighter." www.youtube.com/watch?v=pEIFG7-cmzY.

Spell, Jim. "What City Firefighters Need to Know About Wildland Fires." Tactical Firefighting, Fire Rescue 1. www.firerescue1.com/cod-company-officer-development/articles/what-city-firefighters-need-to-know-about-wildland-fires-8MxFww3qxIslstsX/.

Struzin, Edward. *Firestorm: How Wildfire Will Shape our Future.*

"Ten Standard Fire Orders & Eighteen Watchout Situations." www.angelfire.com/nv/blm/safety.html.

Thompson, Bob. *Fire Story: Vallecito Burning: A Personal Account of the 2002 Missionary Ridge Fire.*

Thompson, Nigel. *Fire Survivor: A Personal Story of the Black Forest Fire.*

Thrace Linq, "Material Safety Data Sheet: woven polypropylene landscaping fabric." http://thracelinq.com/pdfs/msds/Landscape_AL_series.pdf

Tri-Lakes United Methodist Church Emergency Preparedness Group. www.facebook.com/TLUMCEPG , and Wildfire Neighborhood Ambassadors www.facebook.com/groups/1349730358753489.

Washington Fire Services Resource Mobilization Plan. "Type 3 Wildland Fire Incident complexity chart." www.wsp.wa.gov/wp-content/uploads/2018/06/Type-3-ICA.pdf.

ACKNOWLEDGMENTS

Credits

Thank you to these wonderful people for teaching and encouraging me. They've done their best to advise me, but any mistakes and all ramblings are mine.

- Robin Adair – Pikes Peak Regional Office of Emergency Management
- Natalie Barszcz – Our Community News
- Marlene Burkhart
- Mark Hatfield – husband, gentleman, and geographer
- Jayce Martinez – Web Developer
- Sarah McMullen
- Matthew Nelson – Woodmoor Improvement Association
- David Niemi and Kathy Deligianis
- James L. Rubart – Novel Marketing Podcast
- Gordon Saunders – Book Coach, Mediaropa.org
- Barbara Taylor Sissel – Developmental Editor
- Thomas Umstaddt, Jr. – Novel Marketing Podcast
- Joyce Witte – WoTLM Amateur Radio

Acknowledgements

- Larry and Diana Adkins – Tri-Lakes United Methodist Church Emergency Preparedness Group (EPG)
- Stacey and Rev. Jason Baxter – Tri-Lakes United Methodist Church
- Jamey Bumgarner, Tri-Lakes Monument Fire Protection District
- David Futey – Our Community News
- Jennifer Sue Horsey (and Sir William of Williston)
- John Howe – Our Community News
- Tilia Klebenov Jacobs
- Jennifer and Rev. Dr. Bob Kaylor – Tri-Lakes United Methodist Church
- Paula and Jim Kendrick – Our Community News
- Doug Meikle – Community Emergency Response Team
- Ross Meyer – Our Community News
- André Mouton – Tri-Lakes United Methodist Church Emergency Preparedness Group (EPG)
- L. Dow Nichol III, Diana R. Nichol, and Elena Nichol
- Kevin Nielsen – Woodmoor Public Safety
- Shelley Pruett – Tri-Lakes United Methodist Church
- Dave R.
- James Rackl
- Gordon Reichal – Emergency Incident Support
- Allison Robenstein – Our Community News
- David Root – Colorado State Forest Service
- Rebecca Samulski – Fire Adapted Colorado
- Carolyn Streit-Carey – Woodmoor Firewise Committee
- Linda van Noordt and The Leddies
- John Vincent – Palmer Lake Fire Department
- Ben Wester – Black Forest Together

- Irene Wisniewski
- Margie Wood – Mastermind Group
- Jim Woodman – Woodmoor Forestry Committee
- Becky Zitterich – Colorado Estates Wildfire Neighborhood Ambassador

ABOUT THE AUTHOR

Lisa Hatfield shares emergency preparedness ideas so people will be more ready for natural and family disasters.

As we say in CERT (Community Emergency Response Team), we want you to be able to help yourself and others in the middle of chaos...when 9-1-1 isn't coming.

The next novel in the Ready to Go? series is under way. Stay tuned at LisaHatfieldWriter.com where you can see updates or subscribe to my occasional newsletter.

CPSIA information can be obtained
at www.ICGtesting.com
Printed in the USA
BVHW030433061021
618105BV00002B/8